Mack Bolan understood vengeance all too well

The grim fact was that his own journey down the road of his War Everlasting had begun much the same way as Marquis's quest for retribution.

But there was one great and simple distinction between himself and the Frenchman. Marquis didn't give a damn about collateral damage. If innocents got in the way of flying lead, too bad.

When women and children and all other noncombatants became viable targets, or just a mess to clean up, then that fine line between justice and vengeance became aimed straight in the direction of murder. And when the focus of revenge was shattered by white-hot passion and indifference to innocent life, then it was time for the avenger to pack it in, and to be held accountable to the blood standards of ultimate justice.

DON PENDLETON's
MACK BOLAN®

BLOOD AND SAND

A GOLD EAGLE BOOK FROM
WORLDWIDE®

TORONTO • NEW YORK • LONDON
AMSTERDAM • PARIS • SYDNEY • HAMBURG
STOCKHOLM • ATHENS • TOKYO • MILAN
MADRID • WARSAW • BUDAPEST • AUCKLAND

First edition September 2002

ISBN 0-373-61486-1

Special thanks and acknowledgment to
Dan Schmidt for his contribution to this work.

BLOOD AND SAND

Printed in U.S.A.

Vengeance is mine; I will repay, saith the Lord.
—*Holy Bible,*
Romans 12:19

Vengeance is best left to the Almighty. When all is said and done, it's a hollow victory, lacking in meaning.

—Mack Bolan

To the ceaseless efforts of America's justice forces.
God keep.

PROLOGUE

The line of stone hovels at the edge of the oasis wasn't the Casbah, but Max Schneider was ready to rock their world to hell and gone. It was just about time to kill them all, let God sort them out, he thought, then scoot, and he burned inside to get the shooting started. The orders were crystal clear—even the women, down to the smallest child of these terrorist vermin, were history, no exceptions. If it could stand, it was waxed. That was fine with Schneider, since basic combat logic dictated a survivor could run to the nearest army outpost or the camp of another Armed Islamic Group—the GIA—sound the alarm, start the hunt that could leave them all buzzard meat before they made the border. Oh, but he could feel himself edged out on precombat jitters, no doubt about it. He was amazed somewhat that the six of them had come this far against all odds, now stretched out on their bellies along the ridge of the wadi, scoping the village of Bir Khalloubah through NVD goggles. While they watched and waited on the team leader to send the signal to move in over his com link, Schneider pondered both the moment and how in the world he even ended up here in this belly of the beast of North Africa.

He hashed over the serious reservations he'd harbored from the beginning, never voicing them out loud to the others, naturally, but they were moments away from seeing the light at the end of the tunnel—the killing end at least of their targets—or so he hoped. But from the start of this headhunting incursion, the former GSG-9 commando hadn't been real keen on venturing into the most dangerous country on the planet.

Algeria.

He recalled the briefing by their French paymaster back in Paris, the big shot who was shelling out the huge bucks to nail one Mohammed Hahmad, the Syrian terrorist who had brought the Frenchman's world crashing down some years back after a kidnapping of the man's family in Egypt. Schneider had caught some of the scuttlebutt about the Frenchman's past tragedy, never privy to all the pertinent details, and not that it really mattered.

They had a job to do for the pot of gold waiting at the end of their rainbow. They were right then poised to drop the hammer on fifteen terrorists linked to Hahmad, who helped fund the GIA for reasons Schneider could only guess. Terrorist camps, training or otherwise, were spread across Algeria like a growing fungus, and perhaps the Syrian had eyes on more fertile ground for building a future army of suicide bombers. Perhaps. Who knew really, and Schneider didn't much care to rack his brain for the man's method to his madness. Supposedly the

Syrian was on the premises, only none of them had yet to spy the terror mastermind during the past hour or so of sweating out the surveillance. Which left Schneider wondering if he wasn't right then a thousand light-years someplace else, a terrorist reportedly, with more money, contacts and connections than God, or so the rumors went.

According to the briefing, they were now at the bottom edge of a notoriously murderous area known as the Triangle of Death. It stretched away from Algiers, down to the south, through land that was choked with farmland and date trees, but Schneider hadn't seen anything but sand and lunar landscape.

Their LandSat maps told him they were near the vast rolling dune wasteland of the Grand Erg Oriental, where the Sahara began. From what Schneider recalled, the Triangle of Death was nothing more than an endless, around-the-clock killing field, where something like a couple hundred thousand people had been murdered in the past decade by the FIS and the GIA in some ongoing genocidal purge meant to put one or the other in control of the country. And that meant all this blood-soaked real estate was crawling with the armed butchers of the country's two most savage Islamic fundamentalist organizations. Ghosts with assault rifles and long curved knives, those *jambiyas* of jihad lore, ready to flash out of nowhere, phantom killers lurking in the night never far from his thoughts.

He'd heard all about the FIS and the GIA, hordes of murderous thugs who simply marched into sprawling villages, hacking men, women and children to death, slashing their throats, orgies of killing that could go on for days until thousands of bodies littered the countryside in rivers of blood.

Algeria, the second-largest country in Africa, was a land of madness. Hell, everyone, he heard, was fair butcher's meat in Algeria, from foreigner to homegrown fundamentalists. The insanity was so great they especially longed to slaughter teachers, journalists, playwrights and even poets in the Triangle of Death, anybody with half a brain, he suspected, who might rage against the mindless violence. Women who refused to wear the *hejab,* the traditional Muslim headgear? Rape, then cut her throat. He'd even heard the GIA was so whacked out on fundamentalist tradition, they had outlawed belly dancing, claiming it was Satan's way of speaking through body language.

Well, Schneider wasn't planning on hitting any discos in the Casbah for a night on the town. There was a pot of one hundred thousand U.S. dollars per terrorist head to consider right then, any good times on hold. If the numbers were right, the six of them could retire tomorrow, assuming they lived to collect. It was his first outing to attempt to reap the fattest payday he'd ever seen. The other five—two ex-Legionnaires, two former SAS commandos and one of his own kind from the old GSG-9 glory days—had three headhunting ops under the belt. No question in his mind he could cut the muster, but he knew once the bullets started flying all bets were off, and some terrorist's 7.62 mil round could well have his name branded on it. Still, it had been several years since he'd wielded a weapon, much less fired a shot in anger, and it had taken months of drying out just to defog his head, refind the spirit of the warrior that had been buried by self-indulgence, self-pity. A small voice in his mind told him maybe his skills were a little rusty, but once the slaughter was under way he had to believe the old soldier would roar back to former glorious stature.

The reward outweighed the risk, just the same, and he was more than willing to gamble his life he would come out the other side, but the whole venture was full of holes, as far as tactics and logistics went.

Item—the logistics were, indeed, dicey, from getting there to extraction, but any black op that involved outright assassination of a larger force was always fraught with astronomical risk. With little else guiding them once they crossed the border, other than their French paymaster's stolen satellite imagery of the village and orbiting LandSat detailed grids, with the team leader in charge of the GPS module, they were hung out there in a country that was little more than a simmering caldron of murder and mayhem. He didn't trust the Tunisian cutouts, either, grinning Arabs dredged up by the French entrepreneur's shadows from Interpol, to point the way back and forth across the border. The dropoff by the French Aérospatiale-5 chopper at the border had gone off without a hitch, disembarking to find Colonel Bhouri Ayoub had the canvas-covered APC waiting. The Tunisian showed them the quickest and allegedly safest way through a wide hole in the border to skirt past any roving army patrols or fundamentalist goon squads. For his part in helping them get to the back door, Ayoub wanted a cache of weapons and a load of C-4 he'd heard the GIA thugs had stashed away in the village—and how did he come by that piece of intel anyway? Good luck finding it, Schneider thought, they'd have their own problems soon enough, but the team leader had assured the colonel they wouldn't come back with empty hands.

No, getting there wasn't the problem the way he saw it. It was reaching the only suitable makeshift stretch inside the Tunisian border where the British Aerospace C-29A would swoop down to haul them up and away. And if they weren't on-site, give or take fifteen minutes, Schneider feared the extract team would bon voyage for Paris.

It was crazy, all of it, but somehow it fit the dark road his life had taken.

Schneider could have cursed his life right then, his own personal fall that had led to getting the boot from the federal Ministry of the Interior, which was in charge of the GSG-9, but what was the point? What was done was done, but still he was baffled for a moment by his own failures. There had been years, he remembered, of dangling his life on the edge, nothing ever good enough, no amount of adventure, sex, booze ever calming the beast that rattled the chains inside. A failed marriage, destroyed by his fondness for prostitutes and the bottle. There had been some drug use, gambling debts piled up along the way, but he'd always believed any man who was a man, especially one who lived in a world where each moment could be his last, picked up habits that were his business, the warrior among the average man who sought to maintain some lifestyle that would let him wind down after kicking in some terrorists' door and checking them out while under heavy fire. Even back then, though, he'd become sick of being what he'd been, doing what he'd done. Perhaps, he reasoned, he'd forced the hands of his superiors, longing for something more, something else, but when they took away his job and livelihood, he was left twisting in the wind, wondering about his next move.

Enter his comrade, Hans Kruger, and he'd wandered off into this new blood horizon, no questions asked. Seemed Kruger had been hired as part of a private army by the Frenchman, and was often shipped out to hunt down the Syrian or any other terrorists even remotely linked to Hahmad, or any terrorists at all for that matter....

Well, that was all ancient history, and Schneider had jumped at the chance to earn that six hundred thou per terrorist scalp. Naturally, the Frenchman wanted proof, which was why one of them toted a small video cam to film the scumbags, up close and sporting a death mask.

He wasn't about to start counting money yet, since the whole setup tweaked every combat instinct something was about to go wrong. It was quiet below, the only sign of life a sentry who had come out earlier to smoke near the fire barrel on the west of the stone dwellings. Goats and camels meandered near the palm-treed pool of water at the north edge. Three battered military jeeps and a Russian APC were parked near a stone building that sat off by itself. If the cache was anywhere, Schneider suspected it was the solitary structure that seemed to command a prolonged inspection by the sentry, inside and out.

Waiting for the green light was agonizing. Schneider cradled the AK-47, all of them toting the ubiquitous Russian assault rifle, the weapons part of the deal with Ayoub. The Legionnaires were the rocket men, RPG-7s ready to let the warheads fly if the numbers suddenly stacked up, there or on the way out. Despite the nip in the air, Schneider was grateful to be out of the tunic and kaffiyeh, their combat vests loaded down with Russian fragmentation, flash-stun and incendiary grenades, spare banana clips for the AKs, a commando dagger sheathed on his lower leg.

Schneider heard his com link crackle with Worly's harsh whisper. "Heads up, mates, we've got a roach stepping into the light, our way."

Six hovels, a door on each side, two-foot gaps between each structure, Schneider noted. They had their own triangle of death around the village. The Brits on the west, he and Kruger on the east and the ex-Legionnaires to the south. No one had to say it, but it was no accident the teams were paired off according to nationality, which suited him, since he'd trust his life with Kruger, and had in the past. And to get past any language barrier, every man had to know and speak English.

He saw the door open to the front dwelling, light from a kerosene lantern spilling out, enough so that Schneider could remove his NVD goggles, dump them in a pouch, adjust his sight to the gloom. Another smoker, checking out the ridgeline, standing there as if...

As if he sensed they were about to be attacked.

Not good.

Maybe it was his nerves, he reasoned, or maybe...

No way. Ayoub wouldn't have marched them into an ambush.

The smoker vanished back inside, and the ex-SAS team leader came back on. "Check your watches, mates. One minute and counting, starting now. Let's go get happy and earn our paychecks."

Schneider rose, AK-47 leading the way, and headed down, Kruger by his side, into the wadi of death. A moment later, he was aware of the tight smile stretching his lips. He didn't know about getting happy, but he was already counting up the cash.

THE FORMER SAS commando didn't like seat-of-the-pants operations. They got people killed, and that was the bottom line. There was lack of solid intel for one thing, no one even sure of the exact numbers of terrorists here, or if the Syrian menace was even in the neighborhood. Not only that, but they weren't really his men he was leading. Sure, he was in charge, appointed by virtue of age, experience by the Frenchman, but other than Turnbuckle he had never worked close or long enough with the others to know their habits, moves, what might make them do this or that in the heat of combat. He had, of course, run background checks on the others and from what he could tell they were seasoned commandos, nothing untoward in their pasts, with the possible exception of the former Legionnaires. Schneider who'd gotten the boot for "behavioral abnormalities."

And the French foreign legion, even the postcolonial newer, kinder version, he knew, still accepted former murderers, rapists, thieves among its hallowed elite. Bondeloit and Maurier had criminal records with brief vacations in prison, one for manslaughter and the latter for aggravated assault on a policeman. Still, all of them had proved themselves fit for duty, a few commendations among their ranks. They had taken part in hostage raids, or black ops where some diplomat or muck-a-muck had been grabbed by terrorists in Europe, North Africa and Yemen. They had blood on their hands, commando time under the belt, and that had to be good enough for this job.

Problem was, like the others Worly knew he was basically greedy, down on his luck and had gladly put his neck on the chopping block for quick fat cash. There was alimony, agonizing debt that dogged him day and night. There was...

Screw it, there had never been some silver spoon up his behind. Say Hahmad was there, and if he could bring him down he was in shape to collect five mil alone, assuming he made it back to Paris.

He put his mind to the task, AK-47 poised to hit the first shadow that might want to step back outside for a smoke, a piss, whatever. This was a straight bull rush job, nothing fancy or tactically demanding. Kick in the doors, frag them, rush in, spray any survivors.

Keep it simple.

It was distasteful to him to kill women and children, but he reasoned that with each offspring they mowed down here they might save future innocent lives if the children weren't allowed to grow any older to carry on the jihad. With six hovels, each large enough to hold no more than six to a dwelling, it should be a fairly quick and easy slaughter, provided most of the targets were asleep.

Provided, too, every man did his job.

He saw the ex-Legionnaires split up as designed, one to aid the Germans, one to start the sweep from the south on his side. Checking his watch, Schneider counted off the numbers, nodded at Turnbuckle to arm his frag bomb as they made the first door, starting at the north end.

Two, one…

A thundering kick to the flimsy wood door, jacked up on adrenaline, and Worly nearly shattered the thing off its hinges. The grenade was chucked into a murky light that wavered from dancing kerosene flames, voices shouting from beyond in Arabic. Autofire blazed from inside the hovel, Turnbuckle hitting the other side of the doorway, Worly lurching back as slugs snapped the air, chomped off chips of stone near his eyes. He heard thunderclaps from the south, the east, the meshing racket of autofire all around, screams of women and children, and animals braying and snorting in a stampede when his own immediate problems were knocked out of play as the grenade detonated. Worly charged in, peeling off to the left, hacking on the smoke and stench of blood and eviscerated leftovers, his ex-SAS teammate going in low to the right. The blast had obliterated the lamp, spewing kerosene to ignite bodies, blankets, whatever else hungry flames could start feasting on. In the firelight he counted off five mangled shapes, three strewed AK-47s. There were severed legs, a tiny arm....

He felt the bile rise from his gut, but there was no time to spare grief over collateral damage.

Then he discovered a potential fiasco in the making.

A shredded figure was slumped over a radio console, mike still clutched in hand, sparks leaping from the demolished unit.

Make that four terrorists, and he needed Maurier in there on the double to start filming. Close to a half mil already, and they were just getting warmed up. Sure, it was the Frenchman's purloined sat imagery, his contacts in Tunisia that had nailed down this village as a terror haven, but all the sweat and blood would be for nothing if the man back in Paris couldn't view the grim results.

Turnbuckle had to have read his thoughts, because the man shouted above the din of weapons fire, "He didn't have time to sound any SOS."

"Keep rolling," Worly said, and led the charge back for the door.

Something dark and threatening welled up in

Worly's mind, igniting bad combat instincts. He wished to God he could share Turnbuckle's confidence, but he was sure this gig was set to go to hell.

TWO HOVELS WERE a clean sweep, Kruger fragging them out first, then Schneider homing in on the moans inside the boiling smoke to hose down survivors with long sweeps of AK-47 autofire, silencing pleas, cries for mercy or whatever they were wailing and gnashing their teeth about in Arabic. Schneider found himself irritated the women and children outnumbered the terrorists in the first two huts. They didn't get any bonus for bystanders.

Three armed shadows came spilling out door number three, Schneider feeding his AK-47 with a fresh banana mag, when Kruger bought it. He wasn't aware at first where the shots came from, but the manner in which Kruger's backside was torn to shreds, tailbone up...

And there went their radioman, Schneider cursing the lucky bastard who had just severed their only contact to their ride out. Bellowing like some ancient Viking berserker, Schneider flung himself toward the face of the hovel, holding back on the trigger, aware he was stuck smack in the middle of a bursting lead dam, but there was nothing to do but focus on the immediate visible threat. He concentrated the raking burst across the trio of shadows, zipping them left to right as best he could. They were spinning, falling, when he nose-dived away from the hovel, a swarm of bullets gouging up stone where his head had been a microsecond earlier. He was hammering the ground when he saw the silhouettes stagger out of the smoke from door number two. He cursed both his oversight in nailing it down and the fact these GIA goons were proving tougher bastards to kill than he thought.

Maurier was already on it, he saw, the ex-Legionnaire's assault rifle chattering out a bloody death knell. One GIA goon was bowled down, the other terrorist absorbing rounds, but Schneider bore witness in the next instant to the Algerian version of a suicide bomber.

The GIA thug bulled into the storm tearing him up, raging out something about Allah before the grenade in his hand blew.

And went off nearly point-blank in Maurier's face.

Two of their own down and out, and Schneider knew they couldn't afford to leave their dead teammates behind. They could eventually get IDd by Algerian authorities, and with a bunch of dead women and children scattered everywhere...

The Frenchman, he knew, wouldn't want that sort of hassle finding its way to his doorstep. Despite Algeria being known as an outlaw nation, there would be an international hue and cry, a demand for the UN to investigate, maybe Interpol stepping in to open a few closets in search of skeletons.

Schneider listened to the fading of autofire from the other side, moving for door number four, alert for any more shadows lurching outside, when Worly patched through. "Sitrep! Somebody, anybody! Talk to me, dammit!"

Schneider crouched by the doorway, glimpsing the camels and goats streaming beyond the oasis. "Kruger and Maurier didn't make it, sir. I'm clear on the east."

"Grab up Kruger and get that camera. I want this filmed and wrapped! Turnbuckle will cover you inside! We bail in two minutes! Copy that!"

"Roger."

Schneider got busy, draping Kruger in a fireman's carry around his shoulders. It was awkward, bending, retrieving the camera...

Or what was left of it. And Schneider stood, frozen, and cursed the bits and scraps around the hamburger remains of Maurier.

"HOW IN THE BLOODY hell could you have missed them, Schneider? Didn't you go inside and make sure every goddamn cockroach was stepped on? That was your job! Why the bloody frigging...?"

Schneider tuned the man's rage out best he could. He was more concerned with what might show up on the rear of the commandeered Russian transport, as he sat on the opposite bench from Bondeloit, the two of them scoping out the broken lunar hill country they were putting behind. They hit dunes in stretches, rolling up then down, the APC like some mini roller coaster as they barreled hard across the desert for the Tunisian border. The bodies of their fallen comrades were draped over the plastic-wrapped bundles of plastic explosive, Schneider figuring there were three to four hundred pounds of C-4. There were also crates of Russian grenades,

AK-47s, shoulder-fired SAM launchers crated up in the bed. Ayoub, Schneider figured, was about to get his payday, but what about them? Despite his screw-up, Schneider figured there was blame enough to go around, oversights that didn't only just seem unprofessional, but now had them in jeopardy of getting stranded, or worse. As Worly raged on over the com link, the two Brits up front in the cab, Schneider fought back the urge to rail about the team leader's neglect in acquiring backup equipment. Without film of the carnage, it stood to reason the Frenchman wouldn't pay up, despite the fact they'd lost two of their own, proof they'd engaged the GIA thugs. Or maybe the man would take their word?

"Schneider? I'm talking to you. God, what the bloody hell is this?"

They came out of nowhere, those ghosts he'd been dreading all along, and Schneider felt his heart lurch. They had driven in with their lights off, racing in from the north, but now he was counting maybe fifteen pairs of headlights flaring on as the line of jeeps flew over the rise of a dune. The mounted machine guns opened fire next, Worly cursing like a demon now, the canvas ripped away in gaping holes above Schneider's head. He felt them soaring up another dune when the thunderclap erupted from up front. The last thing he heard was Worly's scream of impotent rage. Schneider knew it was over, but he had to try. He was one step behind Bondeloit, flinging himself out of the bed as the fireball seared up his back.

He hit the sand, rolled up, clutching his AK-47.

It was only a glimpse, but he found still more jeeps and APCs rolling over the dune, the cab of their ride having been sheared off by the blast.

Whoever they were, Algerian soldiers most likely, they were playing for keeps.

There would be no fat payday, Schneider knew, not even a trip back to Paris, so he stood, holding his ground, directing a long stream of autofire even as he felt the bullets punching their hot, lethal course through his flesh.

MAURICE CHABEAUX KNEW there was a problem, and he didn't need the pilot to keep pointing at his watch and telling him how late the hit team was for pickup. There was no scheduled check-in from Worly, nothing but radio silence when Chabeaux tried to raise the ex-SAS man, several times over the past hour while they were grounded on the barren plain. Chabeaux stared over the shoulders of the pilot and copilot, reading their dark looks, aware they were thinking the same thing he was.

They would have to bail soon. Colonel Ayoub might be in control of the region, but there were other military outposts near the border, Tunisian officers who hadn't been greased to let foreign killers hop back and forth from Algeria and who might take exception to this unauthorized landing. Chabeaux didn't trust Ayoub, either, the colonel's crafty smile, his continual demands for money and the insistence on the commando team bringing back a cache of weapons warning him the man had irons in fires that could well come back to brand them all at the first sign he might have bitten off more than he could chew. Something had gone wrong—that much Chabeaux could feel in his gut. And it would be the first time in four missions to North Africa that he might be forced to abandon the commandos to whatever fate awaited them.

He kept searching the darkness, urging the transport to show up, when he spotted the line of headlights in the distance. Jeeps, he believed, driving in from the northeast, from the direction, he knew, of Ayoub's compound. Even if they flew on, there was the backup team in Tunis, and he could raise them, after calling Paris, of course, for further orders. Worst-case scenario, the backup team would have to roll down here and sort through the mystery, clean up any messes left behind, maybe even venture back into Algeria if the first team had struck out.

The radio unit squawked with Ayoub's voice. The colonel had the one frequency given him before the mission began, but Chabeaux still flinched, both the man's tone and demands raising his anxiety level.

"Monsieur Chabeaux, this is Colonel Ayoub. Remain on the ground. We will be boarding your aircraft."

"Start the engines," Chabeaux ordered the flyboys. "Quickly! Get us in the air before they plant those jeeps in our path!"

They were rolling, gathering speed, when Ayoub confirmed Chabeaux's suspicions. "Do not leave! There has been serious trouble across the border! You will remain in Tunisia until I have some answers! Respond! Stop the plane or I will shoot!"

"Go! Lift!"

The jeeps became a blur beyond the cockpit window, the nose of the C-29A rising when Chabeaux spotted the flaming fingers of mounted machine guns jabbing the darkness. They were too far out to score the plane, or so he hoped as he strained his ears for the fearful thud of heavy-jacketed slugs drumming the fuselage, the wings.

The pilot, Emile Dupre, heaved a sigh as they rapidly climbed, Ayoub raging still over the radio until Chabeaux snapped off the unit. "They are dead, my friend. Even worse, I fear, perhaps captured."

Chabeaux ignored the pilot, staring at the dark heavens, silently urging more speed and distance. "Just get us out of this godforsaken country."

"You will have to call Paris, inform them."

"I know what I have to do, just fly!"

Chabeaux knew he was looking at the worst of worlds, the future as dark as the sky. Whatever had gone wrong, it could find its way back to Paris. If that happened...

He decided to take his time before he radioed the SOS to Paris. Bad news could wait until they were safely over the Mediterranean. Right then, he needed a trip to the wet bar, a few brandies to get his nerves under control before he called Paris to inform the man the walls had come crashing down.

THE WORLD WAS STILL his to own and bend to his will, but all the trappings of fame and fortune had only brought him grief and misery. And no amount of money and power, he thought, would ever snap him out of feeling like the loneliest, most miserable man on the planet.

Dante Marquis sat alone in the back of his limo, wondering what the future held, if there was any chance at all he might be happy again, or at least free of anguish. A little more than three years earlier, he had set something in motion that he'd known all along could prove both his personal downfall and the ruin of a conglomeration of business ventures that had catapulted him to the top as one of the ten richest men in Europe. If money could buy happiness, he thought, then he should have been laughing at the mere sight of sunshine, partying day and night, living and loving just as he had before.

Before.

He winced at the sound of his knuckles popping, his fist clenching like a vise. There were problems cropping up all over the place, and he knew this moment was long overdue. Money wasn't his problem, but it was the Achilles' heel of the shadow men whose souls he had bought and paid for to help him engineer his vengeance hunt. And there were vultures likewise across the ocean in America who had been licking their beaks behind his back, seeking to pick clean the carcass of his sister company overseas.

Soon Ducloux and Anglerre, up front beyond the glass partition, one of the ex-Legionnaires steering them down rue Lafayette, would settle any problems for him waiting at the end of this ride. The American trouble would be dealt with tomorrow.

He willed himself to relax, but it was impossible. He was waiting for news from Tunisia, keeping hope alive that this time that bastard responsible for his heartache had been found and disposed of like the murdering terrorist garbage he was. He stared at the miniconsole in the well of the limo, silently urging the phone with its secured line to trill.

He gave up, believing no news was good news, then watched the apartment buildings and the hotels pass by without actually seeing them. They were stark reminders now of a past long since dead and buried, as empty in his eyes as his soul felt. Long ago, he recalled, he would walk these streets on the Right Bank of the Seine. Hand in hand with her, so long ago, when they were so deeply in love. They laughed and strolled the parks, never tiring of gazing at the Arc de Triomphe, the Louvre, the Eiffel Tower, whiling away hours that slipped by all too quickly in the cafés, amazed that even after years of marriage they never tired of each other, conversations always lively, the future theirs, every day a new adventure. They would spend nights alone, away from the grind of his empire, drinking and making love in first-class hotels.

And they had their children to consider, also, Nicholas and Monique, a son and daughter he had hoped would one day inherit his kingdom. They might have been shipped off to the best private schools in Europe, but they were never far from his thoughts or heart. Back then he had lived in hope for the future.

Now there was nothing left but revenge.

The glass partition had parted, he saw, Anglerre's broad, scarred visage filling the space. They had arrived in the alley, parked by the private entrance to his club. They were waiting, he knew, in the conference room where he did business with foreign associates or the men from Interpol. Paris, he knew, was a city that didn't sleep, and men of money and power required some private sanctuary where they could unwind, indulge every fantasy their wealth could buy. He provided just such a service, the only secret he'd ever kept from Martique. He wasn't any pimp, but he understood the necessity of mixing business with pleasure, the cold reality of gleaning secret knowledge about an associate that could provide both rewards and a safety valve down the road. In the past—before—he had always entered this place he dubbed Dante's Inferno with great restraint. Only once had he indulged in the pleasures of his after-hours netherworld, felt suitably ashamed and guilty after the fact. Now when he came here he found himself engaged in more pleasure than business. Perhaps, he had often thought following the horror in Egypt, God was punishing him for that one adulterous encounter.

"You are to wait outside the conference room," he told the ex-Legionnaires. "I understand he brought his own security detail." He grunted. "They are not Interpol. I am told they are little more than common street criminals. It tells me not only is he greedy, but he thinks he can intimidate me with cheap muscle. The arrogance of this man never ceases to amaze me. I believe it is time for us to readjust his vision of the future.''

With a double nod, they disgorged. Anglerre opened his door, the ex-Legionnaires snugging their topcoats over the 9 mm MAT 49 subguns in special swivel rigging. Marquis anticipated the meeting would go bad, his adrenaline running hot, Anglerre swiping the magnetic card, the steel door sliding open. It was a short walk down the corridor, light spilling from the conference room as he entered and his men took up position by the doorway.

''Mr. Marquis,'' Agent Euclid Lassere said, nodding in greeting as he rose from his seat at the end of the table. ''A pleasure to see you again, as always.''

Marquis glanced at the two henchmen, sniffed the air as he took up his post, staring them down from the other end of the table.

''Ah, these are my associates,'' Lassere said, ''Doile, and, well,'' the agent said, grinning as if he were eager to deliver the punch line to a bad joke, ''he calls himself Victor Hugo.''

''Let us get down to it.''

''But of course.''

Lassere, Marquis knew, was little more than a thief. He was high up at the Paris division of Interpol, with contacts and connections in the American Justice Department and FBI, with access to classified files and hackers who could crack codes and break through the firewalls.

Marquis needed the man, and he never liked needing anybody for anything, especially when the other party believed he was invaluable and invincible.

"The further along this, ah, operation proceeds, well, sir, I am finding myself acquiring more risk. I am finding myself doling out larger sums to individuals I must do business with. Important men, you understand, who, ah, keep it going for you. Colonel Ayoub, for instance. The colonel was my personal contact down there, and the man, well, it seems he, like most of us, has a lifestyle to maintain. It was most embarrassing, the colonel calling my office to demand a quick transfer of funds to his account, more francs actually than were allotted for—"

"Enough!" Marquis snapped, squeezing his eyes shut, massaging his face, smoothing back his neatly groomed black hair. "You want more money. How much?"

"Well, our original arrangement was twenty thousand, in U.S. dollars, transferred to my Swiss account monthly. Now, I did not anticipate having to dip into my own money to make sure the way was safely paved for your commandos."

"How much more?"

"Sir, please, you seem distressed. This is simply business, nothing personal."

"Do not patronize me."

"Very well. Considering the fact I now have a Justice agent on my payroll, a man who recently came to me and discovered we were hacking into their files...well, considerable—"

"One last time. How much more?"

Lassere squared his shoulders, Marquis noting the

narrowed glance he threw the thugs flanking him.
"To continue this arrangement, I will require an advance of, say, five hundred thousand. Plus an additional fifty thousand per month. This will cover key
individuals who now have their hands out. This
will—"

"No."

Lassere's face hardened, Marquis seeing his
mouth, nearly hidden by his mustache, twitching.
"Did you say no?"

"This is what I will give you. Thirty thousand a
month, no advance. I will not be extorted. If I give
you more now, you will want more tomorrow.
Where does it end? You will pocket my money, and
feed these so-called key individuals bread crumbs."

"You listen—"

"No, you listen. We both have enough dirt on
each other to bury the other one. If you value your
career, if you value your freedom, you will accept
my terms."

"Or else?"

"Yes. I neglected to mention the one thing you
should value the most. Understand, it is business,
nothing personal."

Marquis snapped his fingers. He ignored the rage
bleating from Lassere, turned away as the Interpol
man's henchmen sensed the danger, digging inside
their leather jackets, clawing at the bulges that
hadn't escaped his eye. Marquis swept past his ex-
Legionnaires, the sound of their subgun fire swelling
the doorway, trailing him down the hall. The mes-

sage was delivered, and if the Interpol man didn't rein in his greed...

Marquis had other matters to worry about. He was back in his limo, wondering what might go wrong next when the phone trilled. He picked it up.

"It is me, Mr. Marquis."

"Yes, it is you."

Already he didn't like the agitated tone in Chabeaux's voice, prepared himself for the worst.

"I regret to tell you, we have a problem."

CHAPTER ONE

Mack Bolan looked away from the scene of carnage as Hal Brognola took the remote and snapped off the picture.

"Algerian state-sponsored news, not exactly what I'd call the gospel truth or *60 Minutes* quality, but the CIA confirmed the reports. This little horror show was aired this morning across four different countries in North Africa, the FBI using their own satellite intercept to pick up the transmission in France. Needless to say, the fundamentalist Islamic world is flailing about from Mecca to Morocco, railing about some Western conspiracy to do in their holy warriors in a campaign of genocide."

Bolan had already perused the intel package as soon as he'd slipped into the big Fed's office at the Justice Department, and pieces of a sordid picture were trying to come together. He wasn't sure if there was a mission yet, but he'd been standing down at Stony Man Farm, the ultrasecret covert-ops nerve center in Virginia, when his old friend had called to inform him of a potential crisis situation. The man also known as the Executioner, sitting in the wing chair beside the big Fed's desk, studied Brognola's face, waiting for the Justice man to lay it out. His old friend looked about as relaxed and rested as Bolan had seen in some time, but the soldier could spot the tension building in his eyes. Brognola was both liaison to the President of the United States and in charge of Stony Man Farm, handing out missions that were sanctioned by the Man when national security was threatened, a responsibility that often dropped the weight of the world on the big Fed's shoulders and could age the man ten years in a few short days when Bolan or any of the other Stony Man warriors—Able Team and Phoenix Force— were out there in the trenches. At the moment Bolan couldn't quite find the national security threat, so he waited, listened.

Brognola grunted. "I don't see the Algerians running to the UN and crying foul anytime soon, but this massacre is identical to three other slaughters that made headlines in Egypt, Yemen and Morocco. Same MO. Western commandos swooping down on remote villages suspected of harboring terrorists. The problem is these guys never heard about collateral damage. Women, children, the family camels, these guys give new meaning to scorched earth. They've gotten in and out, bang, bang, clean getaways, which tells me a whole lot of greasing of certain folks in the countries they've hit... Well, we know who they are and who's financing them. The bodies the Algerians are holding on to and parading before the cameras have been IDd by the State Department and the CIA."

"And the buck stops at the doorstep of Dante Marquis."

"Multibillionaire entrepreneur, who, I'm thinking, has acquired his own private army of international headhunters. He inherited his father's winemaking business, then moved on up, branching out and grabbing up chunks of this and that in various takeover deals, fashion, magazines, his own publishing house in search of the next Al Camus. He has his own cable network, his bread and butter, manufactures what are being called 3-D video games, everything from arcades, to CDs for junior's computer and TV. Sex-and-violence stuff made him one of the richest men in Europe. There's a sister company in San Francisco helping the man shape the minds of our next generation.

"On the surface, the guy looks clean, until you start digging around beneath the pond scum. When it came to the FBI's attention the man was hiring former commandos—GSG-9, SAS, a few of our own Green Berets, a bunch of ex-Legionnaires, most of these guys handpicked, looks like, down on their luck and before Marquis watching their last dollar—well, they whiffed up a bad odor, especially when the CIA confirmed the identities of the commandos on their first Egyptian outing. When our people in Paris started turning up offshore accounts, numbered Swiss bank accounts, we wiretapped and monitored the movements of Marquis and associates. The commandos have their own compound-retreat in the French countryside. When they aren't shooting up the hills and the vineyards every day's one big party, booze and high-priced beauties from Paris. My people heard enough to know Marquis is doling out a hundred thousand dollars per terrorist scalp. Apparently after each hit the hunters film the carnage for Dante's personal viewing, proof, I gather, the mission was accomplished. I'd say the man's bounty hunters are doing the world a charitable service if it weren't for the fact they shoot up every innocent in sight beyond the scumbags.''

"I don't see any altruistic motive on the man's part.''

"It's vengeance, plain and simple.''

"The botched kidnapping of the man's family.''

"Right. Wife, son and daughter, on vacation in Cairo. Marquis was supposedly locked up in a major business deal, was about to join them when native Egyptian riffraff snatched them off the street. They were tortured, the wife and daughter raped repeatedly, then their throats were slashed and the bodies dumped near the pyramids. No ransom demand. It must have been some sort of in-your-face statement. I know, you're looking for the national security threat. Here it is, Striker. A Syrian named Mohammed Hahmad who made his own bloody climb to the top of the terror dung heap. Sold Russian hardware, small and large arms, a mover and shaker in the heroin trade, and he was off and running, financing terrorist attacks, setting up camps across North Africa for the next generation of psychopaths. He was confirmed as the brains behind the Marquis incident.''

"And Dante's been looking to even the score.''

"We have it on tape. We also believe Marquis is getting assistance from Interpol. I've got names, a shopping list, contacts in Paris for you. I ran this past the Man, and he'd like you to look into it. It's Hahmad he wants. The guy finances, commands and controls major terrorist organizations from Beirut to Algeria."

"I've heard of him."

"He's a snake, but a big one, pulling the strings from the shadows, and he's believed to be arming and financing Hamas, the PLO, fanning the flames of the conflagration consuming Israel. Forget Arafat—Hahmad, the CIA says, is the spearhead looking to land Syria on the map as numero uno outlaw nation exporting terrorist slaughter machines. And Marquis has all the tools at his disposal to track the Syrian down."

"And you're thinking I latch on for the ride."

"Follow the bullets, one way to put it. I don't know how you'd do it. Maybe you can go to Marquis, offer your professional services."

"That's a thought."

"So, you're in?"

San Francisco

JEAN-CLAUDE LAPIERRE didn't much care for Americans, and thieving Yankees were at the top of his hit list. He would have loved nothing more than to spend some time telling them what he thought about their pseudoculture of mindless violence and rampant greed, where the love and worship of self clearly replaced basic character, but he wanted this sorry encounter wrapped up as quickly as possible. It would take most of the day, he figured, to clean up the mess, drive to the city and dispose of the bodies in the bay, and there were other matters requiring his martial skill. A critical situation regarding the Syrian had been brought to his attention, the primary reason they had been in San Francisco for three days. His security team was on it, rooting out leads to a suspected Hahmad cell while he took care of this unpleasantness, seven hard men with an arsenal at their command, back in the city, bits and pieces of intel outright stolen or "borrowed" from a Justice Department and Interpol stooge.

One butt kicking, one hard lesson at a time, he thought.

The former Legionnaire snorted at the sight of the three luxury vehicles parked in the driveway, mentally reviewed his investigative intel, figured all were present and accounted for. One lawyer, one accountant, one CEO, ordered to come alone, without chauffeurs. Not all the king's men were waiting under the silver domed roof of the estate in San Francisco's wine country, but these three would vanish without a trace, fueling rumors no doubt, which, in time, would have to be addressed during some midnight calling on the others to make sure their heads were right, mouths shut, all the attitude adjustment he was minutes away from shaping up.

The place looked more like a spaceship ready to blast off than the retreat for the charter members of Dante Marquis's American branch of Marquis International Inc. He saw Vice President Gordon Martell standing behind the glass bubble of the viewing room where the second-floor balcony was as spacious as any park in Paris. The sun barely up, and LaPierre noted the VP was working on a glass of wine. Something to calm the nerves? LaPierre chuckled to himself, glanced at Montmarte and told him to park their rented Lexus near the bottom of the steps.

LaPierre gave the bulge of the Glock 17 beneath his cashmere topcoat a pat with a black-gloved hand. "Bring the cleaning materials."

"How come you get to have all the fun?"

LaPierre saw the mean smile dart across Montmarte's mouth, read the disappointment in the former Legionnaire's eyes. "Stick with the plan. Work now, play later. Shall we?"

"You're in charge."

They were out and climbing the stairs, LaPierre taking in the scenery of the vineyards and the distant rolling hill country, looking over his shoulder as Montmarte lugged the large nylon satchel. As he opened the sliding door, Martell, he saw, glass in hand, was strolling through the living room, throwing his partners in crime nervous looks. Binten and the lawyer, Feinstein, were sitting far apart on a white leather couch. LaPierre stood in the doorway, feeling mean and ugly all of a sudden. He had expressly told them to be waiting in the conference room. With the three of them now lounging on expensive furniture, cleanup could prove a time-consuming chore.

Well, Montmarte would just have to put some elbow grease into his janitor duties, he decided.

Montmarte sighed, grinned, gave LaPierre a soft shake of the head, obviously seeing sweat in the immediate future.

"Yes, I know, it's a dirty job, my friend…"

"Perhaps you'll indulge me," Montmarte replied in French, "a glass of wine or two, then."

"I'll even take out the garbage for you. How's that?"

Montmarte clapped LaPierre on the back. "A commanding officer, then and now, you're still all heart."

"A leader leads from the trenches. What can I say. I am not above getting my hands dirty."

"If you don't mind!"

Smiling, LaPierre led Montmarte down the sitting room, nodding at each man in turn.

"You care to tell us the nature of this emergency meeting?" Martell demanded. "This is highly unusual. I would assume if there's some urgent business, Mr. Marquis would be here—"

The VP caught himself as LaPierre read the contempt in his eyes. "Instead of flunkies?"

"I didn't say that. Let's get on with it."

"But, of course, I will waste no more of your valuable time." LaPierre took up post in front of the teakwood coffee table. He gave the spacious room a smile, the walls hung with paintings, modern artwork, he assumed, but couldn't tell what was what. He imagined Monet rolling over in his grave.

"It has come to Monsieur Marquis's attention the

three of you are behind a conspiracy to steal him blind.''

The accountant was leaping to his feet, outraged. "That's preposterous! Who are you? How dare you—''

LaPierre had the Glock out, the air freezing around him with panic. The accountant was first, the Glock cracking and painting a third eye on the man's forehead. One down, and he had every scorching degree of their shocked and horrified attention.

He shifted his aim to Mantell. "The quarterly reports do not mesh with our numbers in Paris,'' LaPierre snarled, annoyed when he saw the glass slip from Martell's hand, spraying a red stain across white carpet, the dark splash hitting the couch igniting Montmarte.

"Why did you have to do that? I have to clean that up! Idiot!''

Martell was shaking, holding out his hands. "No, listen, there must be some mistake....''

"Yes, there was a mistake. Monsieur Marquis regrets his oversight now in neglecting his American company.''

Rubin Feinstein's pudgy bulk was quivering inside his thousand-dollar suit jacket. "But—''

"Shut your filthy lying mouths! I am not here to listen to your lies and your excuses and rationalizations. We have discovered offshore accounts, a sizable gross income from our videos that your accountant pilfered, a bad magic act that made it appear we are losing money. He was not as clever in juggling the numbers as you had hoped. Your offices were bugged, your phones tapped. We know. End of story.''

"Look, we can fix it, we can make it right," Martell whined.

"Too late. This is housecleaning. Goodbye."

They were screaming for their lives, LaPierre thinking how much he detested not only thieves but cowards who couldn't die on their feet when the moment of reckoning arrived, when he tapped the trigger twice. The first head shot made a mess, and he wasn't sure how the area around the accountant would get scrubbed clean of brain matter and blood, so he pumped a round each into their hearts. With the 9 mm rounds blowing apart the vital organ, there was surprisingly little blood, but the bullets found the wall beyond the falling bodies on the way out their backs. In time LaPierre believed the police would find their way here, and other than a gob of drywall mud, a complete paint-over of the walls, they couldn't hide the holes.

"Ah, Colonel, quite the mess," Montmarte groused.

"Get to work," LaPierre said. "We have a long day and much to do. If our sources are correct, we have only just begun making messes."

THE INTERNATIONAL Criminal Police Organization, also known as Interpol, was the weight behind his sledgehammer of revenge. He needed all the intel and resources at their disposal if his commandos were to hunt down and slay the demon and his legions that haunted his sleep every night. Like every military, intelligence law-enforcement agency around the free world, high-tech had rocketed Interpol into the future, steps ahead of most criminals, so he used every conceivable gadget and gizmo and satellite tracking they had at their disposal to steer him in his quest for the head of Mohammed Hahmad in this age of supercomputers, GPS, *Star Wars* wonder toys where even X-ray satellites could damn near watch people through three-foot-thick concrete walls. Interpol was his personal CIA, but his eyes and ears, he knew, could also wear the dirty shroud of duplicity, backstabbing, shadow men playing their own secret games.

Basic nature of the human beast, he decided.

As Dante Marquis moved into the light and shadows dancing from the bank of monitors in his command-and-control center in the renovated hotel that now housed his multifaceted kingdom, he gave it brief consideration that it was always good to keep his friends close, his enemies even closer. Interpol, he thought, had opened the vaults to terror havens like magic, putting his commandos onto the scent of blood, human sharks hungry for cash. But Interpol could prove a giant albatross around his neck unless he continued balancing the high-wire act of cajoling, greasing, monitoring and applying the right dose of intimidating heat when necessary. Cloaked in mystery, from its unorthodox formation in September, 1923, in Vienna to the present, Interpol, he knew, wasn't controlled by any single government. It was a power unto itself, which meant the dark side of men could take over where good intentions weren't backed by iron-clad principle.

Which meant he had to constantly watch his own ass.

Somewhat like the UN, it was a free-roving giant, but Interpol was no paper tiger. Its agents were lions with guns and badges, and sometimes men backed by the law could elevate themselves—at least in their own eyes—to the ranks of gods. Interpol was legitimate and recognized by the Western world as the premier international law-enforcement bulldog, its client list made up of 125 police agencies, but in his mind Interpol was a vast shadow army, with lurking demons behind certain masks of virtue, public and professional fronts he had stripped away, greedy and treacherous beasts he had maneuvered to do his bidding.

Interpol's genesis was as strange, he recalled, as its history, eighty-something years steeped in myth, rumor and innuendo, everything from shady dealings with Nazis to the KGB to drug cartels. In the beginning they hunted down counterfeiters, later moved up to tracking down and bringing to justice Nazi war criminals who couldn't buy their freedom. These days it was skyjackers, terrorists, money launderers, every ilk of international criminal from the bank president who had pilfered seven-figure accounts to drug cartels whose vast oceans of cash were electronically gobbled up in numbered accounts. It was an electronic world, after all, and criminals needed money, which meant Interpol could access any bank account in the world. Bank swindles, fraud, stolen art, tracking fugitives, hijackers and terrorists and smugglers. Whatever Marquis wanted to know about his enemies, known or perceived, Interpol was the next-best thing to the Almighty, he concluded. Unfortunately no institution in the modern world, he thought, where greed could insinuate itself into the blood of even the most principled of men, could claim itself completely on the side of angels.

The founding fathers, he knew, were police chiefs from twenty countries, ratifying some treaty between them that soon left them a combination police force of the Free World, a spy, supersleuth, long arm of the law and bounty hunters sans the cash rewards, and he could be sure they never meant for the agency to be used as one man's worldwide detective agency.

It didn't hurt his cause, either, he knew, that Interpol's world headquarters was planted just outside Paris.

Marquis found Anglerre in the rolling chair, his head swiveling from the satellite monitors, the situation wall map of the world, and a ream of fax papers.

"How many men are we down to?" Marquis wanted to know.

"Thirty-six. And it would appear the good Colonel Ayoub sold us out."

Marquis took the manila folder from Anglerre, opened it to the first of several sat images and felt his stomach clench with hot anger.

"Hahmad?" Marquis said.

"With our Colonel Ayoub."

"Are you sure? We have been duped before by the bastard. We know our men have been left wondering whether they are chasing a ghost."

"Interpol's source in Tunisia confirmed it. Hahmad is there, but believed to be ready to flee the country now that he knows the hunt has resumed. Yes, I know, the Syrian uses cutouts, middlemen, every country he steps into he appears protected by a rogue's gallery of corrupt officials. He has doubles, what you have called 'mirrors,' to throw us off the trail. It is one reason, beyond his obvious wealth and connections, he appears to be in many places at once. Ayoub, I just learned, was funneling the Syrian's arms shipment to GIA cronies in Algeria. He intended to use our people to take back the arms shipment in the village, including plastic explosive, then, I presume, he would have disposed of Worly and his team. And, of course, your money would not have been refunded. A one-shot stab in the back, and Ayoub becomes a reasonably wealthy man by Tunisian standards."

"Our intelligence has been sloppy," Marquis said, seething. "Learning all this now, late in the game, I am thinking I may have to send you back to have another chat with our friends at Interpol. Should this happen again…"

He left the omen hanging, his own voice sounding like a trailing echo as raw emotion took over. It was ugly enough, Marquis thought, the Syrian bastard had engineered the abduction and murder of his wife and children, and often he thought it would have been easier if he simply lost his personal fortune instead of his only living flesh and blood to the most heinous of criminal acts. It was even worse that one of the world's most infamous terrorists could vanish like a thief in the night each time he believed his commandos had him nailed down to a specific location, vanishing without a trace when ultimate justice looked close enough to reach out and grind him to a mass of bloodied and broken flesh blubbering for his life. Now this latest treachery—Ayoub in league with the Syrian, standing beside Hahmad, caught on satellite, both of them grinning, as if sharing a private joke.

It was a mockery of his hatred, an insult to his craving for revenge, flung back in his face, a middle-finger salute from his enemy. Just seeing the hawkish, swarthy features, those cold black eyes made him think of a dozen different torture scenarios he would put the devil through if he could cage him somehow, have him dumped in the remotest region of France where not even God would hear his screams. It was time to up the ante, he decided, offer the hugest slice of his riches to date to the man who could bring Hahmad back alive.

His hand trembled, the sat pics tumbling from his grasp as he stared at nothing. Whenever he stopped and let the fires of hate consume him, the man inside, his very soul seemed swallowed up by a raging vortex. Every time he thought he had the monster in his grasp, fate slapped him in the face with yet another failure. The hatred burned on, the shame welled to bubbling nausea in his belly whenever he recalled the way in which his family had been butchered like sick cattle, their naked bodies, mutilated and dumped at the foot of the pyramids, his women having been repeatedly—

He should have been there with them, would have been had it not been for business, the megadeal that had landed him his own cable network. Fate? Bad timing? Was he cursed, then, by his own prominence and position in the world, building his own kingdom having cost him his family? Was some cruel cosmic entity toying with him?

So he was rich and famous. Did that mean he was to be punished for carving out his own niche, a man of the world who had made it his way brought down from lofty heights to be made painfully aware of life's horrors? Why not take his life? Why punish the innocent? Why cast them in the murderous path of savages, leaving him nothing but terrible memories and imaginings of what their final moments on earth had to have been like? He often lay awake in bed, sometimes the entire night, wondering whether things would have turned out differently if he had been there. But how? What could he have done? Since there had been no ransom demand, he had to assume it was some sort of personal statement, directed solely toward him by the jihad monsters.

Which, somehow, made it all even worse. He could understand greed, and he would have paid any ransom, but to just murder them for no apparent reason other than they were Westerners made his soul cry out even louder for retribution.

"We have the situation in San Francisco to also

consider. The housecleaning was a success, but there is the other matter of the latest sightings.''

''Only if they are confirmed as Hahmad's cell,'' Marquis said. ''And only if this devil manages to vanish from Tunisia. What is the status on Koch and his people?''

''Awaiting orders.''

''Call Koch. Nothing and no one is to stand in the way of their capturing Ayoub, even if they have to burn down half the Tunisian countryside or chase him right into the arms of his GIA cohorts over the border. I want the man skinned alive if that's what it takes to pick up the Syrian's tracks. I want payback for Ayoub's treachery, in fact, I want to hear him scream over the sat link. And I want another team ready to fly out at a moment's notice for Tunisia. Five million in U.S. dollars to the man who can bring Hahmad back to me alive.'' He paused, paced and wheeled back toward Anglerre. ''We have lost six good commandos. How is your search for replacements coming along?''

''I have already combed the various files from our friend at Interpol. It could take time, finding the sort of individual who might fit our requirements.''

''Former commandos and Legionnaires, down on their luck and with nothing left to lose, you mean. I don't have time. I need to field another team. I am thinking of launching several operations across North Africa at the same time, a net of blood and steel that Hahmad will not be able to slither through.''

Marquis felt the fire inside surging to a level of

hate and anger he'd never before known. "Listen to me. I am closer than I have ever been to claiming the head of Hahmad. I will spare no expense, no lives. Fate, God, whatever, has given me the world, but has likewise seen fit to rob me of the one thing I loved more than life itself. I ask myself if the blood of the innocent can be so easily shed...where is God? Where was he when my family was being slaughtered? Perhaps it is up to me to play that role. From here on, I want constant situation reports. I will decide who will live and who will die. The final days of either Hahmad or myself are upon all of us."

CHAPTER TWO

France

There was smoke but no fire. Infiltration of the ranks would be the key, Bolan hoped, that would lead him to the flames of the Frenchman's vengeance machine.

During the flight to Orly, Bolan had sifted through every piece of intel Brognola had handed over, putting names to faces, reviewing past failures and victories, assessing the talent of the opposition. Plowing through all the mystery and speculation, backed up now by certain recent facts and solid intel, the soldier had devised a plan as old as the Trojan horse. He was a master at role-playing, using deception and subterfuge over the years to pave deep inroads into an enemy's camp, often insinuating himself as part of the opposition team while he stalked his adversaries under their own roof before he chose the time and place to bring the walls crashing down in blood and thunder. Of course, there was always great risk involved, wearing a mask of deceit that could get ripped off any moment, becoming a prisoner next, tortured or worse.

No risk, no reward.

For his scheme to succeed it was imperative the Executioner got close to the Frenchman, his martial skills an asset that he planned to sell the entrepreneur, hunting Hahmad while plotting the fall of the house of Marquis. Once it was thumbs-up from Marquis, he would weigh each moment as it came, prepared in the blink of an eye naturally to unleash total war against the Frenchman and his commandos if his ruse was found out somehow and the net came falling. It was never that simple, gaining trust and respect of the enemy, an outsider guarding deadly secret knowledge in his heart while sharpening the knife out of sight. And once he stepped onto the thin ice, Bolan knew it could crack wide open before he knew he was going down and under.

Marquis was a civilian, with no military background, but he had the money and the clout and the motivation, not to mention a kingdom and a life to lose, which could make him every bit as dangerous as his most rabid terrorist hunter. On the surface, Dante Marquis appeared to have it all, aboveboard in his business dealings and lifestyle, until, that was, high-tech had come sleuthing in to unearth the demons that drove the man.

The Executioner understood vengeance all too painfully well. The grim fact was his own journey down the road of his War Everlasting had begun much the same way as Marquis's quest for retribution. A hundred lifetimes ago, it still seemed like only yesterday, and he saw back to the young Special Forces sniper who had come home from Vietnam to find his family had essentially been wiped out by the Mafia. Like Marquis, Bolan had his immediate family snatched away—except for brother Johnny—by cruel circumstance beyond his control. But there was one great and simple and to date clean distinction between himself, the soldier knew, and the Frenchman.

The problem he had with Marquis and his private army of hunter-killers couldn't have been put any better than Brognola had stated back in Wonderland.

No, these guys didn't give a damn about collateral damage. If innocents got in the way of flying lead, too bad. Likewise, witnesses seemed to be a thorn in their side. When women and children and all other noncombatants became viable targets, or just a lousy mess to clean up like the day's spilled milk, then that fine line between justice and vengeance—sometimes blurred so that the two were one and the same—became aimed straight in the direction of murder. And when the focus of revenge was shattered by white-hot passion and indifference to innocent life, then it was time for the avenger to both pack it in and to be held accountable to the blood standards of ultimate justice. In short, the avenger became no better, in truth was worse than the savages whose blood he sought when indiscriminate killing of the innocent was the SOP of the day.

Right then, the soldier could smell the figurative smoke, and the compound was just as Special Agent Hardin had laid out, by mouth and picture. It was a large two-story country house, off the beaten path in the province of Champagne, tucked in a forested valley. Champagne, the next province down from Paris in the Île de France, was a region bathed in more blood down through the centuries than any other stretch of real estate in the country. There was the holy site of Reims where Joan of Arc was burned at the stake, where every French monarch was crowned since about 500 A.D. and where every invading army had to march through the rolling hills and dense forests on the way to Paris. These days it was wine-growing country, Bolan knew, where old man Marquis had launched his business in bubbly, which had eventually left the son wealthy to the point of obscenity—and rendered him a soul tortured by his own past tragedy, a raging demon, Bolan suspected, who had created what he could only think of as murder central.

The fires of the Frenchman's hell—Hahmad—were banked for the time being, but Bolan intended his opening move to make him one of the gang, off and running on a mission that, he hoped, would eventually steer him to one of the world's foremost terrorist savages. Any clean sweep was a long way off and at the moment the angle of Bolan's game plan had some holes in it, but he decided to brazen his way straight to Marquis, plug up any gaps with artful persuasion and cold logic when he met face-to-face with the man.

Or so the scam went.

A thirty-minute surveillance of the compound from the western hills, then Bolan had legged it to a roost on the back side of the compound. Fifteen vehicles were parked out front, everything from Renaults and Peugeots to a smattering of SUVs, a limo that he'd seen troop in the party girls. He was togged in a blacksuit for this incursion, the war paint covering his face, neck and hands meant to make him both as near invisible in the night as possible, and freeze the opposition long enough if they spotted him to put them asleep before they pulled hardware or shouted the alarm.

Enough light spilled from several windows, top and bottom, but the shadows thinned out the closer he'd chart his course in from the hedgerows, vineyards and shrub land. It could go to hell once he was inside their lair, but with any luck at all, a malingering stalk around the premises might turn up a roving commando, or he could slip through one of two bottom-floor windows he'd spotted wide open, each with a shock troop and professional girl earning her fee, going at it just inside the frame for his easy disposal of lovebirds.

The soldier decided to hold on for that wandering commando to get it started, but he wouldn't stay put much longer.

Bolan reviewed the setup and mentally walked himself through it again. Special Agent Hardin had scooped him up at Orly—a military flight arranged by Brognola—and the soldier's gear and heavier firepower were now stowed in the large nylon war bag in the trunk of the rental sedan. The vehicle was parked a good mile down a narrow trail in the woods north. Bolan had walked in, using NVD goggles, searching the blackness for sensors, cameras, trip wires and whatever else might alert the commandos they had unwelcome company. According to Hardin, they were a wild bunch who partied the nights away while they waited to be rotated out for the next hunt, or had returned after a foray for R and R. Apparent disdain for high-tech surveillance, or perhaps they didn't want to part with requisite cash that might cut into the orgy funds, nothing other than a sentry or two might be sent out for a walk around the compound.

The intel had come under Justice Department watch by air, satellite and agents hunkered down in the hills with parabolic mikes, so Bolan was banking on it. Apparently the local police also collected their monthly envelope from a Marquis lackey, and with no one within four square miles of the compound, the commandos felt they could squander Marquis's blood money, free of worry from trespassers or tourists traipsing around the countryside. Even with drunken orgies in full swing under the roof, these men were all professionals from elite special forces, the Executioner knew, and they wouldn't prove easy tags, sated from sex and rubber legged from booze or not. If he could prevent it, Bolan wasn't going for the jugular when he went in to make his presence known.

He was there to test the talent, leave a message and sign on as one of the Frenchman's bounty hunting help.

Hardin, left behind in Paris with the soldier's Justice Department credentials and sat link, stated half

the commando force was housed here, with the
newer additions to the killing elite given room and
board in Paris. Here, they were the more experi-
enced pros, Marquis blessing them with perks and
privilege according to age, combat experience in either the past or on missions they'd already undertaken in North Africa. The tranquilizer pistol, a special request from the soldier to John "Cowboy"
Kissinger, Stony Man's ace weaponsmith, was perfect for the occasion to get the ruse off the launching
pad.

Stuffed in a pouch on his hip, Bolan had two
dozen pairs of plastic cuffs and gags to leave them
trussed up, sucking back their own muffled cries and
anger, wondering what the hell had hit them when
they finally woke. There was pepper spray in a slit
for some unforeseen situation—a sneak attack on his
blind side, perhaps, if he was changing clips for the
T-gun—where he could again avoid the use of
deadly force. Just in case, though, the unexpected
hardmen shot up out of nowhere, going for broke,
the soldier had the trusty and reliable Beretta 93-R
in shoulder rigging, the mammoth .44 Magnum Desert Eagle riding high in quick-draw leather on his
hip. For the finale, the M-79 grenade launcher was
strapped around his shoulder, a 40 mm tear gas curtain call down the chute. Two more sense-choking
bombs hung from his webbing, and one time-
delayed canister dangled on his webbing for an inside plant.

Listening to the drumming thump of rock music
from the farthest upstairs room to the west, the sol-

dier palmed the T-gun. They were having quite the good old time in the rock room. An occasional scoping of the shadows behind the rows of curtained doors told Bolan as many as ten to fifteen merrymakers swelled the far room.

The soldier spied the hedgerow reaching out from beside the back patio. Trellises smothered in ivy stretched close enough to the first solitary window of orgy....

It was time to test the talent, send a statement to Dante Marquis that maybe the big cheese needed a little tougher and smarter hunter on board to tighten up the troops. That maybe he was the guy, just the sort of warrior savior who would make his day in the hunt for Hahmad.

Decision made to move out and in from the direction of the trellises, the Executioner was five steps from cover when the shadow eased onto the patio. The commando lit a cigarette, and Bolan figured he was nailed before he even reached first base. Then the orange winking eye moved away in the opposite direction when the smoker turned his head from the stalking path of the soldier.

Bolan lifted the T-gun, cutting the gap to victim number one in swift strides. The Executioner was ready to crash the party, a silent ghost in the night.

One sleeping commando at a time, he told himself, and took up slack on the trigger.

ROBERT "BUCK" PATTERSON liked a party as much as the next guy, but the orgy inside was enough to make him wonder what in the world he'd signed on for when his former commanding officer had come calling a few months back. It was pretty gruesome to see in his mind what he'd been before this bizarre gig, a damn war hero sitting around his North Carolina cabin out in redneck hell, pretty much twiddling his sphincter, divorced, broke and constantly thinking about eating a Beretta sandwich, when what sounded like the deal of the century was hung like all the cash in Vegas before his eyes.

Patterson wasn't so sure now what waited behind door number one, and the old cliché about if it sounded too good to be true burned to mind.

He was a former Green Beret—with covert stints in Noriega's Panama and the Gulf War that never made the papers, reached the ears of any Senate arms committee or decorated him with much-deserved medals—and, by God, he'd earned his bones, figured respect enough was due him whether he walked among the lions or the sheep. The older war dogs in the orgy house, though, seemed to view him as little more than a snot-nosed cherry grunt fresh out of OCS.

Enough was enough.

Moments ago, he had considered going to Colonel Bill "Bull" Dobson, his CO after the Gulf War when they became part of the Special Forces Omega Program, a black-ops ghost machine so classified and buried so deep it would have been easier, he thought, to find the Holy Grail. He had wanted to shake the old war dog's tree, get a few matters ironed out, such as respect due a soldier who'd put in his time and when the hell he might see some action and a payday. But Dobson was drunk out of his gourd, right then working up a sweat with one of the French whores. Any bitching would have to be done much later.

Maybe it was good to be alone, he thought, regroup. Disgusted with circumstance just the same, Patterson took a hefty drag of smoke, stepped across the patio, checking the hills and wondering about the screwy setup, if he'd get his chance to prove himself like the others and fill his pockets and a numbered account with hefty paper. He needed some fresh air to clear his head, get his thoughts together and maybe calm the seething resentment which, if he wasn't careful, would see him march back in there and go Rambo on his new comrades. Maybe he should put the shouldered Beretta 92-F someplace safe, he thought, cool it, see what happened tomorrow. Maybe he should grab one of the whores, get drunk like the others, shoot pool in the parlor room at least. Trouble was, he didn't have their money to piss away because he hadn't been out on a mission yet, pocketing that hundred grand per scumbag terrorist scalp, which most of the others had raked in on previous hunting engagements. They were heroes, conquerors to the Frenchman, while he was the new kid on the block. And like any military unit, covert or otherwise, he knew he'd have to prove himself in combat before he was truly accepted in the brotherhood. Track records didn't mean squat in tomorrow's killing fields, and kicking around the glory days was for losers and wanna-bes.

It was all getting on his nerves. The rock music

pounding out the far window, the drunken laughter and squealing of whores. Say someone with malice of heart was out there, checking out the scene. How would any of them hear a stealthy approach? No one seemed to give a damn about security, not a single camera watching the grounds and perimeter. But, sure enough, Dobson would volunteer one of them when he could catch his breath or pry his lips off the whiskey bottle long enough to march one of them outside and have a look.

Patterson was pitching the smoke away when he thought he spotted a shadow, charging for his blind side. Alarm bells went off in his head, instinct screaming at him that the black thing materializing out of the night was a pro of some kind.

And with definite malice of heart.

Patterson was clawing for his Beretta, a voice somewhere in the back of his head on the verge of assuring him he could beat the shadow, prove himself....

It felt like a bee sting, his hand shooting up to his neck more out of shock than reflex when the night seemed to melt down, shimmering goo filling his eyes, the black world absorbing itself into his brain before it all took him down into a soundless dark abyss.

THE BROODER MIGHT have caught him out in the open if he'd been paying attention to something other than what was eating him up, dark thoughts clearly distracting him until he realized he was marked, too late, then tagged by a shadow in the night. Bolan would take all the help he could get, and between the opposition's arrogance and drunkenness he held the edge, but he wasn't about to let opposing dulled reflexes or their overconfidence infect the cold professional.

The sulking one hit the ground like a stone, out cold in two seconds flat, just like Kissinger had told him. Neck shots then, close to the brain, full dosage speeding upward and blinking out the lights, no fuss.

Sweeping over his first victim, Bolan rolled him on his stomach, plastic cuffs binding his hands behind his back. A thick nylon gag with fat rubber ball was crammed into the mouth, then Bolan dragged him to the hedgerow. It was a trifle more noise than he cared for, shoving the body into bushes, but the combined racket of music and lewd mayhem took care of the problem.

The soldier was up and angling back for the patio, wondering if this was going to be too easy, when a commando-john and lady friend stepped through the doors, both of them looking up and straight his way. The sight of a black-painted specter, boiling out of the night, gun in hand, nearly shrilled out the SOS from the whore. The bottle fell from the commando's hand, Bolan silently cursing, sure the sound of breaking glass would reach the ears of anyone close enough and in halfway sober shape beyond the doors to send the cavalry running. The vented yap of the whore was a microsecond from rifling the air with a long scream when the Executioner zapped her to sleep first. She was tumbling to the patio, the commando digging out his side arm when Bolan drilled the dart into his neck. He was all over them next, pleased to find the bottle had landed in a flower bed, even more relieved to find no armed figures charging out from what appeared to be a dining room beyond the open French doors.

Sweet dreams for them, but Bolan knew he was getting more locked into deadly reality with each takedown.

Three trussed up and wedged in the bushes, and the soldier was at Love for Sale window one in four shakes. A check of the grounds, all alone, and Bolan found he was still just a rolling bogeyman, with two lovebirds inside the frame.

She was purring and cooing in French, straddling Mr. Love Machine, facing the window. Bolan was close enough to reach and touch them as they went at it on the divan, and when the whore opened her eyes, her mouth going wide at the sight of an armed peeper, she nearly mucked the soldier's play.

The commando was fast, combat instinct coupled with the abrupt end to the humping most likely telling him something wasn't right. Bolan almost lost both of them in the next eye blink, the arm whipping back, the commando starting to rise, when Bolan shot his arm out, wadding up a handful of the lady's bleached blond hair before she could fully dismount. The snarling bulldog was twisting around as Bolan rammed the woman's face to his skull to a meaty thwack and sharp grunts. The love tap bought him a precious two seconds, Bolan hauling the couple out the window, dumping them on the ground, entwining them in anything but passion as the commando started to rage back, thrashing and rising. Two taps of the T-gun's trigger, and Bolan quickly bound and gagged them, put them behind to be discovered in their birthday suits.

The clock was winding down fast now, the soldier deciding to pick up the pace, no longer concerned about hiding bodies. How many more could he take out before he turned the house into a gas chamber? He decided to push his luck. The fatter the scorecard, the better with which to impress Monsieur Marquis one Colonel Rance Pollock could deliver the winning home run when the team was behind.

Moving on, watching his six, the Executioner peeked in on the next union. They were on the bed, fifteen feet downrange, candlelight throwing dancing shadows over their heaving shapes, Mr. Romance whispering sweet French nothings over her face. Two hours under, Kissinger had told him, and Bolan put them to sleep, one dart each to the arm. They twitched, flopped around then went limp together. Bolan left them on top of each other, unwilling to risk entering the room, lose any more precious time or risk the sudden entrance of a few high-priced damsels or drunken commandos who stumbled into the wrong room.

He slipped silently between a thin break in another hedgerow, tallying the sleeping beauties, down to seven shots. Crouching beside a sliding glass door, the thunder of heavy metal rock overhead, and Bolan discovered six commandos had hobbies other than hedonism.

It was a sprawling entertainment room, two pool

tables, a bank of video games, with wet bar and Jacuzzi whirlpool for twelve or more. Everything a commando fresh off a killing expedition would need to wind down. The four commandos, Bolan observed, were sipping beer and shooting pool, the closest targets to entry. In the far corner, two more of the Frenchman's hunters were donning spaceman helmets, whooping it up as they worked the mounted plastic machine guns in a frenzy from the arcade, wrapped in childlike ecstasy over Dante's contribution to popular culture.

Put six more down, and the soldier figured close to half would come around with what Kissinger described as the mother of all paralyzing hangovers.

Time to give new meaning to brazen, the soldier decided. Not surprisingly he found the door unlocked, slid it open enough to squeeze through, the T-gun up and chugging. Two were dropping, hands digging at the steel missiles impaled in their necks, when three and four spotted the big invader and went for shouldered Berettas. Surging ahead, the soldier pumped out the sleep projectiles, the helmets breaking away from the fantasy fun and games just in time to find their comrades heaped on the floor.

Reality check for two more, and they were pitching next in tandem, heads wrenched from helmets, whatever 3-D violence had them so engrossed blinking out to the sleep of babes.

Bolan sensed it was almost time to give it up, wondering if he should just let them lie and exit. He listened to the revelry still in high gear above, checked the short flight of steps leading out of the playroom for incoming. Alone again, the soldier swiftly moved to bind up the six, hoping his luck held long enough to fatten the scorecard.

WILLIAM "BULL" DOBSON was beyond frustration, burning inside as he tried to put out of his mind the image of the whore upstairs. Was that suppressed laughter he'd seen on her face? Mockery? Loathing? Cooing out something in broken English, he recalled, trying to patronize him? Hell, it used to happen that way when he was married, too, drunk and disinterested in the same woman and same routine, always thinking he just needed something new, and younger. Damn near a fifth under the belt, with the best-looking twenty-something Parisian beauty he could have conjured up in his wildest fantasy and there he was, seething and sulking, worried the bitch might spread the word to the other whores who in turn would start the floating rumor...

The wobble left his legs as anger mounted, and long strides took him down the hall, past the so-called feast room where he found Heller was heaping up a plate of shellfish and beef. Not even bothering to use tongs, he just dug in with greedy hands.

Dobson could understand barbarian ways in the field, but lack of manners and consideration for others on the part of a former Green Beret under these circumstances was unforgivable. Dobson balked in the archway at the vulgar sight, briefly considered ripping Heller a new one, then caught himself before he erupted. Taking out his frustration on a soldier who used to be under his command during the

Omega days, especially in the face of his own failure, could come back to haunt him.

The game room then, shoot a little pool, clear some of the whiskey sludge out of his head and maybe he could try again later. Where there was a will, there was always a way, and he'd find it, whatever it took, even if she had to work longer hours.

The ungodly racket above grated his nerves even more, his teeth grinding, rage mounting as he knew the younger commandos were all systems go.

Oh, but when he was a young soldier, he thought, could kick ass all day and play all night. Where had the old Bull gone? Was he dead forever? he wondered. Would the moniker he'd earned, in the bedroom and leading soldiers in battle and black ops, become the brunt of snickered remarks behind his back?

Well, he was still in charge of the compound, with a rep to maintain, and if he wanted to end the party, even out of sheer spite, he could pull rank. He considered doing just that when—

He froze, blinking from the top of the steps to the game room, wondering if he'd had so much to drink he wasn't hallucinating, one of the first sure signs the d.t.'s were right around the corner.

The big invader, camoued with black greasepaint, was darting from the bodies of six of his guys.

No mistake, it was happening, Dobson realized, adrenaline released into his blood, lifting the fog in his brain.

The intruder was binding their hands with plastic cuffs, armed with two holstered side arms, but ob-

viously his commandos were still breathing from
some nonlethal touch. So what the hell was he doing
there? Who was he? Impossible he could have just
come up on six of the world's finest elite commandos, American or otherwise, taken them down, one
by one...

The outrage, from whore to invader, was too
much to bear. He went for his weapon, then found
his hand grabbing at a shoulder empty of holster and
weapon. Chalk up one more slap in the face. Just
not his night—so far—but he felt the commando
dagger nestled on his lower shin. It would be sweet,
salvaging his rep, carving up this ballsy SOB, head
to toe, getting answers while watching him bleed out
and blubber for the pain to stop.

Dobson bounded down the steps, the intruder rising from beside the pool table, on full alert now, the
sneaky bastard plucking a weapon from the floor.
The ex-Omega Special Forces colonel felt all the
frustration and rage burst in one lightning flash.
There was enough raw, ugly emotion and bad mem-
ory to put speed enough to cut the gap in two heart-
beats.

Dobson told himself he wasn't about to lose this
round, then went airborne, grunting on impact with
the invader, but it was pain laced with satisfaction,
and he knew the night wouldn't prove a total descent
into shame after all.

The old Bull was back.

CHAPTER THREE

How he first missed the runaway train that ran him down and knocked him airborne he couldn't quite say. Bolan could venture a few guesses, provided, of course, he survived the blitz. Figure the thundering rock music covering the human rhino's charge, his haste to bind up the six commandos consuming too much time and attention, or the slightest drop in vigilance to his surroundings.

It didn't matter now, for damn sure, knowing better all along, but hindsight and second-guessing were never part of the warrior's program. He was locked into a problem that could cripple—or kill—his entire mission before it was off the ground.

The soldier was flung across the table on impact, falling over the rail, jarred to the bone, the T-gun flying from his grasp. Stars obscuring his sight, he hammered the floor on his shoulders, grunting as fresh waves of pain tore through every nerve ending, another wall of white light blasted in his eyes. The human tornado seemed to fall straight from the ceiling next, two-hundred-plus pounds of fury landing on him before he could roll away, stand and fight back.

The Executioner made out the ugly steel teeth on the serrated edge of the commando dagger, poised above the brute's head and coming down, the snarling cyclone angling the point of entry for his shoulder, it seemed, looking to pin him like a bug to a board instead of going for the straight kill.

With 1001 hand-to-hand engagements behind him, where the soldier had come out the other side, instinct took over. Bolan thrust up his forearm, blocked and swept away an arm that felt made of pure steel. One chance, a microsecond was all he had, and Bolan made the most of it, the pepper spray can out and loosing a cloud that hit the human rhino square in the eyes, nose and mouth at point-blank range. It turned the tide, the brute growling, shaking his head.

Blinded and burned, he was rising from his straddle, lending Bolan one last window of opportunity. The soldier folded back a leg, then slammed a boot heel off the hardman's jaw. He lurched upright, Bolan jumping to his feet. Spotting the T-gun a few short feet away, the brute was growling curses, surging back, blade out and sweeping, when the Executioner scooped up the T-gun and chugged a dart into his adversary's neck. He wasn't sure the human tornado would fall, shuddering a second or two longer than Kissinger's allotted time frame, then he wilted at the knees, joining his sleeping commandos.

Changing clips for the tranquilizer gun, the Executioner listened for any abrupt halt in laughter upstairs that would signal the racket in the playpen had sounded the alarm.

Still going strong. Or were they pro enough to simply not alter the routine, slyly on the move to check out the ruckus in the game room?

Time to bolt, either way, but the soldier decided to risk a check on the hall leading out of the game room for a search ready to clear his exit of any hunters who wanted to chase him into the night. On the move, he watched for shadows in the doorway, senses electrified as a new burst of adrenaline sharpened him to a razor's edge, nose homed in for the slightest whiff of sweat, cigarette, booze.

The hall was vacant of hostiles in both directions, the party still grinding on, noise and soused brains the only things, he surmised, that kept the wolves at bay after the din of his close encounter of the worst kind. Intel couldn't confirm the layout, and Bolan had no intention of trooping through the house for a clean sweep, but it looked to the soldier as if there were no way down from up top other than the two sets of steps on opposite ends. As good as it would get for the curtain call.

He placed the canister on the floor, checked his watch, set the timer for one minute.

His head and body a swiveling compass, the Executioner retraced his steps through the game room, found the way out clear and regained his original roost with ten seconds and counting to spare.

The soldier took the M-79, sighted on a set of double doors on the balcony and sent the projectile flying. The impact fuse was touched off as it burrowed through glass, the noxious cloud erupting, sweeping the party room and creating a racket that was anything but euphoric.

Bolan didn't linger to listen to the startled cries, but spared a glimpse over his shoulder at the shadows flailing in stampede as the soldier melted into the darkness.

ANDRÉ DUCLOUX DIDN'T appreciate being relegated to what he considered errand-boy duty. He was a shooter, a killer, a Legionnaire, not a messenger service.

He was guiding the Mercedes down the main trail for the compound, kicking around resentful thoughts while getting the message from Marquis worded just right in his head. He wasn't happy, Marquis was enraged and Ducloux was coming out to fling some choice language at the commandos, remind them in no uncertain terms what they were getting paid for.

There was anxiety and paranoia back in Paris to spare the greatest tyrants of history, he thought, Marquis holed up in his office suite all night, ranting all of a sudden, according to Anglerre, about some conspiracy swirling dark storm clouds over the operation. Bogeymen, he thought, everything from treacherous Interpol agents to the American FBI and Justice Department on the prowl and eager to swarm the dark citadel. The Algerian fiasco was the primary source of fear, and Ducloux had been seconds away from asserting himself, warning Marquis it was perhaps best to lie low for a while, even slip the commandos out of the country until they discovered the identities of all these shadows the entrepreneur was seeing all over France.

Ducloux had helped in killing the Interpol agent's two thugs, then shoving them through a meat grinder at a butcher shop they used for just such disposal work. He believed someone else, such as a flunky on the payroll, should have been roused from sleep in the dead of night and sent out here to check on the commandos and tighten up the ship instead of one of the man's top shooters. The more he thought about this inconvenience, the more it galled him. But Marquis was insistent in his demands, and Ducloux knew better than to chomp the hand that doled out the fat paycheck. The all-night parties at the compound were notorious for their debauchery, something he could appreciate, since he wasn't above indulging in sins of the flesh. This night, Marquis wanted all whores sent packing from the premises. Marquis wanted the commandos with clear heads, bodies fit for duty in the morning. Marquis, as far as Ducloux was concerned, might as well have asked these libertines to move the Pyrenees.

Still, he had a strong message to relay. The following day a multioperation would be launched, the most ambitious hunt to date. If there was so much legal heat on the scorching way, Ducloux had to question the wisdom behind such audacity.

He was guiding the Mercedes off the trail, out into open field when he saw the pandemonium. He hit the brakes, the wheels sluicing over soft earth, his frame lurching in the seat as angry disbelief dropped over him like a wall.

He couldn't make out the shouted words from the distance, but the manner in which the shadows of commandos and whores were stumbling all over the place, some kneeling and hacking their guts out around the motor pool, warned him the compound had been attacked.

And why were perhaps ten of the commandos staggering around with hands bound behind their backs? If this was a raid, where were all the flashing lights and lawmen?

Ducloux tromped on the gas. He was almost afraid to discover the truth, but sometimes not knowing was even worse, and could get a man killed.

FEAR WAS A CANCER. Once caught, the disease spread rapidly, eating a man alive, mind, body and soul. He'd seen its ravages on rival businessmen who had conquered their respective worlds only to lose them for one reason or another. Bad investments, shady or illegal deals, buyouts or wives who had caught them with mistresses or prostitutes and trooped out a feeding frenzy of legal sharks who only wanted forty to fifty percent of whatever was left to devour.

For men of power there were fates worse than death.

Oh, and he'd seen fear become terror and terror turn to despair when the powerful fell and their worlds vanished before their eyes. Treachery could follow, as fear motivated desperate acts, or the terrified simply caved to despair and committed suicide.

Fear by itself could be a killer.

Dante Marquis wasn't there yet, but he could feel the level of fear rising all around him. The fear was starting to affect his mind, putting him on edge, making him wonder if he was seeing things—shadows with guns—wherever he went. He couldn't sleep, and it was all he could do to try to get his thoughts in order, keep a lid on the boiling anxiety in his belly. He had enemies—he was sure of it—wondering whom he could trust and who might be coming to take him down, especially now in light of the Algerian disaster.

And the phone call from Ducloux confirmed his worst fears that the fissure was cracking beneath the foundation of his realm. As incredible as it sounded, the compound had been hit—by one man. Not necessarily a hit, or even a raid, in the classic sense of a covert military strike, but more like some message that his world could be toppled whenever the attacker felt like turning up the heat to a lethal touch. And whoever the attacker, he was a ghost in the night, striking then vanishing without a trace, which left more questions hanging still. Who? Why?

Why now?

"How is it possible? Are you sure?"

He took the brandy from Anglerre, gulped half of the liquid, then dropped in the leather chair behind his desk. He looked around his study, staring into the dark shadows of the corners, pondering the dilemma.

"You do not believe Ducloux? Do you think he would exaggerate and spout foolish fantasy?"

"I did not say that," Anglerre said, balking at the rising anger in Marquis's voice. "It just seems to me a wild fabrication from a bunch of drunken whoremongers. They gave the report—Ducloux is just a messenger receiving secondhand information. They are all elite commandos, so no one man, no matter how good he is, could have done what we are told."

"Ducloux was told 'one' man snuck in, a big man in black war paint, some stalking silent shadow who, it appears, put down half of our commandos at the compound with some sort of tranquilizer gun, trussed them up like cattle, then chased the rest out into the night with tear-gas bombs. A professional."

"Who?"

"How would I know!" Marquis snapped. "I have the Justice Department, the FBI snooping into my affairs. I am told my phones are tapped, perhaps our businesses bugged even though we sweep the building and my château every other day. I have Interpol agents on my payroll who are not content with their lot and who may be seeking to undermine our operation, feeling heat and their own nerves or anger and seeking to talk and bail to save their own miserable hides. Perhaps one of the commandos has a past enemy they neglected to mention who is hellbent on dogging them to the ends of the earth as badly as I want my own enemy."

"But if that was true, why put them to sleep, embarrass them?"

"Yes, and not just kill them outright."

"If we were found out by the American FBI or Justice Department, if they had concrete evidence against us, there would have been a raid, arrests. What happened makes no sense."

Marquis looked up at the camera monitoring the lobby, half expecting a squad of armed FBI agents to storm the horseshoe desk and corral the security guard, another former Legionnaire, into custody. He polished off the drink, held out the glass for Anglerre to fetch him another round.

"Under the circumstances," Anglerre said, heading for the wet bar, "do you think we should still proceed with the two-prong incursion, what would be our largest and most ambitious operation yet? And with the San Francisco situation so tenuous…"

"You tell me! We have sightings of the monster in both Tunisia and San Francisco. Another Padre Pio act, I am sure, using ringers, aware he is being hunted, smoking out our men, laying ambushes, turning our own contacts against us. Who can I trust? We have this bastard, Colonel Ayoub, breaking it off in my ass and who knows how much he has betrayed me. We have nervous Interpol agents and now we have some shadow threat in our own backyard, humiliating the best commandos money can buy. The whole world is suddenly against us. I ask you, Anglerre, are we men or are we mice?"

Anglerre seemed to consider something, then poured the brandy, nodding. "You would risk everything, then, in your vendetta against the Syrian."

"I believe I was clear on that earlier. What, you

feel the ship sinking, you want off, you want a life raft?''

"No. I am with you.''

"And if the ship sinks?''

"I am sure we can both find a way to swim safely to shore.''

"With sharks in the water?''

"Sharks bleed, too. Sometimes the predator has been known to become the prey.''

Marquis was taking the snifter when the phone rang. He snorted. "Now what? More bad news?''

He plucked up the receiver. "Yes.''

"I understand you're looking for a few good men.''

He sat up, ice walking down a spine going rigid at the strange voice. The voice spoke decent French, but there was something cold and menacing just beneath the tone he would have recognized in any language. "Who is this?''

"I'm the man of the hour maybe,'' the strange voice answered, this time in English. "I'm the man who just ended the fun and games at the compound. You know, those guys really need to tighten up. There's a time to play, a time for business. They made it so easy, it makes me wonder if they do find the Syrian they'll be up to the task of taking him out. I don't think you're getting your money's worth, Dante.''

"Who are you? What do you want?''

"A job. Just so happens I'm in the neighborhood. See you in a few minutes.''

"Wait!" Marquis slammed down the phone, leaped to his feet, stare fixed on the hanging camera.

"It was him, our mystery attacker. He says he's coming into the building. He says he wants a job."

Anglerre was reaching for his shouldered Beretta when Marquis said, "No. Calm down. He is to be let in. Meet him at the elevator. Frisk him thoroughly. There he is."

Marquis heard the exchange as Anglerre went to the phone, dialed the security guard. He saw a big, dark-haired man in a black trench coat, the stranger going to the desk like some stalking lion, radiating confidence and control. Marquis took the remote and adjusted the lens for a close-up. The face was handsome in a menacing kind of way, he thought, then noted the eyes. There was death in those eyes, the same windows to the soul he'd seen on the other commandos who had been on the dishing-out side of violence in combat.

"He's armed."

Something about the eyes, Marquis thought, harder, colder than the other commandos, as if he'd survived the fires of his own personal hell and couldn't be touched by any power on earth. Marquis wasn't sure if he liked what he saw or not.

"He's to leave the weapons at the front desk, then he can come up. He says he wants a job. I suppose it wouldn't hurt to hear his sales pitch."

MARQUIS INTERNATIONAL was tucked at the edge of Montmartre in a ritzy quarter of the Eighteenth Arrondissement. The elder Marquis had made one stab at moving into the hotel business, and the single establishment to his credit had been redone by his sole heir, inside and out, top to bottom, every trace of French craftsmanship, all the trimmings to lure in the tourists gone forever. It was now a seventeen-floor glass, steel and granite monolith, the workforce, legitimate and otherwise, having easy access to any number of fine restaurants, clubs, bistros, museums or, if so inclined, Place Pigalle, where the next Monet could be found painting live nudes.

The City of Lights was an hour or so away from rousing to an early-morning swarm of cars and tourists, so Bolan didn't have any trouble finding a spot to park his sedan near the Boulevard de Clichy, the Parisian version of Times Square. The soldier wasn't there for the sights, and his stay in Paris would only be as long as it took to hop aboard the Frenchman's killing machine.

The Executioner was in the building now, off the elevator and greeted by a lean hardman who put him through a second lengthy pat-down.

"Rance Pollock," Bolan said, hands up as the man patted him down, clearly checking for wires, then digging into the pockets of his topcoat, which the guard in the lobby had neglected.

The man pulled out the bogus Virginia driver's license, passport, examined both in grim silence. The soldier was covered by an elaborate ruse designed by Stony Man Farm. It reached all the way to the State Department, via some cyber planting with a little help from Brognola's contacts, his military background created by Aaron "the Bear"

Kurtzman, covering all bases. Bolan had no doubt it would pass muster when they ran a background check. He got the ball rolling.

"Colonel Pollock, formerly of the United States Special Forces. And you are…?"

"Anglerre. Formerly of the French Foreign Legion."

"I thought they went out of business when you guys got booted out of Algeria."

The smile was flashed, but Bolan saw in the eyes he'd touched a resentful nerve. "With me."

Anglerre kept the ID, silently led Bolan down the wide hallway, past the empty reception bay and through a pair of massive double doors. He found Marquis sitting alone at a round table in an office stripped of any ostentatious trimmings. The Frenchman was a pencil-thin carbon copy of his hardman, but with a crop of wavy black hair, matching turtleneck, sans the hardware. Anglerre handed the ID to Marquis, who gave them a brief perusal, then dumped them on the table.

"Says he used to a Green Beret colonel," Anglerre told Marquis, then stepped off to the side, folding his hands in front of him.

Marquis looked Bolan up and down, then held his hands out. "I'm listening."

"I'll get right to it. I've been in and out of Paris for a few weeks, checking out the sights, hearing things, thinking about my future. I sort of like it here, good food, nice parks, the women…"

"More tourists we hardly need."

"I'm no tourist. By now you know that."

"A display, then, at the compound to show me my people have gotten sloppy?"

"You're looking for Mohammed Hahmad, who murdered your wife and children. You've hired what you think are the best commandos your money can buy to track him down and bring back his head for your mantel. Maybe they are the best, maybe they aren't."

"And maybe you are the best?"

"I didn't say that."

"How do you come by all this information, saying it is even true."

Bolan smiled. "One of your bounty hunters had a loose tongue. A German, GSG-9 commando specifically," Bolan said, watched as Marquis threw Anglerre a look. "Believe his name was Max Schneider. Hey, your boys, they like to party, no secret there. Old Max, he got careless one night at a local watering hole. Twenty-something beers later, a hundred grand, he said, you shell out for every terrorist they take down on one of your black ops. Bring back film for your private screening as proof they earned their francs. But you want Hahmad, only the Syrian keeps on ticking and keeps on sticking it in your craw."

"And what is your story?"

"No story. I'm cash strapped. Maybe I'm looking for my little slice of paradise for my golden years. What I did at the compound was my way of introducing myself."

"Yes, I've heard all about what happened," Marquis said. "Impressive, I must confess. It would appear I need to lay out some new ground rules concerning business and pleasure.''

"A little high-tech surveillance out there might go a long way in preventing any more incidents.''

"Yes. A matter I need to address. It's their compound—they have seen fit to do as they please with their own security.''

"Looks like you need some changes in the program.''

"And perhaps a changing of the guard is in order?''

Bolan smiled. "Something to think about.''

Marquis tapped a slender finger on his chin, Bolan feeling the full weight of the man's stare as he mulled over his own thoughts. "I could sit here and say this is a trap, that perhaps you are FBI or Justice Department. Looking, how do you say, to smoke me out. Entrap me.''

"You have my ID, the way Max told it you can check out any potential recruits with one phone call.''

"Max had a big mouth.''

"I'm not Max, Monsieur Marquis. I'm here to sign on. I need money, but I also like the action. No hard sale, I can get the job done. That's that. Whatever the deal is, I see no evil. Ask yourself this. You ever hear of any G-man who could pull off what I did?''

Marquis grunted. "This is all very interesting, and very unusual. Okay. My associate and I will discuss your future.''

"Don't keep me in suspense. If I have to sit by

the phone too long, I can always sell my services somewhere else they might be more appreciated.''

''It's not a question of appreciation.''

''Security, I understand.''

''Then you understand that if I hire you on and you are not who you claim to be, your apparent martial talent will not save you.''

''That's understood going in.''

''How can I reach you?''

Bolan gave the Frenchman the number to an unsecured cell phone he'd brought for just this anticipated moment. ''Like I said, I'm not the patient kind.''

''By midmorning you will hear from me. We'll hold on to these for now,'' Marquis said, nodding at the ID. ''We'll be in touch, you can pick up your guns on the way out.''

Bolan nodded, unable to read anything beyond their cold scrutiny. They would discuss it when he left, and if they didn't bite his sales pitch he'd find another way. A few hours on hold, waiting for the green light, and he needed to touch base with SAC Hardin anyway.

The Executioner left them alone to consider his immediate future. He had expected more grilling, but sometimes the direct approach, with as few words as possible, worked best. A man in Marquis's position wouldn't be impressed with long-winded sales pitches. One way or another, Bolan determined he was in the game. Either on board or from the shadows, Marquis and his murdering commandos were going down for the count.

"JUST KEEP UP the surveillance," Bolan told Hardin over his secured cell phone. "I'm hoping to be leaving town for a little while."

"And that's it, keep me in the dark. The Lone Ranger rides off into the sunset."

Bolan understood the man's frustration, but the usual legal channels weren't going to stand up against ruthless killers and a man who had the money and connections to buy or murder his way out of any indictments. And the French had proved they would fight extradition, homegrown criminals or otherwise. They had a recent track record for thumbing their noses directly at American authorities who landed on their soil and started demanding they hand over this or that fugitive on the lam.

Clearly Marquis was tagged now as running his own dirty little war, the list of criminal charges adding up the more they learned about the man. And Hardin had just stated the cold facts they had enough to arrest Marquis and his commandos.

"I'll be in touch, Agent Hardin."

"Yeah, and you appreciate my help."

"Look, you're not happy about being cut out of the loop, I understand."

"Oh, now you're sensitive to my personal and professional feelings. Look, this guy's running an ongoing criminal enterprise, shipping out a team of murderers who could incite some international incident that might see Paris become ground zero for every terrorist export east of Pakistan."

"Let's try it my way for now."

"I don't even know what your way is, Belasko."

"Hold down the fort, keep an eye on Marquis. I left my sat link with you, which means there's a good chance I'll be coming back."

"I can't wait. And if I have any problems with you cowboying the action, I can go and bitch to Brognola and all my griping will fall on deaf ears."

"I need you to watch the store." Bolan checked his watch. Beyond the balcony of the apartment rental, a Justice Department safehouse, it was a congested nightmare of drivers leaning on horns up and down rue d'Arcole in the Latin Quarter. It was pushing 0900 hours, and Bolan was growing more anxious by the moment, willing the other cell phone to trill.

"I've got problems on my end, or do you care to hear about them?"

"I'm listening."

"You know the world headquarters for Interpol is right here in Paris. The French have been using Interpol like it's their own CIA for years."

"Meaning you're on to whoever's feeding Marquis what he needs to keep it going."

"We're getting close. You know, without the Justice Department or the FBI's NCIC, Interpol might be just a small fish in the pond. Problem is, once they get their hands on our intel, it always seems to slip through their fingers to the bad guys we're looking to bag."

"The dirt spreads further out to our people."

"Maybe, we're not sure yet. So, while you do your thing, whatever that is, I'll be here doing some weeding. I guess you checking in is all the professional courtesy I'll get."

The cell phone trilled from the coffee table. "It's business, Agent Hardin."

"Yours."

"You said it."

"And the less I know the better, or maybe if you told me what you're really up to you'd have to kill me."

Bolan didn't expect to get into a pissing contest, found himself growing irritated with Hardin's attitude. "Don't tempt me."

"Is that supposed to be funny?"

"I'll be in touch." Bolan severed the connection before Hardin could grouse some more, scooped up the cell phone, punched on. "Yeah."

Anglerre said, "Meet me in front of the Church of Saint Peter. Do you know where that is?"

"I'll find it."

"One hour."

CHAPTER FOUR

The Executioner received the silent treatment from Anglerre when he was picked up by the Mercedes limo. Just a driver and the former Legionnaire for the rendezvous, but it was impossible for Bolan to tell who else might be up front, with black-tinted glass, stem to stern, shielding passengers.

Bolan was blindfolded as soon as he was ushered into the well by Anglerre, relieved of his side arms next, the ex-Legionnaire taking his war bag. He heard Anglerre unzip the bag, rummage through hardware that Bolan expected to at least elicit a remark, a skeptical grunt. Nothing.

The soldier let the silence drag, skipped the routine of spookdom, which, under similar circumstances, dictated the hostage mentally mark off turns, gauge miles and time best he could to later retrace the route to wherever the abductee was taken. The soldier believed if they meant to kill him he would already be dead.

Or maybe not. Maybe they were driving him out to the remote countryside for some sadistic routine meant to make him sing long and loud before they shot him in the head. His hands were free, at least, a definite plus that kept hope alive. But if he sensed bad vibes during the ride, he would rip off the blindfold while going for Anglerre in one motion.

End of game.

If it went that way, the Executioner would burn down Marquis's operation in Paris, storm the palace, an invading one-man army.

Twenty minutes or so later he could feel them gather speed, somewhere now on open road outside Paris. He heard the clack of a lighter, whiffed the smoke as Anglerre fired up. Bolan sensed the ex-Legionnaire was at ease, but kept the spring coiled in his guts, Anglerre directly across on the seat facing him, a three-foot lunge to the man's throat.

"You're awfully quiet, Colonel Pollock. I expected twenty questions, a show of righteous indignation you Americans are famous for in my country."

"You've been dealing with too many tourists who can't speak perfect French in perfect French restaurants."

"I deal with soldiers, Colonel."

Who had proved themselves less than perfect, he thought, in every sense. "I can assume, then, I passed the test."

"With flying colors."

"You make it sound like a dirty thing."

"You checked out." A pause, then, "Almost too good to be true."

The radar screen for trouble began to blip in Bolan's head, his guts knotting up with tension. "Am I in or out, Anglerre?"

"I discussed the matter about bringing a new man aboard with Monsieur Marquis. Pros and cons, the brazen manner in which you appear to have ingratiated yourself to my employer. You have talent—that much is obvious. I also think you clever, perhaps devious, and to the extreme. Since I'm in charge of recruitment, I was against bringing you in."

Bolan cut a mean smile. "Always good to know who my friends are."

"You have no friends here in Paris—let us get that straight. Understand, my employer is under a great deal of stress. I am concerned about his judgment these days."

"Times are tough all over. I've got my own problems, and I told you I'm not a patient guy. In or out?"

"Our background check hit a wall when our people traced certain operations in your dossier that were classified."

"Black ops. Assassination and sabotage by operatives of a democratic government aren't sound bites you'll hear about over the evening news."

"You seem to have all the right answers."

"When you're backed up by the truth, the answers come easy. You never answered my question."

"Quite the array of hardware."

"I'm a soldier. I came prepared."

"Really? You assumed a lot. Mini-Uzis, a Heckler & Koch MP-5 subgun that can be fitted with a silencer. Three dozen grenades in a variety of disabling capabilities, not to mention the assortment for the launcher you must have used on the compound. Garrote, a rather nasty commando knife. I didn't even bother to count all the clips. I'm curious. How did you manage to slip into a country with some of the toughest customs in the world with enough firepower to field a small army?''

"You're kidding, right, Anglerre?"

"I'm very serious, Colonel. As head of security, you can be assured I am deadly serious.''

"I came in by Marseilles, which, as you know, is one of the largest narcotics ports of entry in the world. For the right price you could smuggle in a nuclear reactor down there. Marseilles is a sieve for every pirate and smuggler who has the will to make the way, but I'm sure you know that.''

"Your passport was not stamped.''

"I came in by boat from Morocco, a friend of a friend. What's the problem? I did a lot of dirty deeds in a lot of lousy countries for the Special Forces during my black-ops stint. I have a few CIA pals who owe me favors, one of which happened to be in Marseilles. I arranged delivery through him. Diplomatic pouch.''

"Which would require forged paperwork, evasive dancing around the usual legitimate channels.''

"So it would.''

A long pause, Anglerre snorting, grunting. "Okay. For now I will accept things as they appear. To answer your question, you're hired.''

"How about the blindfold?''

"It stays.''

"I'm hired, you don't like it and you don't trust me. I gotcha."

"Then we understand each other. Just in case you turn out to be a hassle we do not need in the organization...well, you're on a need-to-know probationary period. You will do what you are told, when you are told. Are we clear?"

"Clear as ice."

"Sit back, relax. It will be the last time you will have the chance to unwind. Provided you even return from where you are going. No, that is not a threat. We just lost six men on an operation, and, despite what you saw last night, life for our commandos is not one big grab-ass orgy of fun and games."

"I know something about risk. And I'm not here for the good times."

"You want money, you want action, the former is guaranteed only by performance and proof. The latter could turn out to be more than you bargained for."

"I don't like repeating myself, Anglerre. Once more, I didn't come this far to cut and run when the storm hits."

Anglerre chuckled. "Then I look forward to a weather report."

Whatever that meant, and Bolan sat in silence, hardly relaxed. On edge, he was waiting for the lethal punch line, wondering if he wasn't marked already, lured in by smooth talk, all the brittle welcome-to-the-team bit. Despite himself, he marked time while considering his own pros and cons. It was thumbs-up, or so it appeared, which only opened the gates to a new hell. He would be working, killing alongside professionals he had humiliated the previous night, but that was the least of his worries. There was only one commando who had stood in his way long enough to maybe have gotten a good look, file away particulars that would betray Bolan as the party crasher. Even with black war paint, there were the eyes, the build, features that a seasoned commando would recall with all the discerning eye of a Gold Shield detective.

Stung professional pride might unleash another dimension of grief, but Bolan was taking each second as it came, now more than ever, prepared to meet any threat with lightning lethal force. Wherever he was going—North Africa, he assumed—he would be cut off from any contact with Brognola, the Farm and Hardin. On his own, then, surrounded in some remote hellhole by a group of killers who might turn on him for any one of several reasons, there would be no one to watch his back but himself. The usual, yes, when he wasn't on a mission with the other Stony Man warriors, but this time he had sought out and freely signed a pact with the devil, grooming some degree of shaky trust along the way, intent on proving his mettle soon in an undetermined killing field, but armed with a personal agenda that could turn around and blow up in his face any second.

Instinct warned Bolan his troubles had only just begun.

And with the tentacles of his power reaching all

the way to the top of Interpol or beyond, Marquis might have already smoked him out as a ringer. The soldier had been aware he would leave himself about as vulnerable as he could recall, but he was taking this ride to the end of the line, Hahmad and his terrorist organization the first-prize trophy.

One minute, one battle, one savage at a time, he told himself.

Roughly forty-five minutes later they slowed. After another short distance, they stopped and Anglerre said, ''You can take off the blindfold.''

Bolan did, and the man handed him back his side arms.

''Grab your bag and get out.''

The small airfield, he discovered, was cut into a forested valley. One large hangar stood at the far end of the lone runway, next to what appeared to be a small office. Camou netting was draped over the hangar, and Bolan took in their ride to destination unknown.

It looked a scaled-down version of the American C-130, a black-painted turboprop, lighter load in terms of troops and equipment, but built for speed, Bolan assumed. Marquis, according to his intel, owned a private fleet of choppers, executive jets and twin-engine planes, an airport on the outskirts of Paris, near an industrial park. He was in covert country, the Frenchman's bastardization of the Hercules transport and clandestine airfield nowhere on record. As good a place, Bolan thought, to dispose of problems.

War bag in hand, the soldier was out the door,

squinting as he adjusted his eyes to the bright lance of sunlight when he spotted the previous night's near fatal encounter rolling his way.

"This is him, huh, the fucking new guy?"

Anglerre was smiling, but the mood felt wrong to Bolan as he stood his ground, gaze narrowed, Mr. Friendly bobbing his head, checking out the FNG. The shoulder-holstered Beretta was a new addition since the party.

"This would be Rance Pollock, one of yours from the Special Forces."

"So you told me. Remains to be seen if he's one of mine, mister."

"Meet Colonel Dobson. He's in charge, and he can fill you in from here. Bon voyage, and good luck, Pollock," Anglerre told Bolan, wheeled, then hopped inside the limo.

The sudden departure put Bolan more on edge as he felt his heart pounding, Dobson pulling up, face-to-face now, drilling the FNG with a point-blank measuring. The file on Dobson out of Fort Bragg and State had all the t's crossed and i's dotted, which meant the truth was buried beneath all the praise and glitter of a sterling service record. Commendations and medals, from Vietnam to the Gulf War, the record vanished into limbo a few years back, a dark void with deletions all over classified material. The intel package from Brognola on Dobson filled in the blanks; the former Green Beret colonel had run a black-ops assassination squad that specialized in hunting down major drug traffickers and smaller terror links in the chain to hydras like Hahmad.

Head bobbing again, Dobson held out his hand. He wasn't sure how to read the moment, wondering if the man recognized him, expecting a sucker punch, but Bolan reached out and took the strong grip.

"Let's go step into my office, Pollock. I'll give you a quick heads-up," Dobson said, leading Bolan toward the hangar. "We're wheels-up in sixty minutes, so you'll get the full brief on the way."

Silently Bolan matched Dobson's long strides, closing on the hangar, the hair standing up on the back of his neck all of a sudden. It was too easy too soon, the soldier certain Dobson was putting on an act. Something in Dobson's march, his silence, and the soldier was poised for an ambush as the ex-colonel opened a door at the hangar, beckoned him to go in first. Keeping up appearances that all was well where he was concerned, Bolan stepped into the hangar. The Executioner was giving his surroundings a quick search, turning, when the fist slammed into his jaw.

Tunisia

HERMANN BRAUN LOOSED a stream of profanity in his native tongue when he read the first few lines of the new orders from Paris. Leave it to a Frenchman, he thought, one with no military background, no less, to get cold feet at the eleventh hour. They were going to be stalled, sweet bloody revenge thrown on the back burner as he skimmed the orders again,

trying to focus on the words but seeing nothing but
the red haze of his rage. He ranted for a full half
minute, flailing the fax paper around, the others staring back at him as if he'd lost his mind.

One of the Brits snatched the orders out of his
hand. "In English, mate, since we're all brothers in
arms here. I know you're bloody good and pissed,
but we lost comrades, too, and want to carve the
camel jockeys up every bit as bad as you. Get hold
of yourself. You're supposed to be a professional."

"A simple skinning of Ayoub alive would not
satisfy me."

The detailed sat pics came off the fax modem of
the sat link next, Neaves, Randall and Midge, the
ex-SAS half of the six-man squad, huddling around
the two Germans. The wheelman, Metes, hit a deep
rut, nearly tossing the sat link to the floorboard of
the canvas-covered flatbed, Braun ripping free with
another round of cursing as he was nearly dumped
off the bench, wondering how much more insult to
injury he could stomach. Braun was more incensed
than ever, now with Paris altering the operation this
late in the game. Having lost two of his GSG-9 comrades, not to mention the entire team in Algeria,
thanks to Ayoub's treachery, greed and playing all
sides against one another, his blood had boiled hotter by the hour, the closer they drove to the target.
He took a moment to pull himself together, aware
his fury would prove only wasted energy. Presently
they were twenty kilometers and moving due south
of Kasserine, jouncing across a barren steppe, staying off main roads, Metes using his map to maintain

a course well clear of army outposts and villages. If they stayed the course, Braun knew they would have been on Ayoub's front steps before nightfall. Rommel country, he thought, and felt a flush of Teutonic pride ready to return the cold professional to the moment.

"Unbelievable," Braun snarled, cradling the AK-47 so hard his knuckles popped. "We've been out here, dodging army patrols across half of this dung heap of a country, we're three, four hours away from paying back that bastard Ayoub and now the Frenchman wants us to stop in the desert and hunker down and sweat our balls off the rest of the day. The prick must think this is some picnic we're on! Napoleon he is not! Halting now could be suicide! There's a good chance even we were followed from Tunis! You can't trust these goddamn Arabs! The best thing they are capable of is lying! It's a way of life with them, an art they've mastered!"

"Settle down, goddammit! Read the orders, Braun, with your eyes open and with your Nazi mouth shut for a second," Neaves said. "The cavalry's on the way."

"Thirteen-man backup," Midge said. "Odd number for a squad, don't you think?"

"Thirteen or thirty," Randall said, spreading the grid map of Tunisia on the floorboard. "We're going to need all the help we can get once it hits the fan."

"According to the latest word from our Interpol source in Tunis," Neaves said, "Ayoub and twenty or so of his soldier boys always stray from their outpost when the state-run SNTRI tour bus pulls into this village. Another ten of Ayoub's finest always on-site to guard the goodies.''

"A tour bus," Muller grumbled. "More complications.''

"Well, what we were told," Randall said, "Ayoub's running a little scam on the side, milking the tourists for every last dollar he can get his paws on.''

"Witnesses," Braun said. "A bunch of foreigners traipsing around to sightsee Roman ruins and who could end up having a very ugly story to sell to the media.''

"We'll deal with them just like we have women and children and anyone else before," Neaves said, "who could finger us. Collateral damage. End of discussion.''

"Let's get down to business." Midge circled the area in question in red marker. "Sidi Tazmak. A rather large village, courtyards and souks, intersecting streets, alleys, a mosque. Roman ruins, underground villas. Good hiding places for the opposition, a definite problem area if we have to go in and dig them out, hand-to-hand. And yes, apparently Ayoub doesn't like to be away too long from his personal armory. A plus as far I'm concerned. He's a creature of habit.''

"A bloody arms dealer for Hahmad, it turns out," Neaves said.

"A thieving, backstabbing bastard is what he is," Braun rasped.

"This building here," Neaves said, pointing at

the sat picture of the village, "is where we're told Ayoub houses enough explosives and ammonium nitrate fertilizer to blow up half of North Africa. GIA, FIS, Libyans, Egyptians, seems he doesn't care which side he wheels and deals to or whose throat he cuts to fatten his wallet. Okay, so we're on call and on hold at the moment, mates, the orders say we perch here," he said, indicating a chain of hills on the map, "near this *chott*."

"A what?" Braun asked.

"Salt lake," Midge said. "It's going to be a straight blitz on the village anyway, gentlemen. Our orders state we will be contacted by the others before they jump, their DZ aimed at the edge of the *chott*. We link up, coordinate the attack, which, I assume, will be an encircling penetration after nightfall. We mine the main barracks with C-4, silent kills on the way in, a little knife work to whet the appetite. We know where Ayoub will be."

"Or think he will be," Braun said.

"We'll find his ass," Neaves said. "Even if we have to leave bodies strewed clear to the Algerian border, he's history. Okay, we have the armory, and if I may suggest perhaps torching the goodies to add a little bang to the fireworks."

"We'll run it by the others when they contact us." Midge looked each commando in the eye. "What can we do? Shit happened, but it sure as hell won't happen to us. We have enough RPGs, warheads, grenades and C-4 to blow the village straight to Allah if we have to. Braun, you calmed down enough to tell your comrade there's been a change in plans?"

"Nothing but problems," Braun grumbled, cursed and plucked the tac radio off his belt.

"It won't be long, my friend," Neaves said, "before you get the chance to return the grief."

It couldn't be soon enough, Braun thought.

France

"I OWED YOU ONE. Actually I owe you a few more, but I'll call us square."

The hammering blow had dropped Bolan on his back. Bell rung, he stood, a finger touching the blood trickling from the small split in his lip. Cold, the soldier watched Dobson, wanting to handle it his way—retaliate—but he was taking one on the chin for the good guys.

"Special Forces, huh. Black ops, I heard. You want to bet I make some calls to Smoke Bomb Hill no one's ever heard of you?"

"It's a bet you'd lose."

"That a fact? Okay, hotshot, I'll bite for now. Here it is. Twelve of the best that Frenchy's money can buy, I'm leading the charge. You're along for the ride, but you'll earn your keep. Get you introduced to the team, follow orders, you may come back here in one piece. Turns out this is an acting job, meaning you're CIA, Justice, whatever...get my drift?"

Bolan nodded. "Anglerre already gave me the spiel when he welcomed me to the party."

"Did he? Well, this ain't no disco, mister, and Frenchy's never been on one of our outings."

"And the others?"

"What about them?"

"Do I need a mouthpiece and headgear?"

"You're an FNG, an unproven, it won't be any lovefest, but I'm sure you'll survive any hurt feelings. To answer your question, I'm the only one who knows—far as I know. Maybe you put out their lights before they could take a look at you." Dobson shrugged, grinned, striking Bolan as a Roman eager to toss him to the lions. "They're steamed about last night, embarrassed mostly. I've already reamed them out, once the proverbial shit from the Frenchies started rolling downhill. I'm no bellhop, so pick up your bag and shake a leg."

Spitting out some blood, the soldier hauled up his bag, followed Dobson out the door. Dobson might have thought the score was evened up, but the Executioner had other dark ideas on payback as he angled toward the transport bird, heading for the lion's den.

CHAPTER FIVE

Tunisia

The math was computed again, and there was no changing the bitter results. Twice in his head, three times on paper, and the bottom line looked far worse than Colonel Bhouri Ayoub originally feared. Each time he calculated gains against losses it continued his agonizing journey up an icy slope of terror. It would be a long fall to the bottom, and he was one more stumble from losing everything he had worked so hard to earn, desperation and rage fighting each other for control, both emotional wildfires telling him it was most definitely time to plot a new immediate future. Presently he imagined dire circumstances as nothing but a giant laughing demon hiding in a black hole, swallowing up his cash, bent on leaving him broke, casting him back to the past where he saw the urchin in the streets of Tunis, picking pockets, sneaking into hotel rooms to steal whatever he could from unsuspecting tourists.

He had no desire to return to those wretched days, a starving, desperate petty criminal before he joined the army, aware he had to change something back then in his ways if he wanted to live past his twentieth birthday.

Funny, he thought, how a man never really escaped his past. All his life he'd done it his way, wanting to be something more, better than what he saw surrounding him in the souks and mosques and apartment hovels of common Tunisians, and now he was left dreading a return to what he had escaped.

A nobody, broke and destitute, silently screaming inside, day and night, for a way out of his misery. Personal salvation had always been seized by his own hand, then, and now would be no different.

He had never considered himself a devout Muslim—far from in it, in fact. Always seeing himself as more Western than Arab, he didn't pray, didn't practice the teachings of the Koran. That was for other Muslims, and shunning his religion had up to that point proved a way to get ahead in the world, savor the finer things in life. Truth was, he had unbridled contempt for his fellow Arabs, but he did his best to keep this knowledge coveted in his heart, lest the ones he needed to guard his kingdom took exception and turned their backs on him. Still, he wondered, marveled with condescension about his own kind, their ways and philosophy that should have been buried with Muhammad. If they weren't bowing and scraping to a God who, in his mind, had clearly forsaken them—as they existed in squalor and poverty—they were running amok across the planet, raving at the Great Satan and holding the rich Westerners in jealous rage, blaming the powers-that-be for oppressing them, confining the Islamic masses to impoverished misery, left in the dust of their enemies' ravishing quest for more of the world and all its wealth. It was better to join the Devil, he had long since decided, and live for today, because the world was all he could see, at least in the flesh. If the spirit of the Koran wasn't something he could eat, drink or spend, why bother? He wanted money, and he wanted the good life the Europeans flaunted in his face, in Tunis and abroad.

Tunisia was a moderate Arab country, meaning it was minus the fundamentalist headaches and stringent dicates of religious leaders and suicide jihad killers that littered the two nations that hemmed in Tunisia—Algeria and Libya. There were no bombings, no massacres of entire villages by fanatics, tourism was a flourishing trade in what was once Carthage, and he had carved himself a piece of that action, too, something of a conquering Roman soldier in his own right. However, in recent years Tunisia, he knew, had become fertile breeding ground for the Islamic terror machine to branch out, sell weapons, erect terror camps, plan their holy war while hopping in and out of the country on their way to battles against the Great Satan.

Which meant money in his pocket.

And had dumped a crumbling mountain of trouble at his doorstep. CIA, Interpol, American law-enforcement agencies these days were crawling like rodents all over the countryside, and not even his intelligence brokers had the complete scorecard.

It had been a long, difficult day, losing money,

fielding irate calls, dancing around certain figurative land mines planted his way, and he was hardly grateful the night had come. Darkness might have cut away some of the heat of the most ferocious desert on the planet, but the night could bring unseen dangers, lethal shadows rising in his presence out of nowhere, like the black magic of sorcerers. There were already reports of marauders on the prowl, ghosts lurking about in the desert that meant to do him harm, and with good reason. For the moment the deep leather cushion of the couch in the upstairs quarters of his renovated villa, a glass of French brandy on the floor within easy grasp, and the silence and warm glow in his brain were the closest things to paradise he'd known in days since he'd engineered his own sleight of hand.

He might as well enjoy the moment while it lasted. He wasn't broke, he figured, not by Tunisian or even European standards, but he had to do something to change the course he was on before it was too late. The answer stirred, an ominous whisper in the back of his mind.

He was going to take what he had, in terms of explosives, weapons and cash on hand, and bail. He had buyers lined up in Egypt, a personal transport plane, courtesy of the army, nearby in the desert, fueled and ready to fly. He had contacts and allies in Egypt, thanks to his dealings with Hahmad, who were ready to fatten his account in Sicily for the chance to blow themselves up in a suicide attack against American embassies or military compounds. How to go about bailing, though, and when?

Restless, racked by anxiety and mounting paranoia, he hefted his bulk off the couch, sweating in his desert-brown officer's uniform despite the blast of cold air pumped out by his generator-powered unit mounted in the window. He glanced at the radio unit with all its supposed secured channels, tied in to an assortment of operatives and lower-ranking officers on his own payroll. All news that day was bad news, and it didn't take the word of God to tell him the hyenas were slobbering at the jaws, ready to pounce, tear him to pieces before he could run. The GIA contact was making noise, a thundering bellow, in fact, from clear across the border how he was holding him personally responsible for the attack on the village by foreign murderers. His Interpol connection in Tunis had told him Paris had turned down his request for more money, another stinging slap in the face. Worse than a mere snubbing from Paris and threats from GIA thugs, his operatives in Tunis claimed they had lost the trail of the backup commando squad they'd been watching, but they believed the foreigners had slipped out of the city and were heading his way.

Idiots! Incompetents!

He did the math again, as if there had to be some mistake, adding numbers and weight of ordnance, but also hoping to distract himself from his growing fear. He figured he was paying his operatives and intelligence brokers too much, weekly envelopes of dinars converted into francs, which his underlings ran up to Tunis, greasing the skids, from government lackeys on down the feeding chain to eyes and ears on the streets who kept him up-to-date, tuned in to rumors that fellow officers or foreign agents were ready to move on his operation. He was forced to dip into his own dwindling funds to keep tabs on who was doing what, discover what the following day's action would be, and he wasn't getting the desired results.

Yes, it was time to go when he couldn't trust his own money to buy him comfort and security in his own backyard.

He went to the bar, poured another brandy, silently cursing the fact he'd spread so much so thin to cover his tracks. His men had already checked and rechecked the numbers of crates in the armory at the north end of the village. Buried in catacombs—the more superstitious of his men whispering about evil spirits of Roman soldiers who had long since passed through here—he still had twelve tons of ammonium nitrate fertilizer, six hundred pounds of plastic explosive, primers, detonators, radio remote boxes. Factor in the crates of Russian large and small arms, delivered by Hahmad's henchmen, meant to be sold to Algerian warlords, and he was still in the neighborhood of four million and change—U.S. currency—to see him relocate, change identity, start over someplace far away where his name would simply be a curse word to all those he had duped and left behind in the vanishing act of his dust storm. Another two hundred grand after he sold the load, factoring in the next round of greasing so he could slip and slide on his way for tomorrow's horizon. Naturally there would be no more deals with the GIA, FIS, since he'd had a bloody helping hand in arranging the raid on the village. Hahmad would help him regroup, he was sure, since he had personally guaranteed and seen to the Syrian's safe passage in and now out of Tunisia once word reached him from Paris that a killing squad was once again cut loose to hunt down the man like some wild animal.

Give a little, get a little.

These days, he was giving far more than he could afford. He wanted to blame Hahmad to some large degree for his current state of fear, but he realized he would need the Syrian for sanctuary, a number of schemes already spinning in his head how he might ingratiate himself to the man. He could appreciate all the bad blood that boiled on the Frenchman's part, but Hahmad, he knew, had his reasons for slaying the rich businessman's family in Egypt, and maybe he could work that angle, but how to weave the story without incriminating himself? Without the Frenchman's personal vendetta, the coffer wouldn't be as fat as it was, and there lay another serpent at his feet. The blood feud between Paris and Syria sometimes left Ayoub wondering how he got stuck in the middle of warring factions, but what was done was done. He had played both sides against each other, a slippery tightrope act in the dark, and if Hahmad became wise to his own treachery...

Well, he had only tried to better his lot in life. Who could blame a man for wanting to succeed in the world? It was simply a question of personal pride, reasonable enough.

"Colonel? The bus is arriving."

Ayoub turned, spotted Captain Mourar in the doorway. He looked away, sipping brandy, staring through the double doors at the darkness beyond his balcony. If there was going to be an attack, when? How many? Algerians? The Frenchman's commandos? Tunisian operatives of the government? An eradication squad marched back his way from Hahmad who had learned the dark truth?

If that was the case, he was ready to fight, or at least march out the troops. It wasn't entirely true he was above and beyond the tenet of the suicidal grandstanding that was part and parcel of the jihad when frontal assaults and trading shots with the enemy failed. In this part of the world, violent confrontation, he knew, was inevitable, and he had prepared to slip unnoticed into any winds of war that blew his way. From the beginning of his several business ventures, he had feared the end would come, a sudden flash of fire and bullets in his face meant solely to rob him of his own slice of heaven. Many of his soldiers had large families in the village, and more than a few of them kept the tenets of jihad fanaticism close to home, under their own roofs, in fact. The smallest of children, he knew, had been indoctrinated for future service to the holy war by fathers who openly despised the power and wealth of the West, and who would commit themselves and even sacrifice their own blood if it advanced the jihad. If they came under attack and he gave the order, they knew what had to be done. Of course, if the village came under assault, he would have to flee, leave the fighting and dying to others. There was a future to look forward to, after all, and nature dictated the rich and powerful belonged in the world, to live to fight another day or rule the masses who were simply put on earth to serve and obey the strong.

He tried to push visions of personal doom and attacks by armed specters from the desert out of his head, killing the brandy, but the whispering portent of imminent danger clung to his thoughts. There were a few more dollars to be plucked up at the moment, and the scam always made him feel lighter, more alive, during good, bad or uncertain times. Tourists, with mere pennies to hand over, just the same, but he would do what he normally did when the bus pulled in, which was take his nominal fee from the tourists. He enjoyed the scam and the action as much as he looked forward to their helplessness and impotence in the face of circumstances beyond their control. They were on his turf, bottom line. Oh, they would squawk, argue, grumble about thievery, flap their arms, perhaps even mutter some bigoted remark about Arab fleecing. He would smile, explain they would be given food, drink and shelter, all the creature comforts they were accustomed to at home. He would tell them they wanted to sightsee around this region, very well, but there were bandits, even terrorists and they would need his soldiers for protection. They never liked it, but they always forked over the cash, especially when they saw his men standing like statues at the gates of hell in the night, cradling AKMs.

Ayoub patted the holstered Makarov, aware the hand would never stray far from the weapon when he launched into his spiel. "How many?" he asked, stepping past Mourar and heading down the winding stairs for the sprawling living room.

On the way out the door he listened to the tally. It was the usual mixed bag of foreigners. Two large Japanese families, a group of American students from the University of Maryland. There were elderly British and American couples, a few lone travelers who could be journalists or CIA. All told, twenty-eight sightseers. Not a bad night's take. If he cut back on the portions of fruit and meat, one soda or one glass of wine per guest, the profit margin would be fairly decent.

He walked through the courtyard, found the bus parked in the wide entrance of the stone wall that encircled his compound. He put on his best winning smile, the tourists disgorging, looking around at the contingent of armed soldiers, uncertain. It was the usual spectacle of cameras and tote bags, a flowered shirt here and there, sandaled feet and a few broad-brimmed hats to fight the fury of the desert sun.

"Greetings!" Ayoub called out. "Welcome to our humble village. I am Colonel Ayoub, at your service."

"FILE THAT FAT FUCK'S face away. This sack of dung, too. Moving on, here's how it plays. Listen up, I'm going over this one time. You don't pay attention, that's your problem. No questions when I finish.''

They were in what Bolan assumed passed as the war room, gathered at the bolted-down metal table, the hatches closed now to the passenger hold and cockpit, windows down, leaving Dobson in pale yellow light near the screen and slide projector. There was a bank of screens behind the soldier, state-of-the-art radar, jamming, radio and sat links, a quick scoping when he'd entered the room telling him it was high-tech that rivaled just about anything Stony Man Farm used. Bolan was sandwiched between two of the commandos, having been told by Dobson where to sit for the briefing. Ashtrays were already overflowing with butts, and the soldier caught a whiff of whiskey-laced coffee in the smoke clouds, more than a few of the commandos working off the hair of the dog. It was a bad setup, all around, slated for disaster and certain casualties, discipline and military protocol out the window, a pack of killers now fueled to unleash the savage beast inside on whatever unfortunate victims were waiting on the receiving end. Bolan worked on his own coffee sans the juice.

The transport plane was a little more than an hour in the air, and during that time Bolan had endured the chilly reception as the new guy. Dobson did the intros, no handshaking by the eleven commandos, but a couple grunts, nods, thrown in, then they'd gone back to checking weapons and gear, rigging chutes.

FNG.

No sweat. They were on his doomsday clock.

They were known to the Executioner as Alphas

Two and so on, Dobson announcing he was Alpha
One and the FNG tagged as Alpha Zero. Bolan had
already gone through the military jackets as part of
his intel package, knew them by name and service
record, and he recognized a few sleeping beauties
from the previous night. No more haymakers had
been launched his way, so he reckoned Dobson was
keeping the secret, or maybe the others weren't letting on, waiting it out for their own moment of retribution. In the flesh, they looked many years older
now, some of them scruffy with half-grown beards.
There was a meanness in every pair of eyes, which
told Bolan they had aged badly, desperation and
greed and anger their only true friends during their
own dark journeys to this point on their road to hell.
A part of Bolan wondered where and why it all went
wrong for them. Any number of reasons and justi-
fications would provide the salving trick for their
conscience if he cared to ask. Debt, bad marriage,
substance abuse. Dead-end lives going nowhere but
the martial thirst for adventure wanting to whet the
appetite for combat, a craving to recapture the glory
days. Greed, blood lust, whatever, the bottom line
on what they had become wouldn't see Bolan cut
them any slack when the time came to punch their
tickets. Elite commandos from SAS or GSG-9, they
had once been part of units created specifically to
save innocent lives, hostage rescue usually at the top
of the list. Now they freely stood on the other side
of the tracks, to a man nothing more in his final
analysis but mercenaries who, for money, would kill

anything that moved. They weren't any better—in fact, they were worse in Bolan's mind than Hahmad. At least the Syrian savage was motivated by twisted principles.

Bolan was allowed to keep his own weapons, which had drawn a suspicious eye from several of the commandos, all of whom were bringing Israeli Galil assault rifles to the party, but with Beretta 92-Fs as side arms, Russian fragmentation, incendiary and flash-stun grenades fixed to webbing, Duane Dieter tactical folding blades the choice of knifework for close-quarters combat. It was an odd assortment of weapons, but Bolan didn't let his imagination run wild searching for the method behind the madness. Standard operating procedure for black ops on foreign soil, he knew, called for the use of weapons that couldn't be traced back to the invader's origins. It was SOP the Executioner bucked on most missions, since he was at the top of the charts as an expendable deniable. But if he went down for the count, there was always Able Team or Phoenix Force to come in behind and silence any loose tongues who might flap about Uncle Sam pulling dirty deeds.

The way he read the operation, as Dobson worked the clicker, it began to sound like a straight *Wild Bunch* play. The faces of Colonel Ayoub and Hahmad disappeared, and Dobson flashed through sat pictures of the village in question.

Dobson spelled it out. Link up with a six-man squad already in position near their DZ, ten klicks from Sidi Tazmak. Pile aboard their truck, ride in, disgorge west of the village, then fan out in teams he would assign when they hit the ground and were rolling. Move in, burn it, shoot them up, capture and torture the golden calf that was Ayoub. He informed the group he would take five men with him to Ayoub's villa at the southern edge, grab the colonel and either skin or burn the truth about Hahmad's whereabouts out of him. He skimmed over any specifics, but mentioned the armory at the far north end of the village was to be mined and blown by C-4.

"I suggest the teams in this vicinity make their way as quickly as possible to Ayoub's nest. Ammonium nitrate, more than a few tons of it, according to our latest information...well, you see the problem. Oklahoma City multiplied by unknown math. If the numbers are even close to accurate, I expect half the village will be turned into a smoking crater, maybe more. Problem number two. A tour bus from Tunis will be on-site. Every man here knows what that means, but let me state the hard facts."

Bolan saw Dobson glance his way.

"Man, woman or child, I don't give a shit if your favorite rock band or Hollywood bimbo is with the sightseers, if it turns up, if you find it hiding under the bed, it is to be shot. We're looking at a little more than a hundred bodies in this village, give or take. Scorched earth, you know the drill—or most of you do. That's it. Dismissed. Everyone but Alpha Zero."

Bolan tensed. They stabbed out smokes, rose

without looking at him. He was certain the others had already been thoroughly briefed, roles defined. If he wasn't being cut out of the loop altogether, he was being warned, felt out and dangled over some building fire.

"Number five," Dobson barked, hauling out a small metal bin from under the table. He took the slides, dumped them in the bin. "Torch it, dump it."

When they were alone, as Alpha Five shut the hatch behind him, Dobson said, "You don't like it?"

"Straight blitz, burn it down, shoot everyone. A little skimpy on details, if you ask me."

"No one is. You're thinking extraction."

"It came to mind."

"Getting out of Dodge is my department."

"I almost forgot, I'm on a need-to-know."

"I hope I don't have to remind you of that again. You don't have a problem waxing women and children?"

"Whatever it takes," Bolan said. "Even if my favorite rock band is touring Sidi Tazmak."

But the soldier burned inside, fighting to keep the hot anger and revulsion off his face. When it happened...

Don't get ahead of yourself, Bolan thought. It was their game to lose, and he would see to it, whatever it took, that only the blood of the guilty was shed.

"I'm along for more than just the ride," Bolan said.

Dobson bobbed his head, grunted. "You want money, you want respect from the others maybe."

"I can skip the pat on the back."

"Okay, maybe you want to be the one who nails Hahmad. By the way, I forgot to mention. The snake is worth five mil now—alive."

Bolan kept up the act, grinning, nodding. "Say we take him, kicking and screaming, that's a thirteen-way split."

"Don't get greedy, Alpha Zero. The frog whispered in my ear before we left, says he's paying extra for advanced screening of Ayoub under the knife. This outing, it's not going to stop in Tunisia. Fifty-fifty we even make it back to Paris. But that's life. Shit can happen." Solemn, Dobson took a pull from his spiked coffee. "Get the job done, you, all of us, a few of us, we get paid and tell Marquis he can take this job and shove it." A pause, then Dobson said, "You're dismissed. Your chute pack is in the cargo hold. I'm thinking maybe you'd like to check it out, rig it yourself."

Bolan stood. "Way ahead of you."

"I wouldn't have expected anything else. You're a professional. Now get the hell outta here."

Bolan paused at the hatch, hand on the handle, glanced back at Dobson, but the leader of the killing pack looked away, finished with the FNG. Or was he? A warning delivered? A secret agenda, in the wings, about to blow up in his face? Something felt more wrong to Bolan the longer he kept up the ruse.

The Executioner heard the pounding of his heart in his ears and pushed through the hatch to join men who saw themselves as lions on the hunt, but in his mind were only hyenas.

Strong and predatory, just the same, and soon enough, Bolan knew there would be a feeding frenzy that would break the chain when the call of the wild and the savage blared in battle. It was simply a question of who would eat whom, the lion or the hyena.

The Executioner was nobody's prey.

Bolan was going for the jugular, the whole pack, from the bottom of the food chain to the very top, where they hid in the bush and waited while others did the killing.

CHAPTER SIX

Tunisia

"And just what is your business here in our humble country...ah, Mr....?"

"Ridilson."

Whatever was happening, he knew none of it was good. He watched Ayoub scouring the passport as if he were expecting the mysteries of life to come burning up out of nowhere—and clue him into the true identity of one Jack Ridilson.

They were in some dreary, poorly lit room, no larger than the average jail cell of one toilet, one bunk for solitary confinement. There was the smell of urine and fear in the air, dark stains of dried blood on the stone floor. How many poor slobs had been roughed up here or worse? he wondered.

Ridilson smoked, glancing at the guard boring daggers into the side of his head, the guy acting as if it had been some time since he slapped some poor bastard around, in this bleak cubicle of hell. The door was closed, and for that Ridilson was grateful, almost, but not quite tuned out to the bitch session still going strong. The others were still out there, squawking about giving up fifty bucks for the good colonel's hospitality—a half star, as far as Ridilson was concerned, on a line of five for fine dining. Even through the fat wood door words like *outrageous, usury* and *blatant thievery* still filtered from the so-called banquet room. The spread the colonel had laid out on a cracked and chipped long wooden table consisted of oranges, mangoes and paper-thin slices of roast beef, a case of sodas and two bottles of wine thrown in to wash down the big feast and the day's trail dust. There wouldn't be seconds, for damn sure, and Ridilson figured the portions of food and drink wouldn't even make it the first time around.

"And what do you do for a living, Mr. Ridilson?"

"I'm a writer."

Ayoub finally handed him back his passport. "What do you write?"

"Travel guides."

"Really? And what do you think of our humble country so far?"

It wasn't Algeria—yet, he thought. But things weren't all they promised when they trooped them out from Carthage for a tour of the countryside, tourists from a mixed bag of countries, wide-eyed and bushy tailed, with cameras galore to snap reels of film of what was little more than a godforsaken desert, as far as he was concerned. Oh, somehow the village had been plunked down in an oasis on the world's anus, but beyond the palm trees and what little water allowed man and animal to survive out here, they might as well have been living on Mars. If he really did pen travel books, that would be his report.

Pass Tunisia and go straight to Paris or Switzerland.

"So far, so good."

"For a writer, you are a man of few words. Or are you choosing your words carefully?"

"Just a bit tired maybe. Hey, but I could use a glass of wine to wash down the dust, if you don't mind."

"Yes. But of course."

"If that's all… Are we through, Colonel?"

He watched Ayoub watching the AKM-wielding soldier, beady eyes nearly hidden behind slitted lids. Did they know? he wondered. How could they? God, but he hated these sorts of stints for the Company. Going in, unarmed, he might as well be naked.

He was little more than a spy, an investigator, and if they discovered the ruse, he knew they'd take him out in the desert and leave him for the buzzards and the scorpions. The problem, he knew, was how to go about learning where the ammonium nitrate fertilizer was located. Then there were reports of the elusive ghost that was Hahmad in the vicinity, only no one could absolutely state they'd seen the Syrian. Hell, not even all the combined eyes in the sky, from NORAD to NSA, could track the bastard. It was as if the Syrian could disappear into a sandstorm, ride the winds to the next country of his choosing.

Forget Hahmad. Right then he was stuck, under suspicion, wondering how he was going to do what had to be done. He hadn't expected to be separated from the others as soon as he was off the bus, questioned and peered at like some common child molester. Now his mission might be a wash, traipsing back to the Company's in-country ops, Berbers and shadow agents from Tunis who wanted to know just what and how the colonel was doing what he did down here at the edge of hell—the Sahara.

Impossible to get it done right, on the sly? Maybe not. Say he needed to stretch his legs, ask for an escort around the village. Coldcock the SOB when he wasn't looking, grab his weapon, off for some sneak and peek. There were plenty of jeeps, trucks scattered around, a hot ride out of there and back to his contacts.

"Very well, I believe I can accept that. I hope when you write your book about Tunisia there will also be something favorable to be said about your stay in my humble village. Feel free to use my name. That's Ayoub. A-y-o-u-b."

He heard the smart crack flying for his tongue, but kept it to himself.

"You may go join the others, Mr. Ridilson."

Ridilson ground out his smoke. It was all feeling wrong, and he wondered how he'd let himself get talked into what could be a suicide mission. Worse than stepping onto the cracking ice, there were reports of murderous commandos, the Frenchman's rampaging killers, maybe headed for Sidi Tazmak for payback. Still more ghosts who had vanished while under surveillance up north.

There was going to be trouble that night. Ridilson

would be ready if and when it hit the fan. He'd gone for broke in the past, Algeria and Yemen at the top of the list, and he'd walked out the other side, blood on his hands.

"Thank you, Colonel."

"Enjoy your stay in our humble village."

BRAUN WASN'T BUYING the new guy's version of events. There seemed very little he could do at the moment about him, since they were closing in on the village, on the edge of hell to go down there, blowing things up and shooting everything that moved. At least he was back in the saddle with his own kind on an op, Muller and Metes part of his Alpha squad, good men from the GSG-9 days he could count on to watch his back.

And monitor Alpha Zero, poised to blow the guy away if he was something other than what he claimed.

Through NVD goggles, Braun took in the targeted village, hand signaled for his team to hold up, drop to get their bearings. They were spread out in a skirmish line, shadows falling now into narrow slashes down the side of the incline that led to the village. The truck was ditched in a wadi, one klick or so west, and Braun was grateful to be free of the cramped conditions when the others had climbed aboard after their landing. Comfort was the least of his concerns, but it was good to be moving, pumped up to shed blood, revenge in the name of his fallen comrades.

The village looked true to form according to sat

pictures. Domed mosque to the northwest, then the large block of stone to the north where another Alpha team would penetrate, mine the colonel's goodies and light up the night. Panning on, the dirt tracks cut through four rows of stone hovels, but there were breaks in sections which ran in half circles, archways and courtyards, what might pass as alleys for these people. Meandering camels and goats could prove an additional problem, sounding the alarm at the sight and smell of dark invaders on the prowl, waking up the neighborhood, soldiers running amok. Well, it was a straight-on silent march into the bowels, at least before the show started, and from there all bets were off anyway, since everyone except Ayoub was fair game to go down hard. Dobson and his crew would take down the colonel's palace, Braun checking the illuminated dial of his chronometer, three minutes, fifteen seconds and counting for all of them to get into position. He was about to signal for his team to move in when his com link crackled with Dobson's voice. He keyed the frequency that tied him alone to Dobson.

"I've been thinking about what you said about the new guy's story. How Schneider would have never run off at the mouth, no matter how drunk he was. How he duped the frog. Something's hinky with the new guy, so keep an eye on him. It's your call whether to smoke him. Check your watch, we're going in."

Braun glanced at the new guy. Alpha Zero had the look of a warrior who'd been there many times, could do the job. That alone troubled him. Factor in

Dobson's entire report while the others were still in the air, and Braun smelled an infiltrator. CIA? FBI? Who knew, he thought, but he sure as hell cared.

This wasn't only payback; it was payday.

Time to rock.

Braun keyed the frequency to his teammates. "Let's go. Alpha Zero, take point. You copy?"

"No sweat."

Bolan rose, a stalking shadow moving out from the tight wedge in the slope, HK MP-5 leading them down to the row of hovels closest to the armory.

THE EXECUTIONER KNEW the moment of truth was moments away from becoming grim reality as he made the edge of the buildings assigned to his team. Three killers were on his heels, the tactic calling for him to kick in the door while one of the others pitched in a grenade, go in firing. The whole operation was hardly carved out of the stone of sound surgical-strike principles, but this was meant solely to be a rampage, all hands taking up position, one mass eruption to begin the slaughter. They'd gone over it again while they'd ridden in by truck.

A killing vise, clamping down on selected targets, north to south. Ayoub was the prize, and Bolan was already planning his move to get to the colonel's abode. With eighteen enemy heads spread out, the village would be turned into a raging battle zone of mass chaos, confusion and killing. An earlier perusing of the layout and Bolan knew it would be tricky, navigating alleys, shadowing from door to door, aware it would be hand-to-hand in certain close quarters, armed shadows boiling up out of nowhere. He would do everything in his power to see that noncombatants didn't get mowed down in the cross fire of the commandos. Trouble was, the enemy had plenty of bullets, grenades, RPG rocket teams, and a few them had been eyeing him with questionable intent.

And when that armory blew its load of ammonium nitrate, at least half the village would be lost in a fireball he intended to be far away from, which was the deepest corner to the north where Dobson and company would bag Ayoub for questioning under the knife.

The soldier checked the deep shadows down the street, the buildings all dark blocks, with the exception of two open doorways where kerosene light washed through the openings.

There would be more problems, more potential for disaster....

A check of his watch, and he was counting off the doomsday numbers. Dobson was a professional, and he would make the time frame, Bolan knew, for simultaneous assault work like black magic. Flinging utter shock in the faces of Ayoub and his soldiers gave them the edge, but the soldier also intended to make his own play before the surprise and terror factor wore off and both sides were locked in firefights.

Crouched, Bolan gave the street a final search. Clear.

He glanced at his watch.

Eight, seven...

He saw Alpha Fourteen pluck a grenade off his webbing, give him the nod. Bolan shed his NVD goggles in sync with the team.

The door looked flimsy enough, no lock he could find, but Bolan wouldn't know until he kicked it. If it didn't cave in the first time...

The Executioner lifted his subgun, then drove a thundering blast of boot heel into the door. It was flying in, a shout hurled from the shadows inside as Fourteen tossed the grenade into the maw of darkness. Autofire broke out from inside the room, bullets flaying the edge of the doorway. If that was a soldier guarding his nest, the soldier could only hope any women and children were covered somewhere deep in the home. He had to play it out the way he had mentally scripted, reel the trio into committing themselves, lured to the point of no return he was one of them. Somehow, beyond the racket of weapons fire, he made out the voice shouting in Arabic for his family to take cover.

Bolan waited, heard the distant rattle of autofire cutting loose to the north and south.

Right on time.

He rode out the blast, smoke and fire shooting out the doorway, a searing taint of mixed stinks blown up his nose. His teammates were launching themselves off the wall when the Executioner turned his death sights on the trio of commandos and hit the SMG's trigger.

STANDING BESIDE the archway on the deep side of the banquet room saved his butt. The explosion rocked the house, it sounded, top to bottom. He wondered if more than one grenade had been unloaded on the living room, but the blast of white light from behind him told Ridilson the hitters had dumped in flash-stuns. There was enough concussive force, even still, to knock the man off his feet, the glass of red wine and paper plate of roast beef flying from his hands. Whoever they were, they came in firing, bullets flying everywhere, the gaggle of tourists screaming like banshees. Ridilson was lifting himself to his feet when two soldiers flying past him were chopped to bloody ribbons, dancing around in jig steps, spattering gore over the spread before they dropped like stones.

It could have been manna from heaven, he thought, the diversion he needed to either locate the armory or blow town.

And he grabbed up the discarded AKM, checked the hall ahead, found it clear. The shooting, screaming and dying appeared confined to the living room, but he wasn't counting on the assault to stay locked to any one piece of turf.

Smart money told him the commandos from Tunis had arrived, and they were there to have a few choice words with the good colonel. If it played out like the other killing rampages the Company knew about, no witnesses would be left behind to talk about the horror show.

Ridilson checked his rear, shadows darting through smoke, dark-clad invaders barking at the other tourists to get down and stay down. The soldiers guarding the colonel had to have taken another drubbing, the sound of weapons fire coming from the staircase beyond the archway leading to the living room doused to silence.

Ridilson fled.

THEY WERE IN, Patterson leading the charge, his assault rifle barking out long bursts at the trio of soldiers running out of what appeared some off-shooting chamber in the armory. They were right on time, in sync with Bull Dobson and company, but from there on it would prove dicey.

Especially when the ammonium nitrate was primed and they were trying to beat their own time frame back to the palace. Most of Sidi Tazmak, he knew, was slated to become a smoking crater.

Two more Tunisian soldiers were framed in the kerosene glow in a doorway Patterson assumed led to the underground chamber. The five other commandos assigned to his team opened fire in unison with his own Galil, riddling Ayoub's best, head to crotch, flinging them out of sight and back to where they came from.

They paired up, spreading out to check the circular room. Patterson and Neaves bolted up a short flight of steps that put them on a landing that led to the doorway for the underground chamber, their satchels flopping between their shoulder blades, bulging with C-4 bricks. Randall and Midge had already been ordered to watch up top while Patterson and Neaves went below in search of doomsday.

"You two cover this door," Patterson ordered Mathers and Nilsen. "Let's do it."

It was good to be acting out aggression, Patterson thought, after the previous night's embarrassment. He had put it out of mind up to then, but he was juiced now, hoping for more of Ayoub's soldiers to show up as he descended the flight of stone steps. Someone had gotten the drop on him and the others the previous night, and since he'd been the sentry on duty Patterson had been the unfortunate recipient of a dressing-down by Dobson.

Well, Patterson thought, he had something to prove. Redemption wasn't far off, as he hit the bottom of the steps, and froze for a moment at the sight of what they were supposed to blow.

The underground chamber was huge, piled floor to ceiling with countless crates.

They'd be lucky, he knew, if they didn't blow themselves up in the process, clear back to Paris. Ammonium nitrate fertilizer was volatile enough, but he spotted the drums of fuel in the far corner of the room. They'd dump the barrels on the way out, adding a little extra bang for the Frenchman's buck.

Patterson stole a few moments to check the room for hidden soldiers. They were clear. "Let's get busy and get the hell out of here. Dump it all."

CHAPTER SEVEN

Alphas Fourteen, Fifteen and Sixteen were history. From their military jackets Bolan knew they were former GSG-9 commandos, Braun, Muller and Metes, one-time heroes with more than a few hostage-rescue missions to their credit. Now they were scum, dying on their feet, howling out their shock and rage, not wanting to give up the ghost. Holding back on the SMG's trigger, Bolan stitched the line of commandos, stem to stern and back, riddling their vests, driving them into one another, their assault rifles coming around, chattering for a brief dangerous moment. The soldier felt the hot slipstream of lead, and the way in which they had responded to his attack, quick and ferocious, told him all he needed to know about the others.

Alpha Zero wasn't to be trusted.

Alpha Zero wasn't one of them.

They went down in a heap finally, and Bolan took a second to get his bearings on the street, aware the storm had just broken over Sidi Tazmak, watching to see who came running, who did what.

The easy part was over.

Three gone, fifteen more professional headhunters

to go in search of, blood running as they likewise jump-started the killing. If Dobson called for a sitrep he'd never get from these three, the ex-SF colonel might send out a hunting party, his radar screen already blipping where Alpha Zero was concerned. But Bolan intended to meet any prowling threat head-on. They were all going down, in ones and twos, in the street or at Ayoub's compound or however they showed up. By now the armory would be mined, primed to turn half—or more—of the village into a smoking crater. No way could he make a house-to-house sweep for evacuation of innocents.

Everyone was on his or her own, good or bad.

He saw a shadow barging into the light down the street. The Russian assault rifle was up and swinging his way when Bolan tagged the shadow, crucifying him in the doorway with a lightning stutter of SMG fire before he folded into a boneless rubbery mass.

The war for Sidi Tazmak had only just begun.

The wailing inside the acrid smoke cloud snared Bolan's attention, before he looked back and found still more shadows spilling onto the street.

"Hahmoufif!"

Bolan risked stalling for several more seconds, calling out in Arabic through the doorway, "Are there children with you?"

She loosed a string of profanity, then pulled herself together long enough to tell Bolan the sons of whores killed her husband, but it would have been better if they'd murdered them all since they would right then be in Paradise waiting on a vengeful God to mete out punishment. He made out several voices of small children next, crying over their father, told them to get out of the village, run east, as fast as they could and don't look back.

Whether she'd do it, or could do it…

He had no idea which way the demo team would chart its course to Ayoub's compound. Charge down from the east or the west? The map had shown him the straightest line was down the middle of Sidi Tazmak, through an alley, across a courtyard. The heart of the village, then.

The Executioner hugged the faces of the hovels, flying past doorways swirling with voices raised in panic, alert for armed silhouettes. Another armed shadow was barreling out the next door down when Bolan nailed him with a 3-round burst to the chest on the fly, racing past the body wilting at his feet, spinning in a one-eighty next but finding no takers on his heels. Facing front, the warrior darted into a break between hovels, taking in the street, planning his next move. It was utter chaos now, camels and goats milling and snorting in panic at the far end of the street, women wailing and cradling small children to their breasts, villagers being rounded up by a half-dozen armed soldiers barking out the orders to move. Shadows flew past Bolan, linking up with the other Tunisians.

The Executioner decided to stick on the heels of the crowd, then make a straight run for Dobson and company. If, on the way, he bumped into the demo team he'd wax them on the fly.

It appeared the mob was heading out of town, westbound, then the next round of slaughter broke out.

"YOU MUSTN'T DO this! It is an abomination in the eyes of God!"

It was something Yusuf Sadeh had dreaded doing since the day he first told his son Alif what might happen if the village was ever attacked by infidels. But he was a soldier, not only for the Tunisian army, but a warrior in the jihad, a holy son of God, alone in a world of evil men. Sometimes a man was called upon to sacrifice more than just his own life. This might have been Tunisia, he knew, but there were still plenty of believers who believed the way of the sword was all the devils of the West understood and respected.

The shooting sounded as if it came from two different directions, the screaming and din of weapons fire the next street down nearly right on top of him, with more racket at the colonel's compound, a mixed cacophony of autofire and explosions that seemed to mesh outside, leaving him somewhat undecided which way to go.

He grabbed his son by the shoulders, even as his wife shrieked defiance and outrage. "Hanis! Be silent!" he screamed. She lapsed into quiet sobbing, shaking her head, holding her face in her hands. He checked the bundle of plastic explosive wrapped around his son's chest, then gave Alif the remote box. They had gone through dry rehearsals, and one look into his son's eyes told him he would be proud of Alif when the time came. "You understand why you must do this, my son?"

His son nodded. "In the name of God, the compassionate and merciful, yes, Father. The world is full of devils who wish only to oppress or kill all Muslims. We must strike a blow first, kill as many of them as possible, even if one must give up his own life."

"And?"

"As you have said, if I do it, I will go straight to heaven."

"I will be with you when the time comes. We will both go straight to Paradise."

"Yes, Father."

"You must do exactly what I tell you when I tell you. Understood?"

"Yes, Father."

"Good. I love you. God is watching. God is great."

"Hanis," he called over his shoulder, rising, "take our children and stay behind me. Alif, you stay with me, by my side. Just flick on the switch, then rush them and push that button, just as I have shown you."

"Yes, Father."

PATTERSON CALCULATED three hundred yards, at least, to clear ground zero. There would be a massive shock wave, reaching out for their backsides, no matter what, heat so intense it could melt gunmetal. There would be flying and raining rubble, and they needed both distance and shelter before the world blew up and the sky fell.

That much ammonium nitrate, and he figured they were looking at Oklahoma City times ten, maybe more. He hadn't seen any tombs when he'd been below, but he'd spotted any number of archways leading to chambers that could house tombs. He started to have visions of mummies and shattered skeletons raining down, but any dead Romans unearthed and blown around in the firestorm would have plenty of company soon enough.

According to his watch, they had less than four minutes before the big bang. He wasn't looking for any praise from Dobson when the fireworks went off, but after the previous night's reaming, a quiet job well done in front of the others would suffice.

Kill now, take any praise later.

They were sweeping down a wide alley, Patterson leading the hard charge, weapons up and ready to cut loose, all of them homed in on the chaos just beyond the first row of hovels. They were fleeing, it looked, and Patterson gave the signal to hold up, two three-man teams splitting to take up positions on each side of the alley. Let them run? No, they had a job to do.

Thirty to forty marks, soldiers, women and children, a nice tight mob of flesh, he observed. It didn't get any better than this, he reasoned.

"All of them."

Patterson handed out the shooting orders so the mob was covered, front to rear. It was important, he knew, they drop as many of them in the first few moments as possible. Later, he thought, they could troop back and shoot some film, visions of a fat bonus dancing through his head. Of course, they might have to dig through a little rubble, break a sweat even, when the armory rained down.

Mummies and all.

Not a problem. It was good to earn his keep.

"Line them up. On a three count. One..."

THE EXECUTIONER SAW the demo team had made the scene, twenty yards down, six assault rifles opening up on the unsuspecting mob in chattering unison. Innocent victims were screaming, spinning, a few runners breaking out of the falling wall of shredded flesh, when Bolan made his decision.

Hug the face of the hovel, drop a frag bomb into the pack, mop up whatever was left. It was always destined to be run and gun anyway, so why bother with any finer details as far as tactics were concerned?

It was straight slaughter all around.

The Executioner was heading out when he spotted a small boy rushing the killers. There was something in his hand, an armed shadow bellowing in Arabic and shielding the boy, the Russian assault rifle blazing for a moment before the six-man execution squad nailed the man. The boy dropped next, a dark finger of blood shooting out of his shattered skull. Incredibly the downed soldier rose, grabbed up the lifeless body, clutching the dead boy to his chest.

And Bolan knew what the Arab Lazarus was holding, as he bulled into the flying storm of bullets.

It was a new twist to the insanity, he thought, a father prepared to sacrifice his own blood to take out the attackers. He could only imagine the sick indoctrination to brainwash the boy in the name of God, but there was no time to dwell on the hideous ploy.

There was only time to drop, duck and ride out the massive explosion.

PATTERSON SAW IT COMING, retreated, firing his Galil on the backpedal. They got the soldier first, then the kid, only the stubborn bastard wouldn't stay down.

Now he wouldn't *go down,* fueled by the mindless rage of jihad, even as six Galils were turned on him, chopping him to bloody bits. He was screaming something in Arabic, holding the limp body to his chest, the remote box in his hand, still going strong, coming on.

''Fall back!''

They either didn't hear him or weren't aware of the danger. It was a stroke of blind luck, spotting the side door in the corner of his eye, launching his shoulder into flimsy wood. He was nose-diving for deeper cover, screams of his comrades lost to the roaring blast. Smoke boiled in the door, Patterson wincing as scorching heat blew by the opening. He stood after what seemed like an hour, bell rung, gagging on the smoke, the stink of blood and men gutted by a blast that he was sure had all but vaporized them. Galil in hand, he stepped outside, peering into the swirling smoke, checking for any signs of life from the mangled bodies, but knew he was all alone. Then he saw the tall shadow rolling his way. He was lifting his Galil, then froze, recognizing the new guy.

"Zero?"

"Yeah."

"Where're the others?"

"Same deal as here."

Something in the man's eyes changed in the next instant, but even still he wasn't quite sure what he saw. Something about the new guy now, his mind wanting to tell him he'd seen him somewhere before. Where?

"How's that?" Patterson asked.

"They became less than zero. Just like you."

Patterson was swinging the assault rifle up and around, cursing the treacherous new guy when the subgun flamed and stuttered and he felt the hot lead tearing into his chest. Just before the lights winked out, he heard his own voice from the onrushing darkness tell him this was the second time the bastard had gotten the drop on him.

RIDILSON FOUND the APC in the courtyard. He had made it out the compound, through the back door, prayed now the keys were in the ignition. All hell had broken loose all over the village, soldiers and invaders soon to clash. And since he was now armed he could be sure either side would shoot first at the sight of a lone armed runner. He was wondering how smart it was to have brought a weapon with him.

"Oh, thank you, Jesus," he said, when he looked into the cab, discovered his prayers answered. He was twisting the keys, the engine sputtering to life when he heard the thunder. It was a bang, so loud, so strong, he felt the truck shake as if the very earth were splitting open beneath the wheels. He looked up, momentarily blinded by a rising mushroom cloud all but turning night into day.

It was climbing from the north end of the village, an explosion that size and so brilliant it hurt to observe the blazing mountain of fire, he knew it meant only one thing.

There was another team of invaders in the vicinity, and they had found and ignited the armory, running his direction. It looked like his mission was accomplished either way. He might even claim credit later for torching Ayoub's armory, a career move that would advance him out of the ranks of a mere spy marched out on lonely suicide missions.

Ridilson was about to hit the gas when the sky came crashing through the ceiling.

WHEN THE MOTHER of all blasts shattered the night, Bolan raced beneath a thick archway that led to a courtyard behind the colonel's compound. He hit the deck, threw his arms over his head as a tidal wave of rubble—whole rows of hovels obliterated no doubt by the explosion—flew for his backside. The sky was falling now, a meteor shower of lethal stones in all shapes and sizes pounding everything in sight. He had just spotted the armed figure hopping into the APC before this part of the world blew up. Decked out in a flaming red-and-white Aloha shirt and white slacks, armed nonetheless, Bolan assumed one of the tourists had somehow managed to escape when Dobson and his wild bunch made their entrance.

It didn't matter now who he was, as chunks of stone began a comet pounding of the cab, crushing the roof to crumpled tin.

He was on his feet, ready to take a curtain call for the crowd inside Ayoub's compound when the angry voice of Dobson began calling the troops over his com link.

SO FAR THE MISSION had gone too easy. Whenever that happened Dobson became disturbed.

It had been a clean takedown, top to bottom, Ayoub's soldiers—except one—littering the premises, never to rise. The lone exception was lashed with rope to a chair next to the colonel. For the purposes of persuading Ayoub to run his mouth about Hahmad, gasoline, meant to refuel the tourist bus, had been found down the hall.

"Douse his ass!" Dobson ordered, the soldier squirming against the ropes as Heidler emptied the can over his head. "Save some of that for our host."

He heard one of the tourists wretch at the stink of gasoline, or maybe, Dobson thought, he simply knew how the horror show was going to unfold.

The tourists were the first in a series of problems. According to the driver's count, one of them was missing. Dobson didn't have time or the men to spare on tracking down one AWOL sightseer. To get them to shut their mouths, he had assured the tourists they weren't going to get hurt. It was a promise he would have to break, and he did have enough rounds to spare to silence witnesses.

The floor had just stopped trembling beneath Dobson's feet, the roof still hammered by whatever raining debris had been launched over the village, when the armory went up.

The second problem was radio silence down the line.

Dobson tried both team leaders again, then called out for Alpha Zero.

More silence.

"Weiler, Jackson and Simms, go check it out. Something's wrong."

It occurred to him the missing commandos could have been either shot down by soldiers in the village or incinerated by the blast. Either way he needed answers, but his gut was getting that knot that usually warned him it was going to hell due to unforeseen circumstance.

"Okay, Colonel. One time only. Where's Hahmad?"

"I don't know."

Dobson nodded at the soldier beside Ayoub, then told his commando holding the gas-soaked rag. "Light this one up."

BOLAN SPRINTED for the pulped APC, taking in the courtyard on the run. He wasn't sure what he'd find inside Ayoub's abode, but he was going for broke, prepared to bull his way across the finish line if that's what it took to wax the rest of the enemy. Half of the commando force was eighty-sixed, the odds looking better all the time. Figure Dobson had his hands full between watching the tourists—assuming they were still alive—and grilling Ayoub, and the soldier had to believe his chances were better than fifty-fifty to nail it down.

The Executioner hit the front of the demolished APC, sights set on the open back door when the bone-chilling screams from inside the compound burst and told him the hardball Q and A was in full swing. He thought he heard a groan from inside the cab's shell, then three of Dobson's finest came running out the door.

The soldier stepped out and raked them with a long burst of SMG fire. It wasn't quite the way he wanted to play out the encore, hoping for silent penetration until he was right on top of the others, but the hideous wailing, he hoped, would mask the burping of his subgun, the grunts and curses of men dying hard on their feet.

They never knew what hit them, but better still they never got off a shot.

As soon as the diced human dominoes toppled, Bolan wrenched open the driver's door. The would-be runner was a bloody mess, wedged beneath the steering wheel, a hunk of rubble the size of a Godzilla testicle having landed and missed him by inches.

"Can you move?" Bolan asked.

"I don't think anything's broken. You're one of

them, aren't you? Go ahead and just shoot me then.''

"Wrong. I'm with me.''

"I heard shooting.''

"That was me, shaving the odds.''

"You're after those bastards?''

"I don't have time to explain. Are your tourist friends still alive?''

"Last time I saw, and I'm no tourist.''

"Then what?''

"CIA.''

That took Bolan by surprise, but questions were on hold. He checked the door, the courtyard in both directions, the screams fading now, the faintest sounds of sobbing, puking and a man pleading for his life seeming swept outside on the dying echoes of agony. The CIA man held out a hand, asked for help and Bolan malingered a few more dangerous moments honoring the request. The CIA man grunted and groaned as he squeezed and squirmed his way out from beneath the crumbled dash, dumping himself on his haunches.

"Stay put. It's almost over.''

"Not a problem, guy. Good luck finishing off those animals.''

Bolan nodded, fed his SMG a fresh magazine, then resumed the hunt.

CHAPTER EIGHT

"How can I tell you what I don't know? Please, I implore you! For the love of God, let me go. I will forget I ever saw you."

"Stop sniveling! You're supposed to be an officer, a leader of men! We're professionals here, Colonel, you're embarrassing yourself. I ought to light you up just for cowardice!"

"I always hated officers—well, most of them, present company excepted naturally," Ayoub heard another voice say, chuckling. "When the heat is on, they wilt under fire—most of them, that is—sir."

"Yeah, well, he doesn't start singing the heat will be on."

It was a nightmare beyond his worst fears and comprehension, and he'd give anything, tell them anything to stop the pain.

They were only slapping him in the face, of course, trying to revive him as he kept passing out after they torched Captain Thoubaff, but it hurt just the same, stinging lashes that rang his bell so hard it felt as if hot needles were being lanced into his eardrums. He didn't like pain, no degree of discomfort, in fact, which was why he'd set himself up in grand style and easy living that might have been seen as a sleight to the other villagers. It wasn't so much the pain itself, as it was the fear of pain.

And the fear itself.

Fear of being burned alive.

There was shame, too, as he smelled the vomit and urine soiling his uniform. He heard the whimper escape his parched mouth, licking his lips, hoping to find his voice, if only to implore them to be reasonable.

"Where's Hahmad, Colonel?"

"I told you—"

The slap that came was swift and unexpected.

Then he saw the black-clad commando clack the lid on the lighter, holding up the gas-drenched rag. Ayoub wretched, the stench of charred flesh cloying his nose, swelling his brain, it seemed, with nausea. He started fainting when he was slapped again. The sobbing and moaning of the tourists could have been coming from the next country. Everything was turning hazy, bile like fire in his chest, his rear glued to the seat where he slimed his trousers. Why wouldn't someone help? Were the tourists that afraid of a few men with guns?

"You did business with the man, right?"

"Y-yes. But the ammonium nitrate fertilizer, it came from Libya—"

"We know that. Your precious cargo is gone, Colonel, up in smoke, never to find its way into the hands of some jihad flunkies who might run a suicide truck into an embassy or U.S. military barracks.

What we need to know is the how, when and where on Hahmad.''

''He is not a stupid man. He does not inform me of his comings and goings, his secret routes, his cutouts who help him slip in and out of other countries.''

''He doesn't know anything.''

A new voice, softer than the slapping commando. Yes, yes, he heard his mind scream, he knew nothing. A man of reason was stepping forth. Perhaps there was hope yet. They were mercenaries of some sort, he was sure, which meant, if all else failed, he could buy his life.

''One last time, Colonel.''

''I told you.''

''Hahmad may not be a stupid man, but you certainly are, Colonel. Not only that, but a few of our comrades were stabbed in the back by you. Algeria? Remember?''

''That's not entirely true. They knew the risk—''

''Light him up.''

''No! Wait! I have money!''

''We don't need money.''

''Wait!''

''Light his ass up!''

He saw the commando set fire to the rag, heard himself screaming but knew it was only the first in a long wail he would take to the grave.

THE EXECUTIONER might have tagged them all as soon as he padded into some sort of banquet room, subgun up and deathsights laser-locked on the trio of commandos gathered around Ayoub in the living room.

Might have, could have, should have was for the grandstanders, he knew.

He took it as it came, and it came ugly.

First, they lit up Ayoub in a fireball, the colonel ripping loose with the same bansheelike screams that had torn earlier from the blackened corpse of human pyre number one. It was too much for the tourists this time around, and several tried to break and run for the front door. Any other time and Bolan would have spared a mercy burst for Ayoub, but a commando picked that moment to check his six.

A microsecond of recognition of Alpha Zero registered in the commando's eyes, but it was swept away by pure menacing intent next as instinct warned the hardman he was faced with a clear and present danger.

The Galil was stuttering, a burst of 5.56 mm lead hornets buzzing past Bolan, but the soldier was already stitching the commando across the chest, the SMG chattering on, tagging two more commandos as they sidled into view.

"You rotten, traitorous son of a bitch!" Dobson bellowed, glancing at Bolan, then snatching up a Japanese girl. "I fucking knew it!"

The stampede was under way, tourists bowling into two commandos. Dodging runners, the commandos returned fire, driving Bolan to cover inside the archway, Ayoub's screams knifing the air, adding to the horror and chaos.

''Out the fucking door! Hey, Zero! I'll waste this girl.''

The slugs stopped chewing up the archway a second later, as Bolan made out the chatter of an assault rifle from the direction where the tourists were beating their exit out the front door. Sharp cries of men in pain rang out, and Bolan figured a new shooter had joined the party.

The Executioner went low around the corner, saw the girl's father grab at Dobson's arm. The commando leader snarled, swinging his weapon toward the father when Bolan tapped the SMG's trigger, going for exposed leg. Hot lead sheared off a hunk of Dobson's thigh, the commando's bellow rising in decibels, pain and shock nearly winking out the brain's motor. The girl broke free, Dobson shimmying on his good leg, when the Executioner sprayed the commando leader, throat to crotch with a swarm of 9 mm death.

Down and gone.

Bolan stepped out into the living room, SMG trained on the front door as the CIA man entered, his AK-47 wandering in the direction of the littered corpses.

''I guess the show's over,'' the agent said. ''I don't believe we were ever properly introduced. I'm Ridilson.''

''Alpha Zero.''

''What?''

''That's what this bunch tagged me. Call me Bob.''

''Okay—Bob. Besides good, what are you?''

"We'll skip that for now. I think we need to make tracks."

"I agree. There's got to be a few of Ayoub's soldiers on the loose still, and I don't think the natives are too happy about seeing their village blown back into the Stone Age. If this bunch ran a repeat performance of what we know they did in Egypt, I'm thinking however many of them you iced on the way in didn't much care about the welfare of women and children."

"You could most definitely say that."

Bolan checked the stairs, the banquet room, looked to the front door, listening to the night world outside as he heard an engine grinding to life. Ridilson moved and began tearing through a pile of nylon pouches and satchels in the corner of the room.

"Any chance," Bolan asked, "you can get us out of the country?"

"Way ahead of you. We're covered."

Ridilson stood, checking out what looked to Bolan like a camcorder.

"I need a secured sat link."

"You want a lot," Ridilson said.

"Let's roll."

The soldier gave the abattoir one last look. The tourists had fled, and he found the last of the group bounding onto the bus. A lot of innocent people had died this night, and it burned Bolan to know there was very little he could have done to prevent the slaughter he'd put behind. Time to go, and there was never any time in his world for the blame game. If nothing else, the savages responsible would never kill again.

"Grab some spare clips for that Kalashnikov," Bolan said, and hauled in an RPG-7 for himself.

"It's your party."

"This look like some disco to you?"

"Gotcha." Ridilson held out the camcorder and smiled. "One secured portable sat link at your service."

The Executioner led the way across the courtyard. No armed shadows came running, but he stayed on high alert.

"I saw a motor pool about a hundred yards that way," Ridilson said, nodding at the wall toward the east. "There they go," the CIA man added, looking at the bus pulling out. "This is one vacation I don't think they'll forget anytime soon. Not one for the scrapbooks, you think?"

Bolan let that slide and picked up the pace.

THE SOLDIER LISTENED as Ridilson told him how to unlatch the camcorder, assuring him whatever numbers he punched in wouldn't be cracked by his team. It wouldn't be the first time Bolan had worked with the CIA, and he wasn't about to take anything Ridilson told him as gospel truth.

The CIA man had the wheel of the Land Rover, heading them in a northeasterly direction, lights out as they rolled over the barren plain, the man navigating with the aid of Bolan's NVD goggles. Behind them, Bolan saw the few straggling shadows of villagers milling about in the umbrella of firelight. A mountain of smoke rose for the sky where the earth was cratered from the blast. It had been touch and go the whole way, a few seconds lost here or there, and the soldier knew he would have been smeared in 1001 pieces by the blast.

Small comfort the bad guys were dead, and on that score he had achieved one goal. Marquis was losing killers at a furious pace, but there was more to do, and the butcher's work had only begun. Bolan needed to touch base with Brognola, put their heads together and figure out where it went from there.

Paris could be out, for the time being, unless the soldier wanted to blitz his way back into the City of Lights, risk the wrath of French police, who weren't exactly American friendly and who were most likely in the entrepreneur's pocket. Marquis would eventually learn about the disaster in Tunisia, and with any luck Alpha Zero would be presumed dead, perhaps opening a back door where the soldier could slip through and nail it down.

"To answer your question," Bolan said, "I'm with the Justice Department."

"Uh-huh. Bob from the Justice Department. This where I give all and you give me squat?"

"I'm sanctioned to take down Marquis and his bounty-hunting operation."

"So, you want a ride back to Paris? Collect all the heads for JD's mantel?"

"I'm not sure yet."

"Just get us out of Dodge?"

"You got it."

"Guess you want to know what I was doing tagging along with those tourists?"

"You want to keep me on a need to know, that's your call."

Ridilson seemed to consider his next words, his gaze scanning the vast darkness. Bolan let him drive in silence, both of them watching their surroundings for army patrols.

"The CIA has a lead, or thought they had, on Hahmad," Ridilson finally said. "They sent me down here to take a look at Ayoub's operation, smoke it out and report back. I know, one man, you're thinking. Well, the geniuses running the show in Tunis thought maybe I'd troop into that village on my lonesome and catch Hahmad arm in arm with the late colonel, since the two of them were doing business. Phone home and they'd fly down a black-ops team, bag Hahmad. Thing is, Hahmad's long gone. I knew that, but my so-called superiors are keeping hope alive the bastard's still in the neighborhood. My guess is he's in Libya or Egypt by now. The slippery eel…anyway, Hahmad, I'm sure you know, is one of the most wanted terrorists alive. The Israeli Mossad is in on the hunt, too, and those guys do more than bang on the war drum. Word is they've mounted a first-class black-ops team to burn down Hahmad and his jihad troublemakers."

That was news to Bolan, but he kept his expression neutral, let the CIA man talk.

"Hahmad has an operation in Lebanon, and marches out the suicide troops with greater frequency these days. This thing is going to get ugly if the Israelis start landing a bunch of black ops in North Africa or Syria or wherever they even think Hahmad is holed up.''

''It's already ugly.''

''Right.''

Ridilson lapsed into hard silence. The soldier stayed quiet and alert, eager to get out of Tunisia.

It was hot all over the desert, and Bolan was certain the heat was still on, looking to scorch him before he was on his way out of the country.

''FORGET PARIS FOR NOW. I need you back here, and like five minutes ago, Striker. I've got a major situation, a wave we could catch to shore. Here's the story.''

The hard drive brought Bolan to a series of tents in a wadi. Four armed shadows, Berbers, he assumed, were Ridilson's in-country contacts, hunched now over a fire, AK-47s by their feet. Their ride to Tunis was an ancient Bell Huey, an American pilot who had been introduced as Taslowe cranking up the engine, Ridilson hollering for Bolan they had to go. With the portable handheld sat link, the soldier paced near the tents, rotor wash kicking up dust and grit as the blades spun to life. The plan was to fly to a CIA outpost south of Tunis where a waiting Gulfstream jet would fly Bolan back to the States.

He had already filled in the big Fed, now listened to what Brognola had waiting in the wings. When Brognola finished laying it out, the Stony Man warrior told him he had a few ideas of his own.

A wave to shore, right, he thought. Could be. He was thinking about time lost in the air, but Brognola had his own people monitoring the situation in question, assured Bolan they'd keep the lid on until he arrived.

The Executioner bounded up into the belly of the Huey, settled on the bench. They lifted off, not a second too soon, as far as Bolan was concerned, the chopper climbing into the night sky. With any luck he'd be on that jet within the hour, saying goodbye to Tunisia. It had been a nightmare run, but the Executioner knew the worst was just over the next horizon. Bolan told Brognola he'd call back when he was on his way out of Tunisia, signed off. There was a lot to think about, another battlefront on the way.

"Guess when we make the next taxi stop we'll part company, Bob."

Ridilson held out his hand, and Bolan shook it.

"I don't know who you really are, suppose it doesn't much matter. I'll tell you this, if you hadn't shown up and did what you did, there'd be a whole lot more innocent dead people right now. You're all right, Bob."

"Back at you."

"This thing shapes up the way my people think it might...well, you never know, we might run into each other again."

"You never know."

CHAPTER NINE

France

Dante Marquis was normally a wine man, but the moment called for something stronger, and lots of it. The whiskey went down the hatch again, harsh and burning, a little smoother, though, the fourth or fifth time around, then he moved to the bar and built another double. He could feel Anglerre, perched on his stool, watching him, waiting, wondering, no doubt, where it all went from there.

"If you have something to say, say it. Do not sit there, like a piece of stone, afraid to speak up!"

"Perhaps you should take it easy on that stuff."

Marquis nearly lost it, rage shooting through him, head to toe.

"More than twelve hours, eighteen more men either dead or captured, my world is about to go up in flames," Marquis rasped, nearly topping the glass with straight whiskey, then splashed some ginger on top, "and you want me to relax?"

"Not relax, but think. We need a plan. There is trouble, a lot of it."

"Tell me something I don't know!"

They were alone in the game room of the club, the nightlife beyond the doors gearing up now, laughter and talk rising in decibels with each round of drinks. Marquis walked to one of the two billiard tables, picked up the cue ball, tossing it up and down in his hand. He was feeling very strange, very alone these days. He was torn between mounting paranoia and hot fury, unable to calm himself, and the whiskey wasn't helping to take the jangle out of his nerves. On all fronts it was set to spiral down the toilet. Business was also suffering, Marquis neglecting his daily routine at the office, dodging phone calls, barking at subordinates to handle routine affairs.

"How could this have happened? And now even our contacts in Tunis have pulled up the drawbridge, all but disappearing into thin air. Not even our Interpol people are returning our phone calls! This is disastrous!"

"That is not quite true," Anglerre said, unsure but sounding as if he wanted to appease. "Lassere said he would call us as soon as he learns what happened down there."

"What do we know? Chabeaux did a flyover of the village. They shot pictures of the carnage. Dead men, all over the place, and with the explosion of the armory, all the debris and rubble, there is no way of telling who is who or what is what. We don't know if Ayoub is alive or dead! All we know is they did not make the pickup site! We must assume the worst!"

"We must concentrate on San Francisco. As you ordered, I flew out another squad of men to shore up our forces. They have arrived and LaPierre is waiting for your order to move on the targets.''

''We are losing good commandos so fast we are soon to be without even a security detail!''

''I am presently correcting that situation.''

''How? By going to the street and hiring common murderers and rapists and pickpockets?''

''It will be handled through the usual channels. The men I recruit to replace our losses of commandos will be professionals, I assure you.''

Marquis sipped quietly on his drink. He glimpsed his reflection in the bar mirror, resisted the sudden impulse to shatter the image with the cue ball, detesting suddenly what he saw staring back. He looked old, tired and frightened. What did it profit a man, he thought, to gain the world...?

Screw that. He had the world, but he wondered if that was enough. Maybe it was never enough. Money, fame, love. For all his money he couldn't track down one man and kill him. It was infuriating, maddening, in fact.

''Do they understand what they are to do in America?''

''Yes,'' Anglerre answered. ''They are looking at three separate Syrian families. Should they be forced to kill or torture most of them, they will make sure one adult male prisoner is taken. However, I must caution you on any optimism regarding a prisoner leading us to Hahmad.''

''But the link has been established?''

''Yes. The trouble is, we know the Justice Department is wise to the Syrian cell.''

''And?''

''A run-in, worse, some shootout with American

authorities could only make our troubles worse. A few of our men over there are sort of using the San Francisco office as a base of operations.''

''Sort of? Either they are or they aren't!''

''They are. And with three dead VIPs in the company...''

''Missing.''

''Of course. Missing.''

''Do you know something, Anglerre? I no longer care about my business in America. It can go to hell. I'm not sure I even care any longer about the company at all. If it survives all of this, so be it. If not...I'll leave the country, go into exile. A modern-day Napoleon. The walls are closing in, and I am suffocating on anxiety and fear in Paris. Rumors of Justice agents traipsing all over Paris, I am losing confidence by the hour in our Interpol men. You want a plan, here it is.'' He watched as Anglerre twisted on the stool, intent. ''Any more disasters, no, this is what we do and now. I want Lassere to set it up through his people in Egypt. That is where Hahmad hides when it gets hot.''

''Or Syria, or Beirut.''

''We comb Egypt first...''

'''We'?''

''Yes, dammit, we! Our next operation will see myself in charge, from the trenches, so to speak.''

''But...''

Marquis threw the glass, which missiled over Anglerre's head and shattered the mirror, his right-hand man flinching, looking at him as if he'd lost his mind. ''It is so ordered! Arrange it, a weapons drop, sat recon, Lassere, some clue, even a rumor where Hahmad is currently hiding in the darkness like the cockroach he is. Shake some trees, kick some ass, threaten our Interpol people, pay them more, I don't care. We leave as soon as it is arranged. Are we clear?"

"Crystal."

"Then what are you waiting for?"

California

SOUTH OF Market Street stretched a vast neighborhood of warehouses, industrial parks, factory-outlet stores and bungalows where the free spirits holed up, doing whatever they did to help lend San Francisco its image of artistic tolerance and self-indulgence.

It was also where Bolan planned to start the next leg of the campaign, having run it past Brognola, both men agreeing it was time to crank up some serious heat, send a message of doom back to Paris.

There had been too much lost time in the air, Brognola working out the logistics while the soldier flew in to the States, jetted west, the big Fed getting Special Agent Belasko out to the West Coast and planted as the man in charge of the Justice Department special task force, and the soldier was anxious to jump-start this outing.

It was burn and blitz on the menu. The Justice Department agents were ordered strictly as backup for Bolan, his eyes and ears. He could tell that didn't sit well with a few of them, but the kind of action he was prepared to bring to the city went far beyond SOP in the Justice manual.

Rumor was that Hahmad had landed a terror cell

in the city by the bay, three families of Syrians, most of them male and of fighting age. According to Justice surveillance, Marquis had a shadow army that was aware of the terrorist nest also, as men tagged as Marquis's ex-Legionnaires staked out the targeted Syrian homes and businesses. If it worked out the way he envisioned, Bolan planned to bag one prisoner from each camp, make somebody sing long and loud to steer him back overseas to resume the hunt for Hahmad or wherever Marquis's next round of headhunters would land. A war was heating up in San Francisco, a lot of waiting and watching at the moment, Brognola's people monitoring the target sites from Marquis's American office to the Syrian hiding holes.

The Executioner was going for an end run at Marquis, and he was starting with the Frenchman's warehouse. The idea was to start toppling the man's kingdom from the outside, torching his merchandise, making the security henchmen sweat and wonder as they made their drive-bys of the Syrian homes in question. If it blew up before he was ready to make his final move, Bolan had left orders for Special Agent Bangle to call on his cell phone.

He found a parking space in front of a chain of stores, boutiques, cafés and restaurants, two blocks down from the Marquis warehouse. The loose-fitting windbreaker would hide his standard side arms, plus conceal the mini-Uzi in special shoulder rigging. The pockets held two incendiary grenades, the small nylon pouch slung around his shoulder carrying a block of C-4 meant to get the firestorm started. The large war bag was locked in the trunk, bulging with other hardware and fire-starting goodies he would need to give new meaning to urban warfare.

He was out and moving double time down an alley that led to Marquis's warehouse, blood racing as he knew he was moments away from serving notice to the Frenchman he was no longer welcome in America. Justice had the warehouse under surveillance, but Bolan had spied it on an earlier drive-by. There appeared some questionable activity, lean, grim men in dark suit jackets with visible bulges emerging from the warehouse with large nylon satchels, barking orders at the workforce. Bolan's gut told him he might find more than just video games and CD-ROMs on-site. If the Frenchman had landed a small army in America, then the warehouse could double as an armory.

One way to find out.

The armed guard was out of the booth, stepping up to the chain-link gate when Bolan drew the mini-Uzi.

"Open up," the soldier ordered.

The gate slid open at the touch of an electronic button. Bolan told the guard, "Lose the piece, then beat it. I'm shutting this place down."

"You're making a big mistake."

"It wouldn't be my first. Move out."

The guard did as he was told, tossing the 9 mm Glock, then scurrying past Bolan. Then the Executioner rolled on toward the eighteen-wheeler where three men smoked and lingered while a forklift driver rolled a pallet of crates into the belly of the rig.

When the foursome saw the big man with the mini-Uzi marching straight for them, the smoking stopped and eyes bugged.

"You guys are off the clock," Bolan said. "In fact, you're unemployed as of today."

They remained frozen until the Executioner hit the trigger of the mini-Uzi and drilled a burst of 9 mm slugs into the wall of the tractor trailer.

LAPIERRE HAD temporarily inherited the late vice president's office suite. He had passed the word on to lesser-ranking VIPs that the errant threesome were on vacation, that he was sent by Monsieur Marquis to handle business in their absence. If anyone had a problem with that, he was to feel free to call the man personally.

No takers. What a surprise.

Naturally he didn't intend on hanging around the posh suite any longer than necessary. The truth was Marquis had just called and given the green light to proceed against the Syrians. It would be nice to get out in the field, start kicking ass, not hang around the office catching suspicious looks from the workforce, eyes darting over the noticeable double bulges of the shoulder-rigged twin 9 mm Glocks beneath his suit jacket.

The orders were clear. Bag a Syrian, then phone Marquis when the task was completed for further orders. The man did tell him they were on their way to Egypt, and that made LaPierre wonder for a moment just what the hell was going on. Marquis sounded unusually stressed, on edge, in fact, as if he was intoxicated out of his gourd and going off the deep end. Marquis was becoming more fixated to the point of obsession on his quest for Hahmad's head, and LaPierre wondered about the man's sanity. Not only that, but the man was letting business slide down the tubes, if the books LaPierre had perused were any indication of the thievery going on behind his back in the States.

Well, he wasn't any businessman in a suit, and three thieves would never be heard from again.

He was rising from the deep-cushioned leather swivel chair, checking out the view of the skyline of the financial district, when his cell phone trilled. He punched on, heard the harried voice of the security guard at the warehouse tell him some big guy with a machine pistol was shooting the place up.

LaPierre nearly toppled back into the chair. He told the man to slow down, run it by him again.

It was the same story.

What the hell was this? Who? Why? If it was a raid by Justice or the FBI, they wouldn't just roll in one shooter.

"Do not call the police," LaPierre told the man. "I'll handle it."

He punched off, then rang up Montmarte's number. "We have a problem at the warehouse."

CHAPTER TEN

It took a full clip, winging around the swarms of 9 mm Parabellum hornets over their heads, but Bolan had the stampede in high gear, ten steps into the warehouse, voices flinging questions and curses in fear, on the fly. A fresh magazine in place, cocked and locked, the soldier let them beat their exit through the open rolling door, barked at a couple of paralyzed stragglers to get going, then gave the sprawling warehouse a look when the place was cleared of bodies. Thick plastic was wrapped around video and pinball machines stacked on pallets. There were crates labeled computers; other boxes he found choked with DVDs. Then he spotted three large wooden crates in a deep corner, sitting by their lonesome. Finding a crowbar on a workbench, he went and pried off the lid. Inside he found Uzis, Glocks, spare clips.

Bingo.

The soldier went to work, placing the C-4 charges at strategic points around the warehouse, opting for one meshing blast that would consume all merchandise in a firestorm, legal or otherwise, up in smoke.

He primed them with a radio-activated detonator, all
the blocks tied in to one frequency.

Beyond the open door he heard engines growling
to life, tires squealing as the workforce vacated the
premises. Someone was sure to phone the home office in San Francisco about the armed incursion, but
Bolan was counting on the alarm being sounded
about one mysterious madman on the loose at the
warehouse.

The first stop on his shopping list was nearly a
wrap, no resistance, but armed force would show up
soon enough. Of course word would reach whoever
was in charge of the armed guard in America, which
would go searing overseas to Marquis, the Frenchman wondering who in the world was razing his
operation in America, and why. The idea was to
make them nervous, get them running scared,
flushed out into the open where he could pick them
off, one by one, in groups, however they showed up
in his gun sights.

And there was the Syrian terror cell waiting in the
wings, under watch in the Mission District.

The soldier was wondering how long it would
take to get the enemy troops scrambling his way
when he saw the black Lexus lurch to a halt in the
mouth of the doorway.

Doors opened, disgorging three men who came
out firing 9 mm Glocks.

MONTMARTE DIDN'T understand what was going on,
but he had his orders. One crazy guy was inside the
warehouse, having driven out the entire workforce

with subgun fire for reasons unknown, and LaPierre wanted the ballsy bastard nailed. Any questions were on hold, as the big guy inside the warehouse opened fire on them with his mini-Uzi, the stubby SMG flaming from around the corner of a crate.

Montmarte flinched, ducking for cover behind his door, and triggered his Glock wildly as the spray of lead washed over the Lexus, blasting out windows in lethal flying glass shrapnel. He heard Dubenaux cry out, glimpsed the man toppling back, Glock cracking skyward, blood spurting from his chest.

Who the hell was this guy?

They had only just left the warehouse not more than an hour ago, the latest round of soldiers from Paris having been armed from the stash, marched out to take up positions where the Syrians were hunkered down. Someone was onto them, aware of the deadly game about to go down, or so it stood to reason. Who? Montmarte wondered again as bullets spanged off metal. That was no ordinary law-enforcement officer, blasting away as if he knew what he was all about. That was a soldier, a killer.

It didn't matter either way. He needed to get busy, down to just himself and Chaisson on the other side, trading fire with the bastard who had them outmatched in firepower.

He was looking up, wondering at the sudden lull in the shooting when he saw the steel egg bouncing under the front end of the Lexus. He didn't consider screaming ''grenade,'' warning his companion—no time, he figured—as he dashed to the side, away from the coming blast.

When it detonated, he felt the terrible heat reaching out with a scorching hand, then heard the hideous screams raking the air. Looking back, he found his companion had been lit up into a flaming scarecrow.

IT WAS A WASTE of a good thermite bomb, but Bolan couldn't spare the time, getting bogged down in a standoff, SFPD sure to come flying onto the lot in short order. Besides, he was loaded to the gills as far as ammo and grenades were concerned.

Plenty to spare in the firepower department, with no shortage of enemy numbers on the menu between the Frenchman's army and the Syrians.

The brilliant fireball lifted the Lexus off its wheels, before it bounced down on fiery rubber while angry flames boiled out from beneath the chassis. One hardman cleared the epicenter, and Bolan spared the flaming demon a quick mercy burst from his mini-Uzi. He was racing for the edge of the doorway, peering around the corner, when the surviving hardman scrambled to his feet. Bolan needed a live one, but number three wasn't destined to be his pigeon. The guy stood, wobbly from the concussive force of the blast, but triggering his Glock in a rapid-fire spray and pray, eyes wild, mouth ripping loose with curses in French.

The Executioner marched a line of slugs across his chest, knocked him off his feet.

The tough part would be clearing the scene without SFPD swarming him. Brognola would flex some muscle on his end to get Bolan cut loose if the police grabbed him, but it would be time-consuming, raising too many questions about Justice operating procedure, red tape to hack through, cops grumbling.

The Executioner sprinted across the lot, palmed the radio remote box and thumbed on the red light. He was past the gate, the alley clear back to his ride, when he heard a sound of rolling thunder, four massive fireballs, he knew, that would incinerate everything inside the warehouse.

Dante Marquis was on short notice.

THE ARCADE WAS located between Montgomery and Sansome Streets. Planted in an area that was at one point in the city's history awash in brothels and saloons, Bolan found the atmosphere inside the arcade electric with what he imagined the howling ghosts of frenzy and desire that once haunted the neighborhood when it catered to pirates and cutthroats who came trolling for fun and games.

It was Marquis's contribution to American culture, the arcade chock-full of his 3-D video games, banks of pinball machines, everything catering to simulated violence with busty, semiclad women painted on the score banks for the pinball wizards. The soldier could have skipped this round altogether, but it was on the way to Marquis's office, where the soldier planned on paying the armed guard on-site a courtesy call.

They were mostly teenagers, Bolan wondering why they weren't in school at that hour, but he spotted some gangbangers on the way in from the back door, Raiders jackets open to display semiautomatic pistols, mean eyes glancing his way from beneath the standard do-rags.

Life in the big city, he thought, and marched on for the proprietor, who was hunched at his upraised cubicle, peering at a skin magazine.

"Yeah," the fat guy behind the counter grumbled, not bothering to look up.

"Clear the place out. There's going to be a fire."

Now the guy looked up, attentive as hell, in time to lose the scowl when he found himself staring down the muzzle of Bolan's mini-Uzi.

"What...who...?"

Bolan turned toward the players. "Everybody clear out. The fun and games are over."

The gangbangers hesitated, Bolan watching them as one of them reached inside his jacket. "I wouldn't."

And the soldier loosed a long burst of subgun fire over their heads, the autofire drilling into the ceiling, raining plaster and dust on the stampede. The proprietor was screaming at Bolan he was nuts, when the soldier adjusted his aim, put the guy in flight with a short burst that blew apart his change machine. All clear, and the soldier primed his thermite bomb. He retraced his steps for the back exit, lobbed the incendiary egg in the deep corner of the arcade.

It blew as he hit the door, spewing hungry flames that would bring the place down in minutes.

Bolan was only just getting warmed up to show Marquis what he thought of his contribution to American culture.

"WHAT THE HELL is going on out there? Who is this bastard?"

"How should I know?"

"Describe him!"

The proprietor did. It matched the description of the bastard who had blown up their warehouse.

LaPierre heard himself screaming into the cell phone, a string of curses in French echoing throughout the office suite, the second of two horrifying reports reaching him within a span of thirty minutes. Lomaire did a drive-by of the warehouse, finding the place in flames, Montmarte and his crew dead, one of them burned to a crisp, as if the attacker was armed with incendiary grenades. The backup team had just cleared out when SFPD and an armada of fire trucks rushed onto the firestorm.

Now the manager of their arcade, the latest report of the same lone gunman rolling in, clearing the place out before he torched it with another thermite grenade. Forget the millions of dollars in merchandise, equipment, even weapons lost—LaPierre knew when he was being hunted. Whoever was after them was clearly military issue of some sort, a stone-cold professional with a track record. That kind of firepower, those kind of stones...

"Do not talk to the police. You know nothing," LaPierre snarled at the manager, and signed off.

It was time to do the job he was sent to America for anyway. His team was in place at the apartment building, prepared to storm in and hopefully snag a talking Syrian head.

He stood, frozen at the horseshoe desk for a long

moment just the same. There was no way the late trio of VIPs could have some lone avenger on the loose, looking to even the score. The bodies had been dumped in the bay, and it was too soon for anyone to start thinking foul play as far as the missing VIPs went. Then who? The Feds didn't operate with such brazen violence.

Whatever was happening it was utter insanity, frightening, in fact.

Well, the ship was sinking in America, and it was time to bail, but not before the mission was accomplished. It should have been done sooner, but there were Feds prowling about, easy enough for his men to mark on their own stakeout of the Syrians' apartment complex. Marquis, probably thinking he couldn't do the job himself, had ordered they hold off until he beefed up the forces.

Trouble was the force was already thinned out by three shooters. They were looking at twenty-one Syrian males of fighting age when they crashed through the doors. Then there were family members to contend with, cops and Feds who might drop the net, forcing them to fight their way out of the country.

Oh, but the madness had clearly begun, and it wasn't even by his own hand.

LaPierre flew out into the reception bay, ignoring the bustle of executives and secretaries flying around, glancing at him with startled eyes. Whatever was set to go down, he was sure they would all be out of a job soon. Marquis was finished in America. The police were sure to come knocking on office doors, throwing around questions, digging into their business. He was licensed to carry a weapon, as were all his men, but he could hear the litany of questions already, cops suspicious as hell, wondering why the office needed armed guards lurking about.

And that was just for starters.

He was sweeping past the receptionist's desk when he spotted a big figure captured by the camera monitoring the lobby. A dark guy, all grim business, flashing something in the guard's face, then marching on for the elevator.

He couldn't be positive, but there was something in the big guy's manner that warned him the madman on the loose had just entered the building.

LaPierre hastened his stride for the elevator bank, watching the lights as they flashed and the big guy made his way for the top floor.

He wasn't about to take any chances, searching the corridor, finding it clear at the moment of any watching eyes.

He reached inside his jacket, wrapped a hand around one of the Glocks.

THE OFFICE BUILDING in San Francisco wasn't quite the same setup that he'd found in Paris. Only the top two floors belonged to Marquis. So he couldn't burn down the building, but Bangle's men had the parking garage and front lobby under surveillance, and they had filled him in on the comings and goings of strange faces. The latest face on the premises had been tagged as belonging to an ex-Legionnaire by the name of LaPierre.

Unless the man was completely insane, going for hardware in full view of the workforce, Bolan hoped for a fairly easy snatch of a prisoner.

Of course, the man could have heard by now how the firestorm was spreading his way, driven by confusion, panic and fury.

Then there was the security camera at the guard's desk, an itch going down Bolan's spine that warned him he was made coming in.

No sweat. He'd take it as it came.

The heat was building, the Justice teams were in place and it was time to push the envelope.

He wanted LaPierre in the net, alive and thrashing.

Paris might have been watched by Justice agents, but with disaster dropping on Marquis all over the map, he figured the man would get nervous, perhaps even want to vacate Paris for a while, regroup, add to his depleted force of commandos. And maybe light another fire to the seats of his headhunters, ship them off for another stab at Hahmad, the walls closing in to crush his hunger for revenge.

At this point Bolan needed a prisoner, someone he could turn the screws on, find out what Marquis had on the back burner.

The Executioner watched the lights flash as the car climbed. He wasn't sure what it was, but paranoia flared to life, warning him it might have been smarter to sweat out a long haul up the stairs. He didn't think LaPierre would prove himself a desperate cornered animal....

The doors opened, and Bolan found out just how wrong he was.

CHAPTER ELEVEN

As soon as the doors parted, Bolan read the silent communication in the man's eyes. One heartbeat, and the former Legionnaire told Bolan he knew he was the fire starter come to burn him down now. There was also respect, fear and pure menace staring back at the soldier.

Heartbeat number two, and there was body language to back up the look of murderous intent. The Glock was snaking free of its holster, coming out and around for target acquisition. The former Legionnaire nearly had the weapon drawn on his chest, but Bolan was charging ahead, clamping a viselike grip over the wrist. The problem was the gun was free and clear, cracking out a 9 mm round, the soldier glimpsing his reflection lost in a spiderweb as the slug shattered the mirrored wall of the elevator car. Bolan slammed a head butt off the Frenchman's nose, squelching bone and loosing a faucet of red gore.

When LaPierre didn't buckle or even lose his grip on the Glock, Bolan knew he was faced with a raging bull of an opponent.

The knee speared Bolan in the side, the wind

punched from his gut. The free hand came out of nowhere next, a fist that hammered off Bolan's jaw, adding a light show to the knifing pain in his side. Somehow he held on, coming back right away, matching the Frenchman's tenacity even in the next instant after he nearly faltered from the punishing blows, aware they were going the distance. One lost step, one extra blink of the eyes and someone was down for the count and not getting back up.

The Executioner locked a hand on the man's windpipe as they tumbled into the car, the doors closing. The Glock roared twice as Bolan thrust the gun hand up. The mirrored roof came down in sheets of glass, LaPierre exploding a forearm up and through Bolan's stranglehold. If he let go of the gun hand, the soldier knew it was over.

They spun, glass raining off their skulls, LaPierre reaching out with a clawed hand, fingers seeking to gouge out Bolan's eyes. Swatting the hand away, Bolan shot another head butt into the face of rage. His forehead slashed the man just above the eye, opening a gash like a burst pipe where hot blood instantly ran into the orb. With the eye stung he was half-blinded, and Bolan felt his opponent faltering for a moment where he might turn the tide.

Grabbing a handful of shirt, the Executioner, fueled by adrenaline and driven by his own fear into decisive action, lifted LaPierre an inch or so off his wing tips. A cycloning pirouette, and Bolan slammed the Frenchman into the remaining sheet of glass. The car shuddered as if the building were about to topple from one of San Francisco's famous quakes.

Air belched from LaPierre's mouth, blood flew into Bolan's face, but he wouldn't give up the gun, which rang out another round, the slipstream of hot lead tearing past the warrior's scalp, his ears ringing so loudly now he nearly couldn't hear the retort of the next shot.

He spun the Frenchman again, two charging steps, and rammed him into the other wall. The gun came free, falling, crackling into a bed of glass. Incredibly LaPierre started to bellow, fury lighting his eyes, bringing back the demon, as he slammed an uppercut off Bolan's jaw. The Executioner staggered back a step. He glimpsed the blurring fist, a roundhouse on the way, flying for his jaw through the fractured light, and slipped under it with a microsecond to spare, knuckles scraping the top of his skull. The miss was all the soldier needed to retaliate with a fresh burst of adrenaline-powered might, and Bolan put a pile driver into his adversary's guts. If the man's stomach hadn't been like steel washboard, the blow, Bolan knew, might have scraped spine and started a slow, agonizing death from internal bleeding.

The ex-Legionnaire dropped to his knees with a thud, and Bolan found himself momentarily grateful it was over, and that he was still standing. The guy was a gladiator, a demon.

Bolan stepped back, rubber-soled combat boots crunching glass, and drew the Beretta. He took a moment to suck in some air, shook some of the cobwebs out of his ringing skull. Suddenly he noticed they had stopped, a gasp or some other sound breaking through the chiming in his head. He found the car had stopped at another floor, a crowd of horrified onlookers gaping and gawking into the gladiator arena.

"You folks wouldn't mind catching the next elevator, would you?" Bolan said, and drew in another deep breath.

The doors shut, and LaPierre sounded another war cry. He nearly made it to his feet, when Bolan clobbered him over the back of the skull with the Beretta.

Cautious but quick, the soldier pulled the plastic cuffs. Cop-style, he pinned the Frenchman, facedown and eating glass, with his knee across the back of his neck. When the hands were fastened behind his back, Bolan let out a breath, stood and punched the button for P2.

THE EXECUTIONER expected some form of welcoming committee when he hit the parking garage, LaPierre in tow and jacked along, the soldier's Beretta out and fanning the parked cars, concrete pillars. He was surprised that so far the route looked clear to his rental, but no way would he drop his vigilance when the toughest part could be vacating the garage. If Special Agent Bangle's last report was accurate, then the French hitters were circling the Syrians' apartment, scoping out the scene, probably waiting for the green light to start crashing doors and blasting people. But there could be SFPD on the way to intercept him on his way out, angry cops to deal with, a phone call to Brognola to get him back in the game. And with the firestorms he'd left behind, and witnesses...

No point in dwelling on what hadn't happened— yet.

Bolan keyed open the passenger door, checking the garage, listening for squealing tires, looking for shadows.

Clear.

LaPierre was a little wobbly, but he was making angry grunting sounds, coming around now, spitting out blood. Bolan slung him onto the shotgun seat, slammed the door in his face. Keeping the Beretta in hand, he watched the garage, the doors leading up to the lobby. The witnesses to the headbangers ball in the elevator were either too shaken up to call cops or security or the search was just getting under way.

"Hey! Hold up!"

The security guard, Bolan saw, charging toward him, gun drawn.

Bolan pulled his bogus Justice Department credentials. "Special Agent Belasko. Justice Department. Get that gun off me, or you're going to have a problem you won't be able to handle."

"Let me see that, chief."

"Lose the gun."

The guard did, shoving it into his holster. His strides slowed as he came up to Bolan, peering through the windshield, eyes wide as he scoured the battered face, lips moving soundlessly at the sight of the red ruins staring him back. Finally he gave the ID a lengthy inspection, as if he were thinking Bolan had printed it up himself.

"It's real."

"That may be, but—"

"No 'buts,'" Bolan told him, an icy edge in his voice. "This man's under arrest. If SFPD shows up you handle it. Tell them to contact Special Agent Bangle at this number if there're any questions," he said, and gave the guard the SAC's cell line.

"Okay. I'll bite."

"Bite and swallow. Have a nice day," Bolan said, and left the guard gawking at him a moment before the man pivoted and marched back for his post.

Bolan hopped in behind the wheel. "Here's how it is. Marquis is finished in America. He's going down at some point for good, and that means any of you mercenaries he has on his payroll out and about looking to carve up some Syrian hide. You help me, maybe I can get you a deal."

LaPierre grunted, spit some blood off his lips. "And if there's blood on my own hands?"

"You want to spell that out?"

"I'll think on it."

"How did you know the Syrians were in town?"

"Hackers."

When LaPierre fell silent, Bolan growled, "How's that?"

"Marquis has a team of hackers. Your Justice Department computers have firewalls, but they're outdated, like one giant sieve, or so I understand. We knew about the Indonesian freighter, how Hahmad uses his Indonesian Muslim connections. We knew of your suspicions, your operation, your surveillance of the Syrians. The freighter was how Hahmad smuggled in their weapons and the explosives. Hahmad had a cell planted in San Francisco as long ago as a year. The Syrians were funneled in, student visas, one by one.''

True enough, Brognola had agents who had suspected the freighter in question was one of Hahmad's hot boats, and that the first suspected terror cell had landed on American soil about the time La-Pierre mentioned. The whole operation to take down the Syrian cell struck Bolan at that point as too little too late. There could be any number of reasons why the Feds hadn't moved in on them before now, but the fuse was lit and Bolan intended to be the point-man when the war blew.

''And who knows?'' LaPierre said. ''Someone in the Justice Department might also be taking an envelope in the middle of the night for information. All I know was the information I received from Marquis came from hackers.''

It was plausible enough, and given what he'd heard from Brognola, anything was possible. These days, even the so-called good guys were going for themselves, usually for quick, fat cash. The list was endless, and Bolan knew there were still plenty of snakes out there hiding in their holes. There were CIA guys on the take, there was that FBI guy who'd been living the high life while he marched other agents to their deaths. Bolan despised few things more than a traitor. They were one half step above a child molester.

''And your troops? What's the story?''

''No story,'' LaPierre said. ''They are ordered to go, with or without me. My men tell me the Syrians appear highly agitated, peeking out their windows, others having marched into the one apartment, carrying large nylon satchels. The war for Hahmad, my tough friend from Justice, may have already begun.''

Bolan stowed the Beretta and keyed ignition. If that was true, the shooting had already started. Bangle and the other agents would go in behind the hitters, or maybe the SAC had jumped the gun and bulled in ahead. Either way, Bolan needed to get to the target site.

He gunned the engine, one hand on the wheel, while punching up Bangle's number on the cell phone.

MAHMOUD HUSIF HAD FEARED this day would come since he'd first arrived in America.

They had been discovered.

The worst part of it was he and the others might never realize the dream of martyrdom now, unleashing holy war on the hated infidels since their enemies were out there, everywhere, and coming for them.

For two hours he had been standing near the window overlooking the alley. He had alternated between giving out the orders to his twenty-strong jihad force and watching the alley and the next apartment building. Four of them were now walking time bombs, he saw, wrapped like mummies with C-4. All of them had armed themselves with AK-47s, five RPG-7s passed out to the designated rocket team. There were women and children in the other bedroom, including his wife and two sons, Husif telling them all to stay put, no matter what.

They knew why they had come to America, and even though he knew he'd never see his family again...

Well, they understood he would see them some day again, in Paradise.

"What is it?"

He ignored Dara for a moment, dwelling on the possibility of disaster, personal failure. It galled Husif none of them may even make out the building, as he looked out the window again, staring down at the three black luxury vehicles below, sure they were American law enforcement. The same cars had earlier made three drive-bys down the alley, Mustafa informing him that he'd spotted a veritable armada of unmarked Crown Victorias and sedans across the street when he'd come into the building with the remaining soldiers of the cell.

And Husif spotted the armored snipers, hunched and moving across the roof of the apartment building across the alley, taking up positions to be able to shoot down at the row of their third-floor windows.

He cursed. They were being hit. He was angry with himself for having malingered in America, not acting on his own, waiting for word from Hahmad on what the targets would be and when to move. As if it mattered, he thought, since downtown San Francisco was a wealth of prime kill sites.

It had been easy enough getting into America, setting themselves up in various apartments, Arab families looking for a better way of life, part of the immigrant scenery. Getting their hands on the weapons smuggled in by the Indonesian freighter had gone off just as Hahmad promised.

Now this.

The end of a dream before it was ever realized.

"We have police out there," Husif told them.

He turned, looking at the camera which monitored the hallway. The minicam had been the sole high-tech gift from Hahmad. It had taken considerable effort to install, and he'd thought maybe it had been pointless to expend such time and sweat and worry that maybe the building manager would spot the glass eye above the doorjamb. Now it gave him an edge.

"Ali," Husif barked across the living room, "this is what you are to do."

JACQUES LOMAIRE PASSED the word on to the other former Legionnaires over his tac radio.

"We go. Back entrance. Stick to the plan."

Lomaire couldn't wait for LaPierre any longer. His orders were to hit the Syrians' apartment, and according to his watch it was now the exact time—top of the hour—LaPierre had designated for the green light. Given the mysterious rash of trouble sweeping across the city, their businesses getting burned down, their men getting shot up, LaPierre was nervous and wanted the mission wrapped up, with or without him. If their leader didn't show, he had said, it meant there was trouble on his end. No need to specify. LaPierre was either in police custody or the mysterious one-man army had taken him down. There was the not so little problem of what to do after the hit, getting out of America safely, and such, but he'd worry about escape and evasion after he earned his payday.

Blood first, flight later.

"Let's do it," Lomaire told the four men in the

Lexus, then opened the passenger door. Uzi sub-machine gun in hand, he stepped out, the pockets of his windbreaker filled with grenades. The plan was to place a glob of C-4 on the door of the targeted apartment, blow it, lob in a few grenades, then go in shooting after the blasts did their gruesome work, mop up, and, with any luck, bag a hostage or two for interrogation later. Chances were the Syrians would go down fighting, but he bore in mind they were all getting the same hundred thousand per terrorist head as any of the commandos on the other hunts.

He checked the grim faces of his troops. Twelve shooters against twenty. With grenades and the element of surprise on their side, it should be quick and easy.

Lomaire picked up the pace, heart racing as he knew he was moments away from leading his troops into the slaughter.

"I DON'T GIVE A DAMN if you're two seconds away, Belasko, that French hit team is armed to the frigging teeth and they just went in. I can't wait any longer."

Special Agent Jim Morris softly shook his head. Whoever Special Agent Belasko was, he was sent out here by Washington, the man of the hour, in charge, and his word was supposed to be taken as if it were written in stone. Now Special Agent in Charge Bangle, for reasons Morris could only guess, was going to bull ahead, call the shots on the spot. There was some sort of underlying envy of Belasko, he supposed, since the ongoing operation, culminating now in a raid on the apartment, had been his puppy for months. They should wait for Belasko, if nothing else than not to buck protocol. Going against procedure, leaving out the head man at such a critical moment, could mean paperwork. Lots of it, and explanations to superiors to boot.

"You disappear, leaving me watching the store, and now you want me to sit on my hands...."

Morris looked at the drab apartment building on the corner of Guerrero and Eighteenth. Earlier they had seen twelve Syrians, casting suspicious glances at their unmarked vehicles, toting nylon satchels, and he had done the math even before the last arrival of alleged terrorists. Their Justice Department task force was fifteen shooters, against twenty Syrians. Plus women and children, crammed into the apartment, and he figured thirty bodies were in that apartment. It was a tall order, a raid through the front door, fifteen men against twenty, and if the Syrians were as heavily armed as they believed...

It was going to get ugly.

Now the French hit team, stacking the long odds even higher against them.

"I'm gone. Yeah, yeah. I'll alert our guys you're on the way."

Bangle signed off, hooked the tac radio to his belt, then, looking down the line of parked vehicles where the other Justice shooters were waiting, said, "Let's go. There's going to be shooting, so don't hesitate to start waxing the bad guys, French, Syrian, whoever shows up with a piece."

And they were moving, surging across the street, angling for the front doors of the lobby. There were passersby, Morris reading the fear and anxiety on the faces of civilians as the armored shooters closed on the building.

Oh, but it was going to get ugly indeed, Morris knew, and he had to wonder how high the body count would climb.

He feared more than a few of the home team were going to get zipped up in rubber bags before it was over. He wasn't sure what Belasko would have done, but at least he was another gun.

They should have waited.

HUSIF SAW THEM, twelve men, creeping down the hall, stacked up, Uzis in hand, hugging the wall.

Dead meat.

One of them was pulling out something, and Husif knew it was a glob of plastic explosive after a second longer look. Wait, he told himself, hold on and blow up their world as soon as the raider went for the doorknob.

Their own charge was already primed to the door, Husif checking his troops as they hunkered down for cover behind the couches, pulled to the far corner of the room.

Husif took up the radio remote box, waiting on the raiders for what felt like agonizing eternal minutes but was only a few seconds, smiling to himself as he knew he was about to give them the shock of their lives.

Their final moment on earth before he sent as many of them to hell as possible.

Beyond the blast, the orders were to move out of the building and take their holy war to the streets of San Francisco.

He was going to die soon anyway, perhaps within

the hour, but somehow, some way he would make it outside, find something—a café, business, anything where he could shoot up infidels while his human time bombs blew themselves up.

Husif thumbed on the red light.

LOMAIRE NODDED for Bomain to place the charge. He fell back a few feet, his troops lined out in front of him, against the wall.

He watched as Bomain made the door. The hallway was clear for the moment, but that would change soon enough. It could prove a plus if he was forced to grab some other resident on the way out, use him or her as a human shield against any cops who came flying onto the scene.

Lomaire lifted his Uzi, two of the frontline troops palming frag grenades.

He heard his heart thundering in his ears, then the sound was lost as the world blew up in their faces.

CHAPTER TWELVE

It was impossible to tell how many raiders the blast had eliminated, since the camera lens was lost in the fireball, the screen winking out, leaving Husif to wonder how many shooters were still standing.

Or crawling around, wounded snakes writhing about in the boiling smoke, wondering how the sky had just fallen on them, he thought.

The explosion left his own ears ringing, and he was forced to shout at Ali, "Fire!"

He watched as Ali raised the RPG-7 over the top of the couch, aiming his impact point for the wall on the other side of the hallway. He heard some choking, a groan of someone in horrible pain from somewhere in the roiling smoke, the women screaming from the bedroom, children crying, then Ali loosed the warhead.

And added another fireball to the hallway.

The second blast again rocked the floor beneath Husif, men hollering outside once more, a scream trailing in the deafening wash of the explosion. They had won the first round, but it wasn't enough.

It was far from over, and victory was hardly assured.

The snipers had to go, he knew, and Husif gave the order to blow them off the roof.

The rocket team was up and punching out the windows with the butts of assault rifles as Husif told his men to move out. He lagged behind, no sense in getting too carried away, as six or seven of his jihad soldiers bolted for the jagged maw of the front doorway, forging into the billowing smoke, Kalashnikovs out and searching for fresh kills.

A second later he discovered he was glad he'd stayed put, as he saw the grenade come bouncing out of the smoke wall, roll up at the feet of his men and blow them to smithereens. He ducked as steel bits and wet strips of shredded meat blew over his head.

No, he thought, victory in the name of God was hardly guaranteed.

BOLAN PUT ASIDE HIS RAGE that Bangle didn't hold on until he arrived to lead the charge. There was no sense in second-guessing his detour around town now. Time had been eaten up while he did his damnedest to heap more misery on Marquis's life, and now someone else might pay the price for his personal blitz. Despite that, it wasn't wasted effort. The upshot was he had a prisoner. And if any blame was pinned on anybody it was Marquis, his merc legion and the Syrians.

A war was under way inside the building, the sounds of thundering explosions reaching his ears as he burst out the door, locking LaPierre inside before he rushed to the trunk, keyed it open and took the

HK MP-5 subgun. A few grenades shoved into the pockets of his windbreaker and he was charging for the doors of the front lobby. He had the setup mentally marked. Two ways in and out, front and back doors. Third floor was where the action was, the killing field in high bloody gear from the sounds of it. Twelve French shooters, an equal number of Justice agents moving on the hall from the opposite direction and the Syrians caught smack in the middle, human sharks fighting for their place in the feeding frenzy.

He looked up at the rooftop of the adjacent apartment building and spotted the three snipers.

Then they were blown away by three roaring explosions peppering the roof, one after another, vaporizing the Justice snipers.

The Syrians had massive killing power.

Bangle, he thought, had no idea what he was up against.

The Executioner hit the doors, raced for the steps as he took in the shouts of alarm from above. The home team had taken casualties in the opening rounds, and the soldier felt his blood boil for a moment over the loss of a few good men.

Then he steeled himself to do what had to be done.

LOMAIRE ALMOST CHOKED on his own vomit, unable to decide if it was fear or the stench of death up his nose that wanted to empty his stomach. He looked up, knocked on his back by the first explosion, wondering if things could get any worse, trying to assess dead and wounded, when one of the terrorist bastards blasted another message of doom and gloom in his face.

The hallway seemed to erupt once again in blinding fire and ear-shattering noise. He had nearly made it to his feet, the stink of blood and spilled waste in his nose, when he was floored again, dust and cordite and heat sweeping over him, a force so powerful it seemed to pin him down like a snake under a boot heel.

Lomaire staggered to his feet, Uzi up, the terrible cries of wounded men in his ears. He peered into the choking ball of smoke, found bodies and body parts strewed in the path that led to the door. At least four of the others had survived, two more writhing about and holding in their guts, one of them moaning, a wounded animal on his knees and clutching the mangled limb where an arm had been sheared off below the elbow.

They were in a world of hurt.

"Go! Frag them!" he shouted at any survivors, trying to save the moment, rally the troops to action.

He armed a frag grenade himself, forging into the smoke. Autofire blistered from inside the apartment, Lomaire screaming in French for the others to do something, anything, even if it was wrong.

He aimed his throw at an angle, knowing he wouldn't connect any large numbers with the coming detonation—unless he got lucky—but if he could let them know he was every bit as well-armed as they were...

He chucked the grenade, then heard more screams

as autofire roared from down the hallway. This was a disaster, and he knew discretion would prove the better part of valor.

Cops, he knew, had arrived.

Lomaire fired his Uzi at the helmeted figures, the grenade erupting from inside the apartment, the ensuing screams hardly sweet music to his ears.

The would-be slaughter troops were getting slaughtered.

He wasn't sure if one of his men had added to the firestorm tearing through the apartment, but he was damn glad one of them had the good sense to dump a frag bomb in the direction of the cops.

"Fall back!"

MORRIS THOUGHT it was a bad move, Bangle bellowing from his point position to roll out into the hall and open fire. They were exposed, even as they managed to cap off a few rounds and nail a couple of the French hitters. The Syrians had obviously mined the door somehow, and it looked to Morris as if they had taken out half to three-quarters of the hit team with the first in-their-face send-off.

Number two was a worse shocker, as the wall on the other side of the hall was hammered by another fireball, and God help any occupants who might be cringing in that apartment. Something had blurred in his line of sight for a heartbeat, and he knew they had rocket firepower.

This was more than he'd bargained for, assault rifles going up against bazookas and grenades.

He was pouring on the autofire himself when one

of the French hitters tossed an object their way. It took a moment for his mind to register what it was, but Bangle echoed his horror as he shouted, "Grenade!"

He thought he saw two of their own jerking as slugs slammed into body armor, but he was part of the human wave next as Bangle bowled into him, knocking him back down the stairs. His own momentum created a domino effect as Morris tumbled into the next agent in line. He heard the explosion, a sound that cleaved his senses, but he was more concerned about not getting his neck broken as he was rolled up in a tangle of arms and legs windmilling out of control.

"COVER THE ALLEY!"

Husif began screaming the new orders at the rocket team. They were to blow the luxury cars if the hit team made the alley. It was only instinct, but something in his gut told him the raiders would retreat after taking such a drubbing.

Or would they?

There was only one way to find out, and Husif had no intention of getting pinned down in the close quarters of the apartment while brazen raiders perhaps pulled it together for some bull-rush charge.

"Follow me! We go for the streets! We go down to a man if we have to! Kill as many of the sons of whores as you can before we go to God!"

He took the lead now, autofire seeming to come from two separate directions in the hallway. An explosion from the end of the hall nearest the street?

Two groups of raiders, then, one side shooting at the other? What could this mean, other than they had more enemies than he had originally imagined?

He grabbed one of his human time bombs, jerked a nod toward the street end of the hallway. "Do it! Take them out! Go with God!"

Aldabij nodded, eyes fired up with the glow of knowing he could score a victory against the infidels before he blew himself up to Paradise. He was gone, and running down the hall.

Husif decided it was time to bolt, escape on the heels of the four dogs he saw moving on shaky legs for the alley end of the hallway. They fired as a foursome, driving him to cover for a moment, but with the coming wrath of martyrdom, Husif knew the way would be cleared to take the holy war to the streets.

BOLAN SHOULDERED and shoved his way through the wave of tumbling bodies. He needed to top the steps, get a read on what sort of fiasco they were staring down and start turning the tide of battle somehow. Two wounded Justice agents were down, moaning and twitching on the landing of the hallway. They were crawling over the lip of the steps, Bolan reaching out, grabbing them one by one and slinging them to cover. They were in bad shape, he saw, faces chewed to raw burger by flying shrapnel, and he doubted they'd make it.

Subgun out and ready to blow away the first hardman to show in his death sights, Bolan hunched low around the corner and—

The replay of the horror show he'd witnessed in Tunisia was running straight for their position. The remote box was in hand, the Syrian bellowing at the top of his lungs. Bolan held down the trigger, the spray of lead turning the face of fanaticism to pulpy mush, then he flung himself away from the corner, aware it could be too late to keep the bundle of human explosives from lighting up if death throes flared out final electric impulses to the finger on the button.

He was bounding back down the steps, tripping over an armored body, when the blast roared and seemed to rip apart the entire floor.

LOMAIRE WAS INCENSED. And he was also very much afraid.

The mission was a total failure, disaster beyond his wildest nightmares, and he would have to make an accounting for this fiasco sooner or later. Of course, he might never get the chance to hand off a litany of excuses and rationalizations to Marquis. Right then they were under fire by the Syrians, a whole pack of rabid wolves chasing them down the stairs. They would have to make a savage fighting withdrawal, then, as he triggered his Uzi, clipping two of the Arabs off their feet before he began his descent down the steps. There was no way they could make a stand, four guns against fifteen or so crazed Syrians who were prepared to go out in a blaze of glory for Allah.

He hit the alley, wheeling around the corner, his survivors on his heels. He was looking back, sure the Syrians would be right there, tensed and waiting for the bullets to begin scything him to ribbons, when he slammed into something and hit the alley floor on his face. Looking up, he cursed the garbage Dumpster that had dropped him, then let loose another round of vicious oaths as his own men darted past him, hell-bent on making the cars. What the hell were they going to do? Leave him?

Lomaire was on his feet, gathering momentum, when the missiles began sailing down from the third-floor windows. He screamed in horror, then hit the deck as their escape went up in a series of fireballs.

THE EXECUTIONER BARKED out the orders for Bangle to do three things. Get the wounded help first, split the unit up to cover his back and march a team to the mouth of the alley on the street end. Under no circumstances was any agent to follow him.

He left Bangle to his shock and confusion, forging up the steps, subgun leading the way. Quick but cautious, he charged into the cloying smoke clouds, glimpsed the ceiling and walls riddled with gaping holes, doors on other apartments blown in. Bits and pieces of gory flesh and blood dappled the walls. He made out the sounds of screaming and crying from several battered doorways, then heard the world was rocking from some point in the alley. Peering through the smoke, he made out the last of several heads going down as the hardforce cleared the hallway, the floor littered with strewed corpses, slick looking with running pools of blood.

Voices of panic and anger reached his ears as he made the shattered mouth of the targeted apartment. He wheeled around the corner, took in the threesome by the windows and held down the trigger of his SMG. They were turning his way, chucking aside spent RPG-7s, when the Executioner hosed them down with a long burst of subgun fire, left to right and back, nailing it down. Standing in the ruined doorway, the soldier gave the carnage a hard perusal. He heard the sobbing and whimpering from another room, but no more shooters came running.

Done here, but he stole a moment to raise Bangle for a fourth order to secure the apartment.

Then the Executioner moved out to hunt down the surviving savages.

CHAPTER THIRTEEN

There was nowhere to run, nowhere to hide, and he was sure at that point he wouldn't have wanted it any other way.

Death was preferable to running from combat, even in the face of certain suicide, and thus being branded a coward posthumously by his employer.

As he scrambled to his feet, Lomaire had a sick, sinking feeling that the third time the world blew up in his eyes would prove strike three.

Out.

No problem.

When a man had nothing left to lose, he decided, his life hung over the fire, in his face, when there were no choices left, no options, no friends...

Lomaire grabbed his Uzi, plucked a grenade out of his pocket and primed the steel egg.

Time to return a few grim favors, in spades, in blood.

Evac was definitely out the window. Three expensive luxury rentals, he saw, were up in flames, wreckage still winging around the alley, banging off walls, skimming the ground like angry metallic birds, fiery debris raining from the sky.

Screw it. It had all gone to hell, and so was he, but he could take a few of the Syrians along with him for the ride into the fire. If he was the superstitious type, he could figure some form of divine intervention had arrived, driving another hot poker into the side of Marquis, a big joke, pissing all over his big plans to hunt down Hahmad, telling him—and them—revenge was not to be.

And he discovered he wasn't alone. Incredibly enough he then found two of his teammates had somehow survived the explosive wrath from above, crimson scarecrows staggering out of the conflagration nonetheless, Uzis searching for targets, something on which to focus their pain, shock and horror.

Perfectly understandable.

He couldn't make out their features, since their faces were bloody masks, so couldn't call out their names, tell them it was time to do or die.

And most likely it was the latter.

They seemed to understand that concept, warriors rolling on his way, eyes going wild with a mix of agony and anger.

Better to die on their feet, he thought, than either get wasted on the spot and not score some satisfaction by way of revenge, or spend the rest of their lives in an American prison.

Besides, the mission was down the toilet, and Marquis would hold someone personally responsible for not bagging him a Syrian. In that instance death was certain. The rumor these days was that Marquis was losing his hold on sanity, consumed with nothing else but blood lust for Hahmad. Word was the man was a caged lion in Paris, drunk most of the time, blaming any- and everyone for not being up to the task of finding the Syrian.

Where did the madness end and sanity begin? Lomaire wondered, and thought that was a hell of a thing to have wander through his mind at a time like this.

Death would bring peace, if nothing else. Or would it?

He would find out soon enough.

They came charging around the corner as a group, AK-47s already up and spitting flame and lead. Lomaire chucked the grenade into the heart of the pack, glimpsed a few pairs of eyes going wide as the steel egg rolled up at their feet. He felt the hot beestings digging into his flesh, tasted the blood smeared across his lips, but he was hosing them down, holding on to the last bitter breath, hell-bent on going out with a roar. If he wasn't in so much pain, fire torching his insides up, head to toe, he might have howled in glee at the sight of three or four dropping under his barrage.

The grenade blew, but there was another blast that ripped from some point behind the pack of wolves. He didn't think it was his own men, hurling a bomb into the Syrians, but he couldn't be sure.

The lights were shot out.

JUDGING THE WAY they dogged the French hitters out the door, not bothering to look back at what might be chasing them, Bolan knew they were fixated on a single goal.

Slaughter the ones who had come banging first on their door.

They had blood in their noses, for damn sure, and if there were any more walking human sticks of Armageddon, he could be sure the Syrians meant to go out with a big bang. Which meant they were cranked up to jihad extremes to turn the streets of San Francisco into a personal slaughter zone, take out as many innocents as they could in their twisted vision of jihad before they ate the great worm themselves. It wouldn't be the first time he'd seen jihad erupt on American soil, and he knew if he let them run on—even one or two escaping his guns—dozens, even hundreds of innocent lives could be snuffed out in some moment of madness called jihad.

Bolan was on their six as they surged as a group of twelve around the corner of the alley, firing for all they were worth at what he assumed were the surviving French shooters. The Executioner figured he could knock out half the pack with a well-placed frag bomb, and lobbed a live one into the jihad troops. At the same instant he deposited the grenade into the hardforce an explosion ripped through their ranks.

The Executioner rode out his own blast, hugging the wall of the apartment building, then stepped up to the moaning and the mangled to mop it up.

LaPierre DIDN'T TRUST the big hitter to keep his word about some sweetheart deal of the century. Cops and Feds—if that was what the big guy even was, and he had some serious doubts—tended to lie to perpetrators, jerk their chains to get what they wanted, then leave the guilty twisting in the noose, whining about deceit. And if he came clean with the man about the executions of the VIPs, he was certain he'd be facing a life sentence in some American prison.

No way. He was gone.

LaPierre leaned his body down and over, stretched out toward the driver's seat. A double kick lashing out, and he punched out the window, chipping off the jagged shards at the bottom best he could with the heels of his shoes. Then he sat up and launched himself through the hanging glass teeth, a shard snagging him on the shoulder, but he was outside, on the ground, good to bolt. He was plenty bloodied and banged up as it was, so another gash running with hot crimson didn't really matter.

He was a former Legionnaire, a tough guy, and pain simply came with the turf. So did fear, he knew, but fear was a good thing, a motivator, in fact, if a man knew how to use it as an action tool.

He checked the neighborhood as the explosions and autofire reached his ears from the alley. It was a dreary section of San Francisco, the Mission District notorious for crime, poverty, porn. Surely he could find someone who would help him if the price was right. The Feds were occupied, shooting it out with the Syrians and his own men, and he had to wonder how his own troops were faring. How it had gone up in the flames of obvious disaster he couldn't say. He should have been more cautious, perhaps even prudent since he'd known all along Feds had the apartment building staked out, but he was a leader and leaders had to make decisions. Perhaps he had somehow become infected with the same insanity rumored to have gripped Marquis in obsession, bulling ahead, into the guns, tackling the long odds.

An insanity that told a man, he thought, he was invincible, untouchable, one step away from dwelling among the gods.

He was on his feet, believed he saw a park somewhere to the north. If he could make it there...

"Hey, pal, where do you think you're going?"

He couldn't believe it. The young Justice agent, face like a baby, had come out of nowhere.

"Why don't you climb back in there, ace."

LaPierre felt the numbing claw of despair. He stared at the assault rifle trained on his chest, considered charging the kid, but there was something in the eyes that warned him that whatever this one had just lived through was something he didn't much care to challenge. Baby face and all, he knew combat, and LaPierre knew when a man had just come out the other side and wasn't taking any crap from anybody.

LaPierre choked down a bitter curse.

NO MERCY, no prisoners.

The Executioner didn't know for sure if he had them all in his death sights, but a quick mental tally of the body count, coupled with the Syrian numbers provided by intelligence, and he believed what he saw before him were the last survivors.

A full clip up the HK MP-5, and the Executioner unloaded on the mangled savages, a cyclone of lead tearing into them, sweeping around from all points, locking them in a long dance of death. They were bloodied, face to foot, one of them missing an arm but holding back on the trigger of his assault rifle, firing wildly at some target down the alley. He'd gotten a little help from one of the French hitters, and with their senses cleaved by the double whammy of the frag blasts, it was like shooting rats in a barrel.

Which was exactly how the Executioner saw them.

They went down hard, just the same, absorbing the soldier's barrage of lead mutilators. They danced, screamed and spurted blood. Three, four, five, and they were all history after the warrior burned out his clip, a quagmire of corpses and running blood.

A fresh magazine locked home, and Bolan moved for the corner of the alley. Near the fiery hulls of the wreckage, Bolan took in the strewed corpses.

One French shooter left, barely standing, but turning the Uzi his direction, roaring in rage and pain. The soldier waxed him off his feet with a 3-round burst to the chest.

Slowly the Executioner moved up the alley, taking in the carnage, alert for possums. He toed the dead on the way out, saw nothing but blank stares fixed on the sky.

Heat from angry fire stung his face, and the stink of blood and emptied bowels and bladders swamped his senses. The sky seemed to burst with noise next as he heard the growing cacophony of wailing sirens, closing in from all directions.

It was time to fly, leave the mess for someone else to clean up. The soldier had what he'd come for on this particular leg of the campaign—a mouthpiece to take him to wherever Marquis's bounty hunters would turn up next. And from what he could see, all martyrs were present and accounted for, gone to the great beyond to receive their just reward.

"YOUR NAME IS Morris?"

"Yes, sir."

Bolan looked in on LaPierre. "I thought you were going to be Mr. Cooperation?"

LaPierre grunted, shrugged. "What can I say? I became nervous."

Bolan turned and looked at the young agent. "Appreciate what you did."

"Not a problem, sir. If you don't mind me saying, I think if SAC Asshole had waited on your arrival, this might have turned out a little different."

Bolan wasn't so sure about that, but the way the war had turned out, with friendly dead and wounded, he figured he could use an ally in his camp on the West Coast end. He had come into the operation, taking it over, calling the shots. His orders hadn't been followed to the letter, and he had to wonder about Bangle. Something smelled where the Justice operation here was concerned. There was a leak somewhere, a traitor in the ranks, and Morris had shown some initiative in keeping LaPierre from bolting. The agent might prove useful in weeding out any traitors if that was the case. The fact the French hitters knew about the Justice operation, where to find the Syrians...

There was a definite stink in the air.

Bolan watched as SAC Bangle crossed the street. The big, buzz-cut agent had a thousand-yard stare in his eyes.

"Belasko...I, uh, I...this is a...I understand... Well, we did a head count and all the Syrians are dead and accounted for. No loose time bombs looking for a place to go off. Same thing for the French hitters."

"I'm out of here, Bangle."

"Wh-what? Hey, hold on a goddamn second! You see all these cops around here. You know the shitstorm that just blew in our faces! You know how much—"

"Deal with it. I'll touch base with Washington once I'm in the air, try and smooth the waters for you guys."

"That's it?"

"I came here to do a job, Bangle. It's done." Bolan searched the man's eyes, wondering if Bangle was the leak.

There was that silent communication again, the Executioner certain there was a wolf lurking behind the official mask.

"So I get the big favor of mopping all this up? What am I, a fucking janitor?"

"I may be in touch," Bolan said, and left SAC Bangle standing there in the street, watching, scowling.

"What's that supposed to mean?"

"I may be back this way."

And Bolan hopped in behind the wheel, keyed on the ignition, glimpsed Bangle standing there, muttering. He couldn't quite hear the man, but he read the lips.

"Thanks a lot."

CHAPTER FOURTEEN

When they were aboard the Justice Department's Gulfstream jet, on their way back to Washington, Bolan—seated across from LaPierre, the two of them alone in the cabin—spelled it out for the former Legionnaire. The soldier had fixed the Frenchman a glass of whiskey, given him a smoke, hoping the quasicourtesy would help loosen the man's tongue.

When Bolan was finished telling LaPierre what he wanted him to do, the man stared into his empty glass. "Another, if you don't mind."

Bolan hesitated, saw the ghost of a smile dance over the man's lips, LaPierre making a show of wincing next.

"Hey, come on. I'm in a lot of pain here. You smacked me a few real beauties."

The soldier relented, built him another from the wet bar.

"You make a nice drink, my American friend," the man said as he accepted the glass. "Good and strong. Thank you."

Bolan handed the man the cell phone. "Do it."

"I'm not sure about this."

"Do it."

"Let me tell you something first."

Bolan felt himself losing patience. He needed to set the table for the plan he had in mind, touch base with Brognola, work out the finer details.

"The call."

"About our deal…"

"Only if you work with me."

"I have no problem with that, but I need to come clean with you about something."

"Quickly."

And Bolan heard about the executions of the three executives, the bodies dumped in the bay. LaPierre insisted he was only following orders from Marquis, that the Americans had been stealing money. Surely Mr. Justice could understand.

"Our deal still holds?"

"I'll think about it," Bolan finally said.

"I see. I have blood on my hands. You want to consider me a murderer, toss me into prison."

"I might be able to work around that."

"Mitigating circumstances?"

"Something like that."

"Marquis…he'll become suspicious. Your plan has holes in it."

"Almost every plan has holes in it."

LaPierre sipped his drink, worked on his smoke, smiled. "I think I understand. No risk, no reward."

"You got it. The call."

LaPierre punched in the overseas number. Bolan listened as the man seemed to hit a wall. "I need to reach him immediately. Get in touch with him, Ducloux. Tell him it is urgent. No, it is for his ears only. There was trouble in America, but I have what he wants. Yes—yes. I will call you back in twenty minutes. I don't give a damn—make it happen!''

"What's the problem?" Bolan demanded when LaPierre punched off.

"It would appear Monsieur Marquis is unavailable."

"Word games won't score you any points."

"He's left Paris. That was his second in command of security and recruitment. I am to call back."

"That much I got." Bolan leaned up, put an edge in his voice. "You don't perform, you don't come through, you're going to wish you were simply going to prison."

"THIS IS all most peculiar. Every time we speak, there is more bad news on your end. Why is it everywhere I turn these days there is nothing but bad news?"

Marquis paced around the situation table in the war room of his transport plane, agitated, not sure what to make of LaPierre's sitrep. They had left in the dead of night, and he hoped to have his new team of hunters in Egypt, in place at the enemy's door well before dawn. Not even thirty minutes in the air, and already he was hearing about more problems. It wasn't so much what LaPierre said, as much as it was his tone, edgy and nervous—and what he wasn't saying.

"Let me get this straight," Marquis said, glancing at Anglerre, who looked up from the maps spread around the table. "You are telling me you lost every single man to the Syrians and the police."

"Yes," LaPierre said. "To a man, all of them dead."

"Yet you made it."

"Lucky, I suppose, that I managed to escape with only a few scratches. With a Syrian prisoner, I may add. I am presently booking a flight for Paris—unless you wish me to bring the man directly to you. This prisoner, he claims he can contact Hahmad."

"Interesting."

Marquis didn't like it, and he smelled something where LaPierre was concerned. He had a man in the Justice Department on the West Coast of America, and it would be easy enough to check out LaPierre's version of events. He already knew about the strikes on the warehouse and the arcade, and that smacked of trouble enough. Would LaPierre be setting him up? Had he been arrested by the police, and was now working with the Justice Department? And who had so brazenly attacked him in America, razing his businesses, costing him millions of dollars in property?

"Monsieur?"

"Egypt," Marquis told him, cradling the cell phone to his cheek while pouring a whiskey. "I will be in Egypt. Arrange it so you can get to Cairo. I will send a team of men there to pick you up."

"Cairo is a big city."

"Go to the pyramids. Call me back when you are in the air."

"What is it?" Anglerre asked when Marquis punched off.

"LaPierre. He says he has a prisoner, but they lost every single man during the attack."

"Really?"

"I hear you. It doesn't sound plausible that he somehow managed to escape while still another group of my commandos was butchered."

"Call our man in San Francisco."

"I am considering it. We have four oversize customized Land Rovers aboard. Getting to Cairo, should I do that, wouldn't be a problem."

"And you're going to spare the men and the time for a detour to the pyramids?"

"I am not sure. LaPierre can wait—maybe. If what Lassere told us is true, Hahmad has been sighted in Egypt at this village El Doq."

"A terrorist training camp, down the Nile, more than just a village. However, we are supposed to find this Pharaoh first for confirmation of Hahmad."

"Yes, our contact in Egypt, arranged courtesy of Interpol. This magic man, the eyes and ears of all Egypt. Hiding in a Roman quarry in the desert." Marquis saw Anglerre scowling at the maps. "What is it?"

"You needn't do this. This is dangerous work. We have passports and visas, but we will be in Egypt illegally."

"And I have three duffel bags stuffed with three different denominations of cold, hard cash. We have guns and twenty professional soldiers. If Hahmad is in Egypt, he is dead."

"And if he isn't?"

"Then we go straight to Syria. Or Lebanon or wherever he runs."

"Do you understand there's a good chance that none of us may make it out of Egypt?"

"And?"

"You are more valuable alive than dead."

"My good friend, you need to understand this. I have been dead for a long time."

THE EXECUTIONER DIDN'T like the way the conversation went with Marquis. Listening in on the speaker com, Bolan read the man as suspicious, nervous, paranoid. At least Bolan knew where the next foray would take place.

LaPierre was working on another drink and smoke, shrugging off Bolan's dark look. "I tried. He said go to the pyramids. Call him back."

Bolan dialed up Brognola on the sat link, put the headphones on for privacy. "It's me."

A quick update on the San Francisco front, and Brognola filled the soldier in on what he had. "There's a black-ops CIA team ready to move on Egypt. Ridilson checked out, and I managed to pull a few strings to get you onboard for the Company op."

"And it's definite Hahmad's in the neighborhood?"

"So I'm told. You'll be flying to an American air base in Italy where you'll get the full briefing. A C-130 is set to go, but I managed to stall the wheels-up until you get there."

"Hell, we're still talking another ten, twelve hours in the air. The shooting could be over by then."

"They'll keep. Word is the Company's pleased with the way things turned out in Tunisia, Ridilson coming off, the way I hear it, like the man of the hour. All of a sudden he's a hero in their eyes, and it sounds like he has some pull with this team. What do you want to do with your boy, LaPierre?"

"I'll hold on to him for now. Who knows, I might need him when we get to Egypt." Bolan ran down the conversation the man had had with Marquis.

"My problem is this, Striker. Say Marquis has a man on the inside at Justice in Frisco like you suspect. It wouldn't take much effort for Marquis to find out LaPierre's story is bull. They got their information from somebody, and I don't give a damn what he said about hackers. The whole operation out there only just came across my desk about two weeks ago, which means Bangle, for reasons I have yet to determine, was sitting on all the intelligence. It was only when I started digging around about Marquis's business out there did I learn about the Syrians."

"I may be going back that way if you find or even think there might be skeletons in Bangle's closet. For now we let Marquis keep running, and maybe he'll run me right to Hahmad this time out."

"The Farm 'borrowed' an NSA satellite, and they found that airfield where Marquis's custom warbird was parked. It left about an hour ago. We're tracking it, and it looks like Marquis is en route for Egypt."

"Looks like one big party in the land of the pharaohs."

"And rumor has it a Mossad black-ops team may be in the hunt."

"I'll deal with them if and when they turn up."

"Well, I'm sure you know Egypt isn't Tunisia. Meaning they're a little more fundamentalist than their Carthaginian brethren. The sat pictures the Farm got show a massive terrorist training camp in the Arabian Desert. I'm hearing anywhere from seventy to 120 or so bad guys. I don't know the particulars for the proposed strike, but I was told the CIA might get a little help by way of air fire support from the Egyptian army. Seems the powers that be in Cairo don't much care to have a jihad army in their backyard."

"Yeah. Bad for tourism."

"I hear cynicism."

"I'm going into this with my eyes wide open."

"Trust no one."

"The usual."

"One more thing. Just in case Hahmad doesn't turn up, Bear compiled a shopping list of bad guys and contacts Hahmad is believed to use in Cairo."

"Send it."

"Will do. You know, Striker, this guy Marquis...he's out of control. He's a savage, the smell of blood in his nose and the fact that he sends these commandos out to kill anything that moves makes him a priority to waste."

"In due time."

"For my money it can't be soon enough."

MARQUIS FELT his nerves tweaking out, adrenaline racing, skin clammy. He wondered if it was fear or anticipation.

They were in Egypt.

By the time they deplaned, however, loaded up the Land Rovers and were rolling, using the GPS module to guide them across the barren sea of rock and sand, he could see the first dirty light of dawn breaking over the Arabian Desert. Anglerre had mentioned the problem of a daylight strike. It irked Marquis to think they might have to hole up, malinger the day away, then raid the camp at night.

In the passenger seat of the point vehicle, monitoring the GPS himself, he looked at Anglerre, who had the wheel. In the distance the transport plane was vanishing to the north. When he'd first begun the vengeance hunts, he had bought up patches of real estate, erecting private airfields for hopping-off points and refueling. There was one in Malta, another airfield in Crete. The plane would land this time in Crete, the shortest distance between the two airfields, his pilots on standby, the plane refueled and ready to fly back for pickup.

Marquis didn't plan on leaving Egypt without the head of Hahmad in a satchel. In fact, he had told himself he would die in Egypt rather than continue to feel the cancer of his hatred and rage eating up his guts.

"Nine kilometers," Marquis told Anglerre. "Hold this course, due northeast."

He sat back, felt his heart pounding like a jackhammer. This was a land stained with the blood of his family. This was where, he determined, he would finish it. He was prepared, just the same, to dog Hahmad straight to the gates of hell if that's what it took to hunt down the bastard. He didn't care if they violated airspace, engaged Egyptian soldiers in combat. He didn't care if they all went down in blood and thunder. He had armed himself with a Glock, nestled in a shoulder holster. When the time came, he would pick up a Galil assault rifle himself. He was no stranger to weapons, having often worked out with the commandos on the firing range at their compound. Only this time he would be shooting at live targets.

It was good, he decided, to be out there, with warriors, in the hunt.

Leading men into battle.

Could he do it? Did he have what it took to pull the trigger when the time came?

He told himself he wouldn't be there unless he was willing to go all the way.

The Imperial Quarry loomed in the distance, a terraced heap of granite rising against the gray smudge of a dawn sky. The Pharaoh would be waiting, according to Lassere, on the wadi side of the quarry.

Dante Marquis felt his anticipation rising, aware all of a sudden he was eager to begin shedding blood.

CHAPTER FIFTEEN

Egypt

General Abu Sayyid didn't like the fact his country was crawling these days with human parasites. There were terrorists, arms dealers, even drug runners using the ancient land for nefarious purposes. The way of the criminal world, he thought, wasn't the way of the Muslim. Infidels worshiped their greed and ill-gotten gain perhaps, but for a Muslim to resort to crime was a sin punishable, he believed, by death.

And then there were the so-called information brokers, greasy little men who played all sides for profit, not caring who got killed as long as they fattened their wallets. They swarmed Cairo, hustling, lying and cheating, buying and selling information and selling out. They were worse than mere criminals in his mind, since they never had the backbone to do the dirty work themselves. They were a disgrace to all Muslims, and he would just as soon kill them as look at them.

Nassir Ghanni was the information broker in question at the moment.

"So, they call you the Pharaoh. If you ask me, I see very little that is majestic about you."

The tall, lean, swarthy general ran his hands down the front of his uniform, staring down at the bearded, portly Ghanni. Sayyid had undertaken this particular mission on his own, bypassing usual military protocol and channels. Cairo didn't know he was down there in the Arabian Desert, thirty soldiers at his beck and call, APCs, jeeps with mounted .50-caliber machine guns at his disposal. Whatever was going to happen in the coming hours, he would be there, prepared to clean up a mess that this information broker and the foreign commandos intended to make.

And then there was a reported sighting of one of the most wanted criminals on the planet.

He had been hearing about this Pharaoh for years, how the man always had his ear to the ground, lurking all over the country, learning things about this individual and that, bartering intelligence even on military operations with the fundamentalists who were giving Egypt a bad image these past few years with their murdering of tourists and mass slaughter of simple peasants who worshiped in mosques. Now he had him, this snake who sold lives as easily as any vendor would sell fruit in a souk.

"What is it you want?"

They had the man lashed with rope to the tent's pole. The chill of the desert hadn't been quite burned away as the sun rose, but the man was sweating, nervously licking his lips.

"I, like you, also have my own sources of information," Sayyid told the information broker. "I have learned some interesting and disturbing things the past few days. I hear you have been in contact with a cutout for a group of Frenchmen who are on their way here to meet with you about one Mohammed Hahmad. The same Hahmad who, I hear, is presently hiding in a camp for terrorists nearby. I hear that this Hahmad is planning some major operation to be launched in Cairo and other cities across the Middle East. I understand you have been in touch with Hahmad. I understand you have sold him out to these same commandos who are on their way to meet with you. How much are they paying you to take them to Hahmad?"

"I don't know what you're talking about."

Sayyid didn't have time for games and lies. He stepped up and slapped Ghanni across the face, draped a hand over the 9 mm Makarov pistol holstered on his hip. "If I have to repeat myself again, I will start shooting you—from the feet on up."

"You needn't do that. I will talk, but only if you give me your word I can keep the money when they arrive. I have gone through considerable trouble and risk to stage this hunt for the French. Two hundred and fifty thousand dollars—American cash."

A quarter million.

It was a hefty round figure, and even Sayyid was considering helping himself to some of that money. He was looking forward to retirement soon, and it was time to start planning the golden years before it was too late. Perhaps it was better to be a fairly wealthy Muslim by Egyptian standards than a poor worshiper of God.

"When are they arriving?"

"They should have been here by now. Well? Do I have your word?"

"When they arrive, I will talk to them. Perhaps we can renegotiate the price for your treachery."

IF THE NUMBERS on the terrorists at the camp in El Doq were even close to accurate, Anglerre feared they were headed for just the same disastrous end that had consumed the two previous hit teams. Try telling that to Marquis, though, he thought. Twenty guns against perhaps a hundred heavily armed fanatics. Sure, they had LAW rockets and C-4, but even with the element of surprise on their side, he couldn't envision anything remotely close to a clean sweep. Yes, there was going to be a massacre, all right—it was simply a question of who would do the slaughtering.

"There. Down the gorge. Another quarter mile."

Anglerre drove through the gorge, looking up the terraced face of the mountain wall where stones had centuries ago been carved out by prisoners of Roman penal colonies.

"If I may—we have not even discussed a plan of attack yet."

Anglerre waited for Marquis to respond. "In due time. First I need this Pharaoh to get us to the camp. I will take a look at the enemy, and decide then how to proceed. It will be full daylight soon, and I think your suggestion to wait until nightfall would be the wisest course of action. What do you suggest about an attack plan, now that you mention it?''

"Go in under the cover of darkness. Any sentries, silent kills, then mine the camp with plastique. Four five-man teams, closing in from all points, swarming whatever survivors there are.''

Marquis nodded. "Sounds like a plan.''

He cut the wheel, bounding over uneven ground and guiding the minicaravan into the wide mouth of a bisecting wadi at Marquis's directions.

And right away Anglerre knew something was wrong. There were more APCs, jeeps with mounted machine guns than any mere intelligence broker should have had on hand. He was supposed to be alone in the wadi. If Marquis was concerned, he didn't show it. Anglerre feared an ambush. He was beginning to wonder if Marquis had a death wish.

"Park it here. Let's get out. There he is.''

Anglerre watched as a short, chubby man in a white tunic stepped outside the large tent. He fit the description of Pharaoh, based on intel they had received from Interpol.

Taking up his Galil, Anglerre parked, opened the door, checking the jagged slope of the gorge. Something felt terribly wrong the longer he looked up the slopes on either side of the wadi. About the only upshot he could see on this hunt was that he was surrounded by professional soldiers, all of them French, no Brits or Germans to play ego games with.

If there was trouble they would shoot their way out, no questions.

"Pharaoh?" Marquis called.

Before the man could answer, Anglerre saw a dark man in a brown uniform, festooned with medals, sweep out of the tent. There was a pistol in his hand, aimed at the Pharaoh.

"Put down your weapons!"

Anglerre saw them rise, armed wraiths from behind boulders up the slope. Egyptian soldiers, he knew, fifteen on each side of the wadi. And they were training assault rifles on them, looking antsy to cut loose with a volley that would drop Marquis and his commandos before they could even attempt some fighting withdrawal.

"I am General Abu Sayyid. There has been a change in plans."

And Anglerre knew they were all in a world of crap as Sayyid walked up to the Pharaoh, stuck the muzzle of his pistol in the man's ear and blew his brains out.

THE COMPANY MAN in charge of the black op called himself Hardball. He was fifty-something, military background, Bolan thinking Special Forces, Delta, Rangers with combat experience to back him up. Lean and mean and buzz cut, he was nearly a carbon copy of the twenty younger shooters who were destined to kick terrorist ass.

Sitting in the webbed harness that passed for a seat, Bolan was once again the odd man out. It could have been a replay of the briefing given onboard by the late—and in the soldier's mind unlamented—Colonel Dobson. They were decked out in combat blacksuit, which told Bolan they were going for a night hit. The weapon of choice was an M-16/M-203 combo, and the Executioner had taken one for himself. He held on to his standard side arms, combat vest with pouches fitted with an array of grenades and spare clips. Surprisingly enough nothing had been said to him by Hardball about one Colonel Pollock holding up the show in Italy, nor was there any mention about Bolan's prisoner coming along for the ride.

By his calculations, factoring in the air miles to Egypt and the C-130's top speed, as he listened to the rumble of turboprop engines swelling the fuselage, he figured they should be landing at the CIA outpost near the Nile River within three, four hours tops.

The briefing came complete with slide projector and Hardball with remote clicker. Hardball had a raspy voice that had seen too many cigarettes and too much whiskey.

"This is a keep-it-simple surgical strike, people," Hardball began. "When we land, we will be transported by chopper to the target site. Gunships will soften up the playing field, then we drop down, four five-man teams with our Colonel Pollock going in with me. Red, Green, Blue and Black teams. A swarming attack. Pinch them in from all sides and hit them with everything we have."

Bolan glanced at Ridilson, the CIA agent chainsmoking. He needed a few words alone with the man at some point, had already hinted they needed to speak. Beyond the terrorist camp—as Bolan watched Hardball click through the sat pictures of the target—the Executioner had a shopping list for suspected Hahmad cells and terrorist lackeys hunkered down and doing business in Cairo. As long as he was in Egypt, he figured why not slay a few more snakes.

"We're looking at a little over one hundred terrorist scumbags. I'm hoping our flyboys can knock it down to less than half that number by the time we go in."

It looked to be a sprawling camp, with dozens of tents, draped with brown camou netting. Hardball went a little too fast for Bolan's liking, so there was no way to count up the machine-gun nests, APCs and jeeps.

"They've got it all to train the future jihad prospects in this little corner of the Arabian Desert. The village itself is believed abandoned, and they use the hovels for training exercises. We have an obstacle course. We have generators and fuel bins that will be knocked out in the opening moments. We have an armory, which, we believe, is loaded with various chemical and bio agents. A HAZMAT team is on standby in Egypt. Snipers will be in place on this ridge, and they will drop any jihad scumbags who make a break for the armory, maybe thinking they can light up our world. The Egyptians have given us the thumbs-up to do whatever's necessary to wax these bastards. Should Hahmad turn up, he is to be captured, if possible. Seems this situation is some-

thing of an embarrassment to Cairo, since they still
need Uncle Sam's wallet and military presence in
the region to maintain the status quo, whatever that
is, and don't ask me. Egypt, folks, ain't what it used
to be. They're friendly with Saddam for one thing,
and during the past few years we've seen an infiltration of fundamentalists who want to use the country as a springboard across North Africa, spreading
the word of fanatic Islam. Bottom line here—it is
kick ass and take names. Whatever is left standing
after our gunships drop the hammer we go in, mop
it up.

"Any questions? Good. Colonel Pollock, I need
a word with you."

Here we go, Bolan thought, rising out of his harness, trailing Hardball up the fuselage.

"I can't say I appreciate being held up while
waiting for some hotshot from Justice—if that's
what you even really are." Hardball softened his
tone next, adding, "I heard what you did in Tunisia,
and that's the only reason I agreed to letting you on
board. I could use the extra gun."

"Hey, I'm here to help. It's your show."

"I'm glad we agree on that much. What you don't
know is that there may be a Mossad black-ops team
ready to move even as we speak."

"I've heard something to that effect."

"I'm no politician, no diplomat bullshit artist."

"Sounds like I'm in the right kind of company."

"That you are. We're soldiers, and that's the way
I read you. What's the deal with the prisoner?"

"No deal. Maybe you've heard about Marquis and his bounty hunters."

Hardball glanced past Bolan at LaPierre, who was once again cuffed. "So, that's one of them?"

"He's leverage maybe. A way for me to get to Marquis."

"If this Marquis wanders into the game, his ass is grass."

"No problem. I want him myself—if possible. Whoever gets to him, he's history."

"And Hahmad?"

"First come first served."

"I caught you talking to Ridilson earlier. You want to share?"

"There's a few snakes up Cairo way I'd like to see trampled. The way Hahmad operates, he seems to be able to cut and run when the heat is on."

"Yeah," Hardball grunted. "Vanishes off the face of the earth. Means he has escape valves."

"And plenty of help."

"And plenty of money. You know he has connections to some big-time money men?"

"I've heard."

"Which is why I'd like to bag the SOB breathing. He's a gold mine of intelligence. Cutouts, their operations, what traitorous vipers might be in bed with them, helping to keep the terror machine running."

"I can understand that."

"But you won't take a bullet for him."

"Not my style."

"Okay, Pollock, fair enough. This time let's try to keep that armory from getting blasted clear to the

Mediterranean. Yeah, yeah, I know you weren't responsible, but we can't go in, lumbering around in NBC space suits.''

"What's there?"

"Nerve gas. Botulism. Supposedly made to order for a suicide charge. Backpack stuff. Goes off, catch a good wind…''

"I've got the picture.''

"So, let's do this by the numbers.''

CHAPTER SIXTEEN

If he couldn't get what he wanted, then Dante Marquis was prepared to throw his life away in a final moment of insanity. He pulled out the pistol, locking target acquisition on the Egyptian general.

"I wouldn't," Sayyid rasped.

"I would. Drop it."

"I see that you are serious—and insane. Perhaps we can come to some arrangement and avoid unnecessary bloodshed. I know who you are."

"Do you?"

"You are Dante Marquis. Your wife and children were murdered by this animal, Hahmad."

"And you stand there, making it sound as if you're so much better—and after killing my contact in cold blood."

"He was a thief and a liar. If it's help you want, I can perhaps give it to you."

"And I can trust you?"

"For a small fee."

Money. That was something, as a businessman, Marquis understood.

"Or you kill me and my men?"

"You are surrounded. We have you outnumbered.

You will all be cut down before you get off the first shot.''

Marquis looked up both sides of the wadi at the small army of Egyptian soldiers, then glanced at Anglerre, read the same grim intensity that told him the man would go the distance. If they engaged in a shooting war—well, he realized he would never taste his revenge.

"How much do you want, General?"

"You were prepared to give this snitch a quarter of a million—American. I want twice that."

"And for all that money you are prepared to do what in return?"

"I know where the camp is. We can provide escort."

"Thirty or so soldiers," Anglerre piped in. "A known terrorist and murderer in your own backyard and you're going to stand on the sidelines and let us do all the dirty work of killing and maybe dying."

Sayyid shrugged. "Perhaps I will do more than stand around and watch the show."

"Yes," Anglerre said. "For a half-million dollars I would think so. I am looking at six jeeps with mounted machine guns. I'm thinking perhaps we could use two or three of those when we hit the camp. Maybe some extra rocket launchers."

"It can be worked out."

Marquis called to one of his men over his shoulder. "Get the money. Two bags, the black ones. Lower your weapons," he then told his commandos.

"Stand down," Sayyid ordered his soldiers.

"So, when do we leave?" Marquis asked.

"It will take several hours just to reach the camp. There is a gorge from the top of which you can have a look at this camp for yourselves. Determine how you might want to proceed."

Marquis watched as the ex-Legionnaire walked up beside him with the two large nylon satchels. "Give me a few minutes to count out your money. I warn you now. If this is a trick, if you are leading me and my men into an ambush..."

"No tricks. If this animal is among the terrorists, I wish to see him every bit as dead as you do. He's a blight, a scourge, and I want the stain of this animal removed from Egypt."

"He's far more than just that."

THE GUNSHIP ARMADA consisted of two Kiowas, two Black Hawks and a lone Apache AH-64. As he trailed the CIA men from the parked C-130, Bolan took in the air firepower. The Apache alone was a known tank killer, but with the miniguns and Hellfires and TOWs he saw fixed to the other gunships, he was beginning to think the terrorists didn't stand a chance. Of course, once the shooting war erupted and the element of surprise was erased, anything was possible in the chaos and confusion of battle.

Bolan marched on, M-16 slung across a shoulder. Rotor blades were already spinning to life, Hardball barking out for all hands to claim the Black Hawks. It was show time.

Bolan caught up to Ridilson. "Did you think about what we discussed?"

"Let's get this one in the bag first. I can hash it over with Hardball and maybe work out some arrangement to get us into Cairo—and out in one piece."

"You look dubious."

"Nervous is more like it. The names you mentioned are protected by more than just some mindless street thugs."

"Telling me they've got clout with the local authorities?"

Bolan forged into the grit whipped up by the rotor wash. He gave the makeshift airfield a quick search, wondering who or if any of them would be back this way. It was a fly-by-night Company outpost, arranged with the Egyptian military. It was a big, bad desert out there, and he knew that soon enough the sands of Egypt would turn red with blood. He saw two tall brownsuits with HK-33 assault rifles with attached scopes rolling from the large tent. Snipers.

"I'll help you, Pollock," Ridilson said. "Fact is, I want to be there when you start kicking down doors and blowing away bastards the CIA's been after for years. Hell, every time we get together it seems like my career is moving on up all the time."

Bolan let that slide as he bounded up into the Black Hawk. Career advancement was hardly his goal, but whatever worked for Ridilson to get the job done was all he was asking for.

Egypt was alive and crawling with human vipers. The Executioner wasn't going to leave until more than one nest was burned down.

Bolan was wondering about the sudden sense of

urgency to make the camp and start dropping the sky on the terrorists. It appeared a night hit was out the window. Going in to strike during full daylight, they might as well paint a bull's-eye on the back of their blacksuits.

As if reading his concern, Ridilson told him, "Hardball just gave me the word. An Israeli black-ops team—IDF but Mossad sponsored—is ready to move on the camp. We just learned about it, and we're trying to reach our Mossad source now to find out who's in charge. If we start tripping over each other, and shooting each other up in the cross fire…"

Bolan kept his expression neutral. This surgical strike had all the earmarks for disaster.

COLONEL ARI SHAIB of the Israeli Defense Forces gave the order for his force to saddle up. Twenty-four black-ops soldiers, sweating out the morning in the Sinai and they didn't have to be told twice to grab up their Galils, move out from the tent and board one of the two armed Black Hawk gunships. Shaib looked at the two Apache choppers, hoping between the fighting birds and twenty-four of the best-trained guerrilla fighters on the planet it would be enough to slay the terrorist demon that was Hahmad and his savage horde.

According to his Mossad contact, the CIA was right then en route to raze the terrorist camp across the Red Sea. A check of his watch, factoring in their jumping-off point at the southern edge of the Sinai, and he figured something in the neighborhood of ninety minutes before they started shooting the camp up themselves.

If the CIA was on-site, he'd deal with them. Intelligence had it that Mohammed Hahmad had been picked up by satellite at the camp. Shaib wanted to take Hahmad alive, torture him about ongoing operations, but if the Syrian got wasted in the coming apocalypse it was simply one less butcher his country would have to deal with.

Shaib despised Arab terrorists of any nation, but the Syrians had some of the deadliest—and in his mind most cowardly—butchers in the Middle East. Syria had troops and terrorists spread and hunkered down all throughout neighboring Lebanon, practically owned the country for their own military and terror exports across the border. Lately the attacks against Israeli citizens and soldiers were escalating. There was a disco bombing the previous week, two more suicide bombers in the streets of Tel Aviv, a bus of schoolchildren even blown up by a Syrian reported linked to Hahmad's organization. There had been rockets launched on Jewish settlements, toppling entire homes and killing whole families.

Enough.

It was time to make a stand, and a statement against the Islamic savages.

Shaib hopped up into the belly of the gunship. "Lift off!" he ordered the pilot and copilot.

MOHAMMED HAHMAD NEEDED the big one. In his mind only massive and multifaceted blows against his enemies would put him at the top of the Islamic

world as the number-one freedom fighter for all op-
pressed Muslim peoples. He'd come a long way
since dealing heroin. He was now in the business of
mass destruction, both selling it to his freedom
fighter brothers, and carrying out operations himself.

The lean, muscular, bearded Syrian stepped out
of his tent to check on the surrounding desert. There
had been some sort of trouble with the Algerians,
the Tunisians and the whispers were floating his way
via cutouts that the GIA and the FIS were holding
him responsible for the attack on the village in Algeria.

He had lost merchandise, contacts and a springboard across Algeria to Morocco if he was being
branded a backstabber by the Algerians.

Which was why he needed a big victory, perhaps
even a series of astonishing blows against the infidels to put him back in the game, grab world headlines and shine in the spotlight of jihad. It was in
the works, in fact, several planned strikes against
American and other Western embassies in Egypt,
Tunisia and Morocco. He even wanted a twin-billed
suicide run at the American air bases in Egypt and
Italy.

He looked to the armory, a low-lying stone block
stuffed with the fruits of his labor. They were called
backpacks, and could be strapped to a man—a jihad
soldier who was willing to martyr himself for the
cause—and set off by remote control. There was
nerve gas, botulism, the deadly agents capable of
being dispersed for several city blocks when the explosive was touched off by radio frequency. With a

strong wind whipping around a targeted city, he envisioned thousands, perhaps even tens of thousands dying agonizing deaths.

Like most of the weapons he sold to various Islamic fundamentalist groups, the backpacks were created by the Russians. He had no problem dealing with the godless pagans of Russia, since they always went deaf, dumb and blind whenever Americans were attacked overseas. If not for his dealings with the Russians, he perhaps would have no real shot at seeing his dreams become reality.

He strode away from the tent, watching as the black-clad warriors jaunted around the obstacle course, climbing ropes and swinging down the monkey bars, showing stamina and tenacity even under the broiling noonday sun.

In just a few short hours he was prepared to select a group of twelve martyrs. Some would be transported to Egypt after he worked out the final few details of attacks on embassies in Cairo, using his cutouts in the city to get men and matériel in place. Some would fly with him back to Syria in the Learjet that was parked and hidden in the chain of golden brown hills to the east. There, they would get assignments to penetrate Israel and set themselves off in glory, gas and bio clouds sweeping over streets and settlements, bringing in a new age of jihad.

Glory, in the name of God and all that was Muslim and sacred in his holy eyes, was just over the next horizon.

There were other rumors flying about Egypt also, and he tried not to be disturbed by reports the camp may be attacked soon, as he envisioned future triumphs over his enemies. It was, however, confirmed that Western commandos were again hunting for him. They had been identified as belonging to a private army of the man whose family he'd had his minions kidnap and kill long ago. He thought about that day now, when the woman and her children had been marked and abducted off the streets of Cairo. He had been in Cairo at the time, but had played no active role in the abduction. As usual he had given the orders, waited out the mission from a distance in a safehouse in the old Islamic quarter of the city. It had not been a senseless or barbaric exercise in futility, as far as he was concerned.

It was a message to a rich Westerner that he was not above and beyond the reach of jihad, that no amount of money could insulate or save him or his family from divine Islamic retribution.

So he had enraged the Frenchman. It was war, after all, so let him march out his commandos and try to hunt him down. He had far greater matters to concern himself with than some vendetta that would never be realized by the infidel.

He strode back into the tent, heard his primary Egyptian contact ranting over the radio. He listened, his fear mounting with each word he caught. He only caught one side of the heated exchange, but he knew there was trouble on the way. Now what?

Flight or fight?

"This is incredible!" Gezirah raged. "Why have we not heard about this sooner? If we survive this, you can believe you will make an accounting. I will

skin you alive personally. You are paid good money,
perhaps too much money to watch our backs. Now
you warn us.''

Gezirah slammed his fist on the console, stood
and wheeled toward Hahmad. ''We have a problem.''

''I gathered as much.''

THE EGYPTIAN HAD GIVEN the orders to park the
vehicles in the gorge and climb the trail by foot to
the top of the mesa. It made sense to Marquis, even
though it appeared they could have driven up the
weathered spine in the sloping western face of the
mesa. A cloud of dust billowing from the mesa
would signal his hated enemy they were coming. He
had come this far, so the hard way from there on
was no problem.

It was a fifteen-minute hike to reach the top, just
the same, sweat drenching Marquis. It was hotter
than Hades, but his insides matched the furnace
beating down on his face. Marquis, his commandos
and the Egyptians jogged across the mesa.

''Low, stay low!''

Marquis again followed the Egyptian general's orders, crouching as he neared the edge of the mesa.

And he saw the sprawling camp, a quarter mile
or so to the east. He took up his field glasses, adjusted the lens to the distance and took in the terrorist camp. He tried to will his breathing to slow
down, but his adrenaline was racing too hot, too fast.
He could feel it now—sweet, blissful revenge, right
below him, in his hand for the crushing.

Still, it was going to be tough, he knew, for a mere twenty men to go down there and take out what he believed were at least one hundred terrorists. A large contingent was working up a sweat in the obstacle course, while more black-garbed terrorists in black kaffiyehs were shooting up the target range. A few were milling around the tents when...

A smallish figure swept out of the largest tent, flailing about with one arm, then firing his AK-47 in the air.

And Dante Marquis felt his heart freeze to a block of ice in his chest. He would know that face anywhere, had seen it in his nightmares every night.

"He is there. Go, go!"

"Wait."

Marquis scowled at Sayyid, who was surveying the camp through his own binoculars. "Wait? For what?"

"Keep your voice down. It carries in the desert. I do not want to be surrounded and trapped by these animals on this hill. He is looking north, issuing orders. I do not understand. He is agitated."

"Could he know we are here?"

"No. And I resent the implication. If he knew, he would be looking our way or sending out his killers in this direction!"

Marquis looked to the burning sky to the north. He couldn't see anything but a cobalt sky, more hills, more desert. How could anything, man or animal, live out here? he wondered. He went back to scoping out the camp, watching as the terrorists began surging in large groups from the target range and obstacle course.

"There! Gunships!"

Marquis looked from Sayyid, who was pointing north, and whipped his head in that direction. They were black specks at first, then grew into winged flying warbirds, as they lowered, skimming the desert.

"They are being attacked!"

"By whom?" Marquis raged.

"I don't know."

"You don't know! Anglerre, move out, go, go!"

Anglerre was rising, but told Marquis, "Remain here. I suggest you radio our pilots and have them fly back immediately."

"Go and get that bastard!"

"And you, General?"

Sayyid seemed to think about something. "Take fifteen of my soldiers. I will remain here for the moment with Marquis. Take the jeeps."

Anglerre sneered at the general. "Good luck and good hunting."

Sayyid returned the look with a dark scowl. "You may regret those words and your tone of voice later."

"I doubt I'll be around later."

Marquis had no problem staying put for the time being. Those gunships were going to unload the works on the camp. He feared, for the most part, that Hahmad would get vaporized by missiles, and he'd never see the man die with his own eyes. Later, when the rockets finished their red glare, he would go down, move in and search for the body of Hahmad. With any luck the bastard would be wounded, crawling around in his own leaking blood and guts.

Marquis watched as the gunships streaked on.

"WE'VE GOT company on the mesa."

Bolan watched as Hardball stepped out of the cockpit.

"We're out the door on the north end, ride out the storm. Two teams, fan out. Here's the deal."

Hardball quickly reorganized the squads into Blue and Black teams. They would disembark, split up, Blue racing east and going down from the north, while Black—Bolan's team—would become the other half of the scissors.

It was going to hell, he thought, and the first shot in anger hadn't even been fired. Factor in a black-ops Israeli force, which no one on either side had bothered to alert the other side about...

Bolan took up his M-16, glanced at Ridilson, who scowled and looked away.

"Not good," Ridilson muttered, repeating himself.

The unexpected always happened in combat, Bolan knew, but this sudden shift in the whole game plan was probably about to give new meaning to snafu.

The Executioner felt the Black Hawk lower, the black ops up and moving for the door.

"Go!" Hardball roared.

And they were gone.

CHAPTER SEVENTEEN

The lightning attack on the terrorist camp by an unknown force filled Marquis with rage. It struck him as wrong beyond reason, nothing short of a disgrace, an insult to his vengeance. All he had endured, the suffering over the loss of his family, the astronomical amounts of money shelled out, the risk to his name and fortune by hiring out what were essentially paid killers...

It was going up in flames right before his eyes. Someone else—some unworthy opposition in his mind—was about to steal his thunder.

It just didn't seem right.

The missiles streaked away from the Apache, minigun on the nose turret cutting loose with heavy metal thunder next, and there was nothing he could do but watch as the explosions began ripping apart the terrorists as they scrambled for cover inside the tents or raced for the motor pool. Some stood their ground, dying on their feet, shredded by the black choppers as more blasts scythed their ranks, hurtling torn scarecrow figures in all directions.

It was a massacre, and he had to wonder how his

own men would fare under that kind of killing power.

"This can't be happening!" Marquis screamed, searching the hellzone for any sign of his hated enemy through the field glasses. "Who are they?"

"Who knows? CIA perhaps, or Delta Force."

He looked at the Egyptian general, wondering why the snotty smug bastard didn't know more about this strike. "They're not yours?"

"No."

"How could this have happened?"

Sayyid shrugged. "It is a mystery."

"It's more than that—it's a disaster!"

Marquis went back to his desperate search for Hahmad, spotted the Syrian scraping himself off the ground, another terrorist grabbing him by the arm and pulling him inside the tent.

As if anyone could escape the hellfire that was raining down from the sky.

"Come on, where are you!" Marquis cried out, mentally urging his own commandos to hustle up and get the hell into the combat zone where he hoped against hope one of them could grab up the Syrian. But then what? How would they get the hell out of the country? Even when their transport plane flew back they could be chased down by the gunships and blown to scrap and broken bloody slabs of meat before they even got off the ground.

The choppers began scissoring back and forth over the terrorists, taking small-arms fire but those warbirds, he figured, were armor-plated and nothing short of a SAM would bring them down.

Then a few of the terrorists raced out of the tents, lifting RPG-7s. North, Marquis saw the blacksuited commandos charging toward the tents, two groups, it looked, one farther west and going for a pincers lock on the enemy. A search of their faces, and he could tell they were Westerners.

The mystery force took their first casualties as a pair of rockets winged skyward, vanished inside the fuselage and a ball of fire blossomed out the doorway.

That was good, he decided. One less gunship to fear later on.

Marquis would see how the next few minutes panned out, let them savage each other, then he would decide whether to venture down there in search of Hahmad.

He was scouring the faces of the mystery commandos again when he came across a familiar face.

Colonel Pollock.

Marquis snorted. "Why am I not surprised?" he muttered.

What more could possibly go wrong? he wondered. Whoever Pollock really was, the man had duped him, and Marquis could be fairly certain now the bastard had played no small part in the annihilation of his men in Tunisia.

First Hahmad, then he'd deal with Pollock in due time.

HAHMAD FIGURED it was better to live to fight another day than to get spread in a hundred chunks of bloody flesh across the Arabian Desert. There was too much to do, too many infidels to kill that day. Snared in a sneak attack by Egyptians or Western-ers, it didn't really matter who the attackers were, although he was sure they were some sort of black-ops team from the West. It wasn't as if he was going to go ask them for ID, much less stand his ground and fight and risk his life. There was a future to think about. If he died, a lot of dreams, he knew, would die with him.

He bolted inside the tent at the urging of Gezirah, the Egyptian shouting he needed to get to his jet.

That was fine. The trouble would be finding his pilot. Abuzah was in the next tent down, he be-lieved, but for some unknown reason—he figured it was pure terror—he found his legs carrying him into the command tent after Gezirah grabbed him by the arm. All around him their warriors were dying, screaming in rage at the gunships, firing AK-47s at the monster birds for all the good it would do them. Finally a few of his men had the good sense to bring one of the winged demons down with RPG-7s.

He was running for his life, and that was all he was concerned about. It was a hasty, panic-fueled exit that nearly cost him his life.

The canvas behind him was chewed up by mini-gun fire, slipstreams of the big steel-jacketed pro-jectiles searing past his ears, the radio console dis-appearing in sparking ruins. The deafening barrage told him the gunship was hovering just outside, rid-dling the tent with hundreds of rounds of heavy minigun slugs.

It was nothing short, he thought, of hell on earth.

Gezirah cried out, and Hahmad turned in time to find the Egyptian had unwittingly saved his life, the man a crimson shield in his wake, gouted and blasted open by the minigun fire.

On the run, Hahmad scooped up an AK-47. He had no intention of going back the way he came or engaging their attackers. Best to leave the fighting and the dying to others, but he didn't know if he'd need a weapon. A leader, he reasoned, had to live on in order to lead the devout followers of Islam to glory and victory. Still he hoped God would carry him safely from this madness.

A moment later, as he charged for the flap at the far end of the tent, the world blew up in his face, flinging him off his feet, the hammering nosedive filling his mouth with grit. He was sure he was dead, then a few eternal moments later, the lights came back on, and he found he was incredibly still in one piece. He checked his limbs. All there. Just a few scratches on his face.

God, he figured, had blessed him. Would his luck hold?

He was out the tent, saw a dozen or so of his freedom fighters bouncing off one another in a pell-mell dash for the motor pool.

"Abuzah!"

His pilot, he saw, peeled himself away from the stampede. Another gift from God.

Surely he was meant to live to fight another day.

"THE MONSTER IS getting away!"

Marquis watched as Hahmad joined the race for

the motor pool. It was too much to bear. Why weren't the gunships lowering the boom on the motor pool? Or maybe they would, waiting until the rats were running, easy targets crammed into vehicles.

Marquis watched as Anglerre led the charge of his commandos, the .50-caliber machine guns opening up on the terrorists as the jeeps bored in from the western edge of the camp.

Of course, he realized Anglerre couldn't possibly know the Syrian was fleeing, hoping that somehow his force survived, one of his commandos bagging an important prisoner for questioning later. It was a crazy thought, he knew, since there was a good chance none of his commandos would survive the coming hour.

It was going to be a day of fury, a day in hell, he knew, and decided he needed to do something other than stand around and watch the massacre.

Marquis turned, began running across the mesa.

"Where are you going?"

"To do something more than spectate, General!"

He cursed the Egyptian for cowardice or indifference, and it didn't matter which was keeping Sayyid rooted to the sidelines. Marquis had his man down there, and he wasn't about to let him just drive away. Marquis snatched an assault rifle away from a soldier, kept on running.

INTO THE FIRE they charged, and they got busy killing the enemy.

Not missing a beat, Bolan joined the other members of Black team, opening up with his M-16 on the terrorists as the enemy vaulted a low retaining wall near the hovels. Tapping the trigger of his M-203, the soldier blew a fireball downrange, and two more blasts from other Black team rocket men decimated another dozen or so terrorists. More terrorists kept coming, one wave after another.

"Goddammit!"

Hardball was looking skyward where the Black Hawk had been turned into flaming junk, its fiery hull floating to earth, hammering down with a sound like rolling thunder.

"Pull back!" Hardball roared over his com link. "Circle wide, then come back on the motor pool," he ordered the pilots. "I'm not losing another chopper to these assholes!"

Bolan claimed the far outside left flank of the skirmish line as Black team rolled across a wide stretch of no-man's-land, triggering M-16s on full-auto slaughter. Black kaffiyehs vanished in hunks of shredded cloth as still more terrorists tried to leap the wall and intercept their attackers. For every ten or twelve that were mowed down, Bolan found they were replaced by an equal number of shooters.

By now Bolan figured the other team would be in position, coming up on the blind side of the surviving terrorists. It was impossible to take a head count under fire, but Bolan had to figure at least forty to fifty terrorists were still standing.

And it sounded as if a fair number were opting for flight.

Feeding his M-16 a fresh magazine, the Executioner gained the wall with his teammates, shooting two more terrorists off the edge. Looking up and over, he saw the first of three jeeps spooling dust and charging for the desert.

Runners, and he wondered if Hahmad was in the group.

"TAKE THE GUNSHIPS DOWN!"

Hahmad figured he could at least bellow a few orders, hope the freedom fighters could hear him over all the shouting and racket of autofire.

Again the gunships seemed to concentrate long, sustained bursts of minigun fire on the tents, a few missiles erupting fireballs and adding to the ravenous barrage of lead hellstorms. It was impossible to tell how many of the terrorists were dead or how many were left, but a few came running out of the tents, raising RPG-7s, locking on the gunships.

"Fire! Bring down those damnable choppers!"

Hahmad hung back, instinct warning him the gunships were going for the motor pool as rotor wash swelled the air above and behind him. He hit the ground when the first wave of missiles vaporized a half-dozen jeeps and APCs, torn bodies sailing from the fireballs, things that were barely recognizable as human shooting through the air in all directions, minus arms and legs and heads. He rode it out for a few more moments, wreckage winging around his head, ricocheting off the ground.

Then he was up and running, looking back over his shoulder—and smiled at the sight of yet another of the enemy's gunships turned into a roaring mushroom ball of fire.

He made the jeep, Abuzah claiming the wheel. The driver fired up the engine, popped the clutch and sluiced the vehicle around, plowing through the fiery hull of an APC.

Hahmad kept waiting to be incinerated, and when the missiles never struck he silently praised God. It was only a few short miles to the jet, but it was far enough to keep him praying for a miracle of deliverance.

"I'LL BE A son of a..."

Hardball was caught up in shouting another round of orders to his remaining flyboys, hunched down behind the wall while Bolan and the other members of Black team did the shooting. The way it sounded, Hardball was ordering the gunships to fall back, forget about the runners.

What passed as a narrow street between a line of hovels was now littered with corpses, Bolan saw. There were pockets of shooters, hunkered down in the doorways of the hovels, and Bolan knew the dicey part was on the table.

They would have to move out, a door-to-door weeding of the savages.

No problem.

And there was no point malingering.

The Executioner saw the commandos of Blue team taking up firepoints at the far end of the dirt strip, their M-16s chattering and flaming, two terrorists crying out and toppling from doorways.

"Suggestion!" Bolan said to Hardball.

"Yeah, what?"

"We need to get this up close and personal."

"Load up your grenade launchers and let these sons of bitches have it good!"

A 40 mm grenade down the snout of his M-203 and Bolan lurched up over the wall, triggered a round that sailed on, joining about six or seven other missiles on the fly. Bodies were lost inside the line of fireballs, but that didn't mean, Bolan knew, all armed resistance was crushed.

The Executioner was up and over the wall when something to the south caught his attention.

The Frenchman's commandos had made the scene. And the uniforms of Egyptian soldiers didn't exactly inspire Bolan with confidence that every one was on the same page. If Marquis was getting aid and comfort from the Egyptians...

The hell with it, Bolan told himself, and charged ahead for the first row of hovels.

At the moment he had a full plate of problems. Terrorists, ex-Legionnaires or Egyptian soldiers, he'd take them all as they came.

CHAPTER EIGHTEEN

Anglerre already feared the worst, and he hadn't even fired a shot in anger yet.

It was a losing proposition, hopeless to even think he might live to see another sunrise. The heavy thunder from a sweeping triburst of .50-caliber machine guns ripped into isolated packs of scurrying terrorists, chopping them, gory human dominoes, off their feet. From the shotgun seat of the jeep—as Martineau held back on the trigger of the .50-caliber man-eater, turning still more terrorists into dancing sieves up and down in front of the tents, several of which were being eaten up by flames—Anglerre took in the slaughter zone.

The mystery commando force was in the village, surging out as a team, moving in on the stone huts for some hand-to-hand combat with any rats hiding from the wrath of total war, or dug in for some final suicide stand. Two gunships were still hugging the skies, but they had flown out to the north, the commander of the mystery force obviously not too keen on the idea of losing any more choppers, faced now with the possibility of getting stranded.

Understandable, he thought.

It was a nightmare vision that faced Anglerre.

He barked for the driver to slow down, keyed his com link and gave the order to fall out. "I want a prisoner, if possible."

Someone asked about the mystery opposition.

"Fair game."

And so were they, he knew.

Anglerre leaped out, Galil up and tracking. He tagged two wounded terrorists, mauled by shrapnel and bleeding profusely head to toe, out of the gate, forged on into the swirling smoke, hot, dancing flames pasting him in sweat in seconds flat.

The .50-caliber rounds kept chewing up live ones, and that was the good news. For as far as he could see the camp was littered with corpses, a sea of dead and dying. How long before he joined the dead?

He rolled over a wounded terrorist, without a left arm. He could have left him to bleed out, but Anglerre spared a mercy round to the chest. He saw figures darting inside a tent at the far edge of the row of camouflaged terror nests.

He had no idea how in the hell Marquis figured on getting them out of there in one piece. Maybe it didn't matter, he decided.

A warrior, he knew, was always prepared to face death head-on. And it was best if the warrior died in battle, not from old age, he thought, or getting mashed by a drunk driver in the streets of Paris, which he would probably never see again.

Galil chattering, Anglerre zipped a barrage through two terrorists, flinging them into a wall of flames consuming some of the motor pool wreckage.

The stink of roasting flesh, emptied bowels and bladders, choking smoke and burning fuel was a poisonous cloud, swirling nauseating fumes up his nose.

He couldn't get an accurate fix on the numbers of the mystery commandos, but if he could avoid engaging them, so much the better.

They were pros, and the numbers he'd so far seen left the opposition ahead by a few guns.

Not good, he thought, none of it, then told himself it was a good day to die.

MARQUIS SLAMMED ON the brakes. He was behind the tents, most of which were on fire and coughing out thick plumes of black smoke. Several armed figures came running from breaks in the walls of flames, searching wildly for a ride out of there.

He could provide one. The price, of course, would be steep, but it was time to do or die.

It was a dangerous moment, just the same, hurling himself into the fray, and he knew he was no soldier, but that didn't mean he couldn't pull the trigger on the assault rifle. He was out of the Land Rover, holding back on the trigger, remembering how he was shown to start firing low since the weapon tended to rise. He nailed two of the bastards, watching as blood spurted from fist-sized holes in their stomachs and chests. It bolstered his confidence to draw his first blood.

Hahmad, he knew, was gone, but the knowledge his hated enemy was beating a hard escape across the desert provided fuel for his fury. There had to be a Syrian somewhere in the vicinity. If he could bag one, make him talk...

He'd have to round up Anglerre and the others somehow, risk chasing Hahmad across open terrain, worried the whole time one of those gunships would blow them off the face of the earth.

Two went down under another raking burst of his autofire, and he was jogging toward them. One of them was still alive, thrashing around, holding in his guts. Marquis shot his face to pulp.

"No more!"

What the hell? Marquis couldn't believe his eyes. A terrorist was stepping from the flames of a tent, hands held high.

"I surrender!"

"Are you Syrian?"

"Wh-what? Y-yes."

"Do you know where Hahmad is going?"

"Yes."

"Then you live."

BOLAN HUGGED the edge of the doorway, heard scraping sounds from inside the hovel. He primed a frag grenade, glimpsed Blue team taking the row of stone huts, a door-to-door sweep, coming down from the west end of the village to link up. Autofire sounded from inside several of the huts, a commando pitching in a frag bomb, riding out the explosion, then two-man teams rushed inside to mop up.

Bolan did the same, whipping his arm around the corner as autofire blasted the stone off the door frame. The blast cleared the way, but he saw a shredded figure staggering in the far corner, lifting an assault rifle. The Executioner nailed him with a 3-round burst from his M-16.

Three more down, he saw, stretched out in pools of blood and leaking guts.

"Hey, Pollock!"

Bolan met Hardball at the door, the smoke of death boiling after the Executioner.

"You saw the new players?"

"That would be Marquis's bunch."

"Yeah, it would. They're sticking to the tent end of the camp. I'm seeing Egyptian soldiers, helping those bastards clean it up."

"You asking how to play it?"

"I'm thinking we're going to have some problems getting out of here without the Egyptians having something to say about it."

"I think diplomacy went out the window as soon as we hit the ground."

"I think you're right. I think diplomacy's going to come out of the barrel of our guns. Let's clean this up down here. Problem is, I'm down to two gunships and they pretty much blew their loads."

"We're on our own."

"No shit. Let's rock."

HAHMAD KEPT silently praying to God to spare his life. The mountains of the Arabian Desert were looming in the distance. In the gorge the Learjet was hidden, fueled and good to fly. A few more minutes and he would be in the air, on his way back to Syria.

It looked as if he would have to stay out of Egypt for a while, but he had contacts and jihad soldiers in the Egyptian Islamic Front in Cairo who could carry out his plans.

The dream of a massive jihad strike on different fronts had to live on. *He* had to live on.

He searched the desert and the skies behind them, felt his eyes bugging out of his skull.

"We are almost there!"

Azubah gripped the wheel, knuckles stark white, driving them fast and furious over the hard-packed earth.

Behind them, Hahmad spotted three jeeps from the camp.

"They're ours!"

Hahmad nodded. He had an idea. He could use those men to cover their escape if the enemy chased them down. The problem would be getting safely in the air, but there was no sign of the gunships—yet.

It felt like an agonizing wait, but minutes later he saw the mouth of the gorge. Just as they were rolling at an even harder pace for the finish line, almost vanishing into the gorge, Hahmad looked north, felt his heart skip a beat. More black gunships came streaking over the ridge of the mountains, flying low and hard toward the camp. The same sort of gunships he'd seen razing the camp, and it made him wonder exactly who they were. One team came from the north, the latest mystery force flying in from—

The northwest? It couldn't be, he thought. Israelis perhaps.

"Faster!" he yelled at his driver.

And Hahmad kept on praying in silence.

SHAIB NEARLY SHOUTED in rage when he saw the camp in flames, under attack by a large force. He was standing in the doorway of the Black Hawk, fairly certain he knew who was down there, shooting up the terrorists, having pretty much blown the camp to hell.

Someone had already seized center stage, stolen the show.

He moved toward the cockpit hatch, asked his flyboys, "Can you find the frequency to those gunships?"

"If they're CIA, I believe so, sir."

"Do it and fast."

Shaib searched the battlezone through the cockpit Plexiglas. Blacksuited commandos were tackling the terrorists in the village end, lobbing grenades through doorways, then barreling inside to mop up any wounded or armed resistance. Pros. There were brown-uniformed soldiers and more blacksuits attempting to clean up the terrorists in the flaming ocean where the tents and motor pool had stood. Egyptian soldiers. If nothing else, he decided, they had come here, it looked, to clean up a terrorist mess in their own backyard.

"Drop us down in the middle at the west edge of the village!" he ordered the pilot.

He needed to alert the commandos he was there to assist in the killing end without seeing himself and his soldiers getting tagged by friendlies. CIA or whoever, they had the same goal in mind.

Destroy the camp, and waste every last terrorist. That was good enough for him. It would be a tall order, searching out Hahmad in the carnage, assuming the Syrian butcher was still alive.

Either way, Shaib was ready to dig in and join the fight.

ANGLERRE LED EIGHT of his commandos into the one tent that was only just beginning to burn. He saw four terrorists on the move, charging for the back flap, dark figures swathed by black smoke. Anglerre took the lead, cutting loose with his Galil while his men chipped in with a long fusillade that tore up the foursome, skull to buttocks.

He had just given the order for the other half of his team to watch their backs, engage the mystery commandos if they came charging. He wasn't sure exactly what was driving him—other than instinct—to make his way out back. He had heard shooting, cries of pain and alarm and a familiar voice.

He was stepping through the flap when he saw Marquis manhandling a prisoner toward the Land Rover, an assault rifle in his hand.

"Hold up!" Anglerre bellowed in French.

"We're bailing!" Marquis yelled back.

Anglerre was surprised for a moment at what he found on the man's face. There was a wild and savage look in Marquis's eyes, the man having obviously just killed, tasting his first blood in combat.

"We need to talk about that, sir!"

"Quickly, then! Time's wasting!"

"What do you mean?"

"Hahmad's gone. We're going after him!"

"What do you want me to do about the others?" Anglerre asked, leading his men toward the Land Rover, then searching the motor pool, finding that one lone APC was still intact.

"Do? They stay and fight!"

Anglerre didn't like it. Leaving his men behind to fight and die while they fled galled him. But there was a look of insanity in Marquis's eyes, and he knew better than to challenge the man. Then there was the gunship problem, or maybe they'd get lucky, the opposition tied up here while they bolted.

"And guess what?"

"What?" Anglerre said.

"Our Colonel Pollock is on the other commando team."

Anglerre cursed. At least he knew the score. The sneaky bastard was something other than he had claimed. But what? And did it really matter right then?

"Get in that truck!" Marquis shouted. "We're out of here!"

CHAPTER NINETEEN

It took a few more grenades tossed through the doorways of the stone huts, commandos under fire from hostile occupants within, then a few of the smarter terrorists apparently didn't think martyrdom was such a great idea after all.

They were hollering in broken English, "Surrender! We give it up!"

"No shoot! No more!"

From his perch beside a doorway midway down the row of hovels, Hardball was shouting for them to come out, hands up, when Bolan saw the latest batch of gunships landing on the western edge of the village, the soldier briefly wondering now what?

"Hundred bucks," Ridilson said to Bolan, "those are Israelis."

A trio of terrorists shuffled outside, but Bolan knew there were still problems to tackle. There was autofire from the burning ruins of the tents, as the Frenchman's commandos and Egyptian soldiers were hosing down the surviving terrorists.

It wasn't over by a long shot, the soldier knew.

Hardball ordered the prisoners to get on their knees, hands on top of their heads. A lean, hawk-faced man in brown camous, Galil in hand, was leading the new arrivals from the grounded gunships.

"I heard!" Hardball called out. "You're Colonel Shaib."

"IDF. Looks like we're late for the party."

"We got to clean up, and we've got prisoners here to interrogate. The fat lady ain't singing yet."

"They're Egyptian soldiers," Shaib said, looking toward the pocket of ferocious fighting, .50-caliber machine guns apparently doing the bulk of the cleanup chores in that direction, jeeps sluicing around in billows of dust, the man-eaters sweeping away runners and bowling down those jihad troops who chose to hold bloody real estate to the last bitter breath.

"And some commandos hired by a vengeful Frenchman named Marquis," Hardball informed the Israeli colonel.

"I've heard the name. I see spectators up on the mesa."

"We need to nail this down, Colonel. You want, I can coordinate a flyover of the shooters. They shoot at our birds, wax them. No, they lift a piece in their direction, unload the goddamn sky!"

"Sounds good to me. I'm glad you see fit to share some of the leftovers."

"Hey, maybe if our side and your side didn't try to cowboy the action…"

"I understand. I am not here as an adversary or looking to steal anyone's thunder. Our Mossad and your CIA sometimes don't understand the need for communication—or honesty.''

"You're here to help, okay, but I was told there were runners who made it out into the desert.''

"Really? We saw no one on the way in.''

"Then Hahmad may be gone. Word is he bolted.''

"You have prisoners to question. However, Mossad has a line on Hahmad's Syrian compound. We may have another surgical strike in the near future.''

"Sounds like we can do business.''

"I certainly hope so.''

Bolan was checking the village, watching as the commandos kept moving for a house-to-house check for more terror nests. The only shooting now came from the forces near the tents. It was a wrap, at least in the village end.

"Let's move out, Colonel, your guys and mine,'' Hardball said. "One big, happy family.''

Bolan listened as the Israeli colonel keyed his com link and ordered his pilots to make a run at the surviving combatants.

"Come on, Pollock,'' Ridilson said, falling in beside the Executioner. "I'm sticking to you like glue—with the winners. We've still got that gig in Cairo in the wings.''

SAYYID FIGURED it was wisest at that point to move down into the killing field and make an appearance. There was his reputation to consider as an officer and a gentleman, plus a half-million dollars to get banked somehow. His problems, he feared, may only just be starting, but this was his country, and they were foreigners, armed invaders who had barged into Egypt without any permission he was aware of. If he had to pull rank, flex some muscle, he would if they started pointing accusatory fingers his way about the French commandos. He had powerful friends in Cairo, and he could be sure these commandos weren't looking to create some nasty international incident.

They were Western commandos, he was fairly certain, but the latest force was a mystery. They toted Galils, which indicated they were Israelis, but it was hard to say unless he exchanged some dialogue. The French had Israeli weapons themselves, so the choice of hardware really didn't mean much, since black operatives tended to use weapons that wouldn't point to their country of origin. The new commandos flew the same sort of gunships, then again, America sold weapons, aircraft, high-tech firepower to their Israeli friends. He couldn't say who was who, what was what until he drove in and started some exchange that would sound congratulatory or conciliatory at worst.

The good news was that the fighting was winding down. The Frenchman had fled with eight or nine of his commandos, stranding the others to either wipe out the terrorists—his own soldiers standing their ground and joining the slaughter of the jihad killers—but then what?

The Western commandos were moving out from the village proper, weapons poised as they closed in a large group on the final battleground. Surely, he thought, he could hand off plausible explanations to the foreigners about his involvement with the French. No need to mention the money, of course, and who could blame him—an Egyptian general, a commander of men, a protector of his country—for coming here and helping to lay waste to murderers of women and children.

Sayyid barked the orders for the remainder of his soldiers to fall in, move out and be ready to shoot, reminding them, of course, this was their country and they would take no nonsense from foreign invaders.

HAHMAD WORKED UP a terrible sweat pulling the camou tarp off the Learjet. By the time he was finished, drenched, sweat stinging into his eyes, he found a group of eight freedom fighters—half Syrian, half Egyptian—looking toward him for answers.

He was only in the mood to give orders and fly out of Egypt as quickly as possible.

"You are to remain behind and cover our flight out of here. There may be infidels on the way. Your duty is to stand and fight. This is jihad. Go with God!"

It was plain to see they didn't like it, but they didn't have to. He didn't hold the stares of his own people, brought with him from Syria to help train the Egyptians in the EIF. He would miss those men, certain they were soon to die. They seemed to understand, lifting their AK-47s, falling into a phalanx and moving for the mouth of the gorge to defend his exit.

The turbofans were screaming to life, and Hahmad raced up the ladder. One last look, finding two of the Egyptians arguing among themselves and Hahmad spotted the dust clouds in the distance.

He bellowed through the open cockpit doorway, "Go!"

MARQUIS SAW the sleek jet wheeling out of the gorge, the clever bastard having secured his own way out of the country ahead of time.

"How many rocket launchers do we have?" Marquis screamed over the tac radio.

"Six," Anglerre answered.

"Blow that jet out of the sky!"

"We may not make it in time. They'll be out of range by then!"

"No excuses! Do it!"

"I will make the attempt!"

"You will succeed!"

Marquis floored the gas, nearly lost the Land Rover to a sudden hard dip in the desert floor, the wheel trying to rip itself free from his grasp before he corrected his course and got himself steady and back on line.

"What is your name?" Marquis shouted at his prisoner.

"I am Gazi."

"Listen to me good. If he flies on, your life depends on you being able to get me to where he is hiding. Do you understand?"

"Yes."

What was that look, tone of voice all about? Marquis wondered. The Syrian sounded almost eager, as if he couldn't wait to steer them straight toward Hahmad's homegrown compound.

The jet was out and rolling fast and hard down a packed stretch of sand and gravel.

Marquis slammed his fist on the wheel, heard Anglerre patching through. "There are troops in the gorge. It's an ambush."

"Blow them away!"

HAHMAD WATCHED through the cabin porthole as the APC and the Land Rover cut the gap to the gorge, angling toward the jet. A few more yards and they would be wheels-up, then he saw figures, armed with rocket launchers, no less, spilling out the back of the transport truck. One of them was lifting a tubelike object for the jet, Hahmad praying they were out of range but he wasn't sure.

The tube locked on, then the figure was falling, the projectile streaking away, well above and beyond any intercept point.

Hahmad heaved a sigh as the jet lifted at an angle, quick and hard enough to dump him in the seat.

"No!"

Marquis shook his fist at the jet as it rose and vanished over the ridgeline of the mountains. One of his commandos had the bastard pegged, or so it looked, locked on with the LAW, then he was eaten up by the leadstorm pounding out of the gorge.

Marquis held back on the trigger of his assault rifle, shielded by the door, winging around long bursts at the shooters in the gorge. As luck or fate would have it, the terrorists had only assault rifles, apparently leaving behind anything more potent in their haste to escape the hellzone of the camp.

LAWs began chugging out deadly payloads, his commandos dumping five rounds on the mouth of the gorge.

"Stay here!" Anglerre told Marquis. "Watch our prisoner!"

Marquis held his ground, peering into the smoke drifting down the sides of the gorge as his commandos charged ahead. It was over in the next minute, two solitary wounded terrorists rising from the ashes, only to be cut down by autofire.

"We're clear!" Anglerre radioed. "Now what?"

It would be several hours before their transport plane returned. The wait could prove an eternity, if those gunships decided to track them down.

Marquis scanned the mountain range. He had his GPS module, and their pilots would be able to pin down their location.

"We move on the other side of this mountain range and wait," Marquis told Anglerre. "If those commandos come for us…we die where we stand."

THE FRENCHMAN'S COMMANDOS began firing skyward as the gunships swooped down for the finale. On the fly, Bolan loosed a 40 mm hellbomb, dumped it in a jeep where the machine gunner was blazing away with the .50-caliber machine gun, the heavy slugs sparking off the armored hull of the Apache zeroing in, pylons already flaming away with the Hellfire missiles. The Executioner's explosion took one jeep out of play. Black and Blue teams spread out in a skirmish line, the Israeli black-ops team on the far left flank, all of them triggering long, sweeping full-auto bursts at the French commandos. The Egyptian soldiers, however, began throwing their weapons down, holding their arms and shuffling away from the Frenchmen as fast as they could, as if they might catch some disease.

They would catch something, all right, Bolan thought. Death. Even still, with the fireballs eating up the ground near them, a few of the Egyptian soldiers became casualties, ripped apart by flying debris and stray bullets.

With the combined ground and air attack, it was over in the next few moments. The Egyptians were now sprinting away from the falling wrath of Hellfire missiles and minigun bombardments, a few of them hitting the deck and covering their heads.

A wall of fire erupted down the surviving French commandos, obliterating man and machine, adding yet another inferno to the holocaust. The sky became thick with shooting bodies and severed limbs and twisted metal shards. Flesh and amputated limbs began raining the earth in front of the Executioner.

Bolan picked targets, stick figures staggering out of the smoke and flying wreckage, dropping two more as Black and Blue teams came in on the survivors in lockjaw attack.

Hardball and Shaib passed on the orders to fan and check the area for wounded or any sign of Hahmad.

Bolan rolled ahead, saw a possum crabbing along, and drilled a 3-round burst into the back of his skull.

And the soldier saw the next round of arrivals, a caravan of vehicles rolling in from the mesa—the watchers from above, whoever they were. The soldier figured they were the Egyptian army. There was no sign of hostile incursion as the vehicles slowed near the ring of fire. They did everything, Bolan observed, but wave a white flag.

It took a full twenty minutes, but the Executioner made the walk through with his teammates, noting Ridilson never strayed too far from his side.

They found nothing but the dead.

It was a picture of total and utter destruction they waded through.

And the home team had taken casualties, the gunships smoking but burning out now, the stench of the torched flesh of the flight crews swamping the already scorching air.

Bolan had a feeling, though, that a new round of trouble was right around the corner. The Egyptian military, he knew, hadn't exactly invited them here to wipe out a hundred or so terrorists who may or may not be hunkered down in the desert with the permission of the government in Cairo.

Bolan walked down the line of flaming tents and burning wreckage, saw a lean figure with a blouse festooned with medals hop out of the passenger seat of a jeep.

"I am General Sayyid. I think we need to talk about this situation."

CHAPTER TWENTY

"Nice of you to join us, General. Did you enjoy the show? You got any popcorn left?"

Bolan, with Ridilson on his hip, stepped away from the hungry lakes of fire, sidestepping the strewed corpses, closed in as Hardball approached the Egyptian general. Hardball's voice dripped with contempt, the black-ops commander thrusting his hands on his hips, flicking his tongue and making spitting sounds like a cobra as he looked the general up and down, something he'd stepped in and wanted to wipe off the bottom of his boot. Bolan listened, felt the tension rising as hot as the consuming fires around him, poised—as he was sure the rest of his teammates were—to start shooting at the first hint Sayyid intended to get ugly.

The soldier gave the killing field a hard look. The prisoners had been rounded up, hands bound by plastic cuffs behind their backs, forced to stay kneeling, surrounded by Hardball's hitters. Hardball had already given the order to secure the stone building to the west, the perimeter around the armory with its ordnance of mass destruction guarded by black-suits. There were problems to work out, Bolan knew, the least of which might be the fact Hahmad and Marquis were both missing. Where to go, how to proceed from there? Bolan knew what he wanted, but he needed a conference, in private, with Hardball. However, the Egyptian situation took precedence for the moment.

"You want to explain yourself, General?"

"What's to explain?"

"Plenty. Like how you allowed a bunch of murdering commandos to ride in here and nearly muck up our play."

Sayyid shrugged, and Bolan got a bad read on the guy. He was about as trustworthy, he thought, as a cobra, the soldier left wondering when the man would strike.

"What can I tell you? I only recently learned of this terrorist camp. What, you think my government would allow butchers of women and children to hide out in the desert and play war games and plot the destruction of perhaps even my own countrymen?"

"You tell me. You saying we get a free pass here?"

"A free pass? If you mean will I report this to Cairo and seek some sort of action against you, the answer is no."

"That's mighty big of you."

"And these other commandos? Who are they?"

"Israelis. How do they rate?"

"You're all free to go."

"Not quite. I've got to clean up here, bodies of my own people to dig out of the wreckage once the flames die down. I don't know how you operate, but

I don't leave my guys behind for the buzzards and the hyenas.''

"You sound bitter. Need I remind you to look around and see that I lost soldiers also?''

"A lovefest this ain't.''

"Lovefest.'' Sayyid chuckled. "Hardly.''

"I was being smart.''

"I see. So, your mission is not finished in Egypt.''

"You in a hurry to get rid of us, seeing as we did all the shooting and dying for you? Except for the few of your guys who happened to get caught up in the storm.''

"What would you have me do?''

"Cooperate. Make sure we get that free pass out of the country. At worst, stay out of my way, let me do my job. You're right, though, we're not exactly sanctioned by Cairo to be here.''

"I will help you any way that I can.''

Bolan sensed the powwow was over, stepped up to Hardball and said, "You have a minute for me?''

"Sure.'' Hardball wheeled, walking Bolan away from the Egyptians. "Something about that guy isn't kosher. I don't know what it is....''

"I'm thinking Marquis dumped off some cash for another of those free passes you mentioned,'' Bolan said. "I'm thinking he knows a hell of a lot more than he's going to say. I'd keep him here until we're on our way.''

"Do you mind if I join you, gentlemen?'' Colonel Shaib called out.

Hardball glanced at Bolan, who said, "He's part of the team now.''

"One big, happy commando family," Hardball muttered.

Ridilson wasn't invited to the brainstorming session, but insinuated himself in the circle of soldiers as Hardball gave Shaib the nod.

"Ask those scumbags about Hahmad," Hardball ordered his commandos.

Bolan heard the commandos question the prisoners about Hahmad, but they began firing off their answers in Arabic.

"What the hell, I need an interpreter here? Son of a..." Hardball growled.

"He said Hahmad's gone," Bolan said, and Hardball looked at him. "I know some Arabic."

"I know he's gone, but what's his plan? How's he think he's going to get out of the country? What the hell, he going to swim across the Red Sea?"

Bolan put the question to the prisoners, listened to a long response. "They say they're Syrian. They came here with Hahmad in his private Learjet. They were training EIF terrorists, something about how Hahmad had several operations on the table. EIF is waiting on a green light to move on two of the operations."

"Terrorist attacks, they mean," Hardball said. "Anything else?"

"This jet, it's hidden in the mountains out in the desert."

"And he's had a half hour or more head start," Hardball snarled.

"He's flown on, I'm thinking," Bolan said.

"Back to Syria," Shaib said.

"And this Marquis? Hell, you saw what happened here," Hardball said to Bolan, staring the soldier down as if either expecting a challenge or a reprieve. "I couldn't spare any more gunships to go chasing them down."

"No one's blaming your call," Bolan said.

"We pick up the pieces," Ridilson chimed in, "pick up the pace and resume the hunt."

"Suggestion," Bolan said. "Marquis will probably call back his own plane ride. He's nowhere to be found here. I'm thinking he went after Hahmad, and he's out there with whatever's left of his commandos, hiding in the mountains. The man's possessed by his craving for revenge on Hahmad. That's all he's living for, and at this point I read him as not caring about who lives or dies as long as he sees Hahmad dead. He's over the edge, out of control. My guess is he'll go after Hahmad."

"And so will we," Shaib stated.

"This is Colonel Pollock," Hardball said, then introduced himself with his handle, finally nodding and grunting at Ridilson. They shook hands all around, then Hardball said, "Now that we're all nice and friendly, we need to figure out our next move."

"I need to get into Cairo ASAP," Bolan said.

"How's that? And why's that?" Hardball wanted to know.

"The Egyptian Islamic Front," Shaib answered for Bolan. "Mossad has a line on a terrorist organization in Cairo that was responsible for helping Hahmad set up this training base. Is that it, Colonel? These terrorist operations you mentioned?"

"And I intend to blow their house down before they do whatever it is they're going to do."

"How you going to manage that?"

"I need a chopper ride to the outskirts of the city. Ridilson here, he's already told me he has contacts in the city who can get me in and out."

"Get 'us' in and out," Ridilson said.

Bolan felt his mouth tighten. He didn't need any extra hands—a solo act would work best—then he thought it through. Maybe Ridilson could assist.

"Hey, without me, guy," Ridilson said, obviously reading the taut expression, "you could get snapped up by Egyptian authorities. You ever been inside an Egyptian jail? I have. They make any big house in the States look like the Holiday Inn. I know what you're going to do, Pollock. You're going to hit the EIF and you're not swinging for singles. You want the grand salami."

"This is crazy," Hardball said. "I mean, hell, you handled yourself like a pro, Pollock. If I—we," he said, glancing at Shaib, "are going after Hahmad, chasing him straight into Syria, I can't afford to lose you."

"You won't."

"You seem pretty sure of yourself."

"It wouldn't be the first time I've done what I'm proposing to do."

Hardball peered at Bolan. "I'm almost thinking you were ready to use the word *insist*."

"This mission is far from over," Bolan said. "I'm thinking you and the colonel are going to need a few hours at least to clean up here, maybe fly back to your Company outpost, put together a plan, gather some intel, refuel."

"He's got a point," Ridilson said, smiling.

Hardball scowled at Ridilson. "Lose the smirk, pal. I lost good men here, and I'm not in the mood for comedy or smart-ass routine. Colonel, you can see I lost two choppers."

"You need a lift, then."

"It would be much appreciated."

"We will need to gather fresh intelligence. I will need to contact Mossad, have them track Hahmad's plane, monitor the area in question. We know where it is, but if we go in, we will need a little more than a few gunships."

"Meaning?" Hardball asked.

"A plan has been in the works for a while now. My government has been intending to send in a squadron of F-15Es, and simply blow Hahmad's known compound off the face of the earth. They have stalled for reasons I am not privy to, but at this point, knowing what we know about what happened here, Mossad will push the operation through. I want to see the bastard dead with my own eyes. Your country and mine have worked black ops before. With amazing success, I might add."

"Ground troops, guns blazing in, the way softened up by death from above," Hardball said.

"Just like here," Shaib said. "Only this time we will unite our forces."

"First come first served on this Hahmad, is that how it's going to fall, Colonel?" Hardball said. "I mean, you're not looking to take this animal alive, put him in a Mossad cage and pick his brains?''

"No. He is only wanted dead. The problem has been he has people in Lebanon, namely Beirut, and often he slips across the border, hiding among his minions, plotting his attacks on my country. The Syrian army, they also protect him, are equally responsible for helping him mount his attacks against Israel. If we go, we go all the way, understand that.''

"Oh, but do I," Hardball said.

"That means even if we have to wage a small dirty war against the Syrian army.''

Hardball heaved a breath, fished a pack of smokes out of his combat pouch, torched one up with a lighter. "We've got our work cut out for us. Okay, since I read the good general as shady and holding back, I did the same. We cleared this operation with Egyptian intelligence before we came in, shooting the shit out of this camp. There was the usual bitching session, back and forth with a shitstorm of accusations, but we got our way for a solo act until Colonel Shaib made the stage. I've got people myself in Cairo, Pollock, I can contact and help you if you need it. Maybe Ridilson here can play the hand of God, but if you get jammed up…I can spare you the Kiowa. We can work out the logistics before you hop aboard. Thing is, I want you in constant contact with me.

"Here's the time frame. Four hours, in and out. By then it will be night and our combined forces need to be wheels-up and on the way for Syria. If we can do this by the numbers, if the colonel can iron out any wrinkles on his end, we can hit the bastard before dawn, about the time, I figure, he's just landed on his home turf. Of course, I need to run this by the brains up top, but they want Hahmad as bad as the colonel, and I'm thinking they're ready to go the distance, fuck all that international-incident noise. Hahmad's going down. Okay, gentlemen, that said, I've got a HAZMAT team I need to get down here from the outpost and secure this ordnance.''

''Speaking of which,'' Shaib said, and Bolan heard an edge to the man's voice, ''I would like my own people to take a look at these backpacks of mass destruction. Yes, Mossad has known what Hahmad stored here.''

''You're not telling me you want the stuff for yourself?''

Shaib shook his head. ''Not all of it.''

''Whoa...''

''Just a few samples for my own people to take back and examine. What was it you said, Mr. Hardball? We are all one big, happy—''

''Yeah, yeah. Okay. You've got it. How do you plan to ship the stuff? You got space suits?''

''Lead containers. I trust your own HAZMAT team will assist in transporting the samples?''

''We'll work it out. Okay, Pollock, let's brainstorm a few more minutes about the particulars.''

''What about the general?'' Bolan asked.

''What about him? He stays by my side, I don't let him out of my sight. Four hours, Pollock, you hear me?''

The Executioner nodded. "Let's shake a leg, then."

"Right, time's a wasting."

"You'll let me know when I'm on the clock?"

"You bet."

MARQUIS READ the sullen anger on the faces of Anglerre and the others. He brushed a sheen of sweat off his forehead, cursing the terrible heat, the sun a fireball that seemed to suck the very life out of his parched body. Fortunately Anglerre had seen fit to dump canteens in each of the Land Rovers.

They were squatting, sitting or hunched in a gully on the west face of the mountains, staring out at more vast and empty wasteland. The desert, the heat, the emptiness, Marquis brooded, fit his mood. Hot, ugly and promising only death.

"What is it, Anglerre?"

"You want the truth?"

Marquis snorted. "I believe I can handle whatever truth you wish to speak."

"Very well. I don't like leaving my men behind to die."

"Nor I. But had we remained, we, too, would be among the dead."

"That doesn't make it any better."

"Are you angry with me? Do you blame me?"

"I don't know."

"Meaning you haven't decided."

"I don't know. I'm here, I am a soldier, I am paid to do your bidding."

"And you think us going into Syria after the bastard is suicide?"

"Possibly."

It was time to up the ante, bolster morale, Marquis decided. "Listen to me, all of you!" he barked, heads jerking around, Marquis riding out the silence for a few moments. "Any man who flies with me, who helps me track down and kill Hahmad, will be paid five million U.S. dollars apiece. No questions, cash on the spot once we return to Paris."

"Could you say that again?" the commando named Martain asked, his jaw going slack.

Oh, but now he had their attention, repeated the price. When this was done and Hahmad was dead, they could retire, they were cut loose, free to go live their lives. They would be rich, and if they pulled it off he was considering padding the price with a bonus.

"Five million," he said once more.

And he saw morale come back to life, eyes lighting up, minds burning by the one thing most human beings understood.

Greed.

It got them every time, Marquis thought.

CHAPTER TWENTY-ONE

Beyond the heat, the stink of car fumes and basic reek of desperate poverty and body sweat, the problem with Cairo for Bolan was its nightmarish congestion.

Human traffic alone was a vision of Armageddon. Tack on the endless seas of cars and meandering herds of camels all over the tight-packed streets of squalling vendors in jammed souks, groaning buses choking every main road, then throw in teeming hordes of beggars, and it seemed crazy on the surface to expect a successful blitz against the EIF here, in time to meet Hardball's deadline—at worst, capture by the authorities, thrown into that pit of hell for a jail that Ridilson had mentioned. At last count, Bolan heard Cairo was a city of fifteen million people, something like seventy-five thousand bodies per square mile.

Getting in would prove a tall order by itself. Getting out and making the rendezvous for the Kiowa pickup at the pyramids of Giza...

Well, Bolan was forging on, aware he was risking it all, prepared to crush the EIF on its home turf, whatever it took, rolling the dice, hoping the gods of war smiled on this incursion.

The Executioner had claimed the back seat, Ridilson in the shotgun seat, while the Company incountry contact manned the wheel of the rattletrap Volkswagen van. The contact's name was Ahda, a thickly bearded dark man who had been right on time for the pickup near the pyramids. Whether he could be trusted remained to be seen, but Bolan knew he had little choice but to go with Ridilson's program. If nothing else, addresses and numbers of EIF opponents jibed with the Farm's intel.

The weapon of choice for this blitz was a mini-Uzi, one each for Bolan and Ridilson, stowed in special shoulder rigging beneath their long, loose-fitting robes. For the crash and burn of the EIF headquarters, then the known apartment safehouse for another bunch of terrorists, the Executioner and Ridilson had enough frag, incendiary and flash-stun grenades to bring down a small army. He could expect to find fifteen or more EIF thugs hunkered down at their base of operations in Old Cairo, just north of the Roman fortress of Babylon, another six or seven at the apartment near the Southern Cemetery known as the City of the Dead. The Beretta 93-R and .44 Magnum Desert Eagle rounded out the hardware picture for the soldier, spare clips in the pouches of his combat vest for all three pieces.

After some give and take with Hardball, before departing the ruins of the terrorist camp in the Kiowa, the black-ops commander had relented and extended Bolan's deadline to make it back to the CIA outpost to five hours.

He saw he would need every last second he could manage to steal if he wanted to be on board for the proposed surgical strike into Syria.

As soon as they came off the pyramids road and began crossing the bridge over the Nile River, traffic was jammed thanks to a camel herder leading an army of his animals for the slaughterhouse.

Ahda cursed.

"Back it up. There's another bridge…"

"Yes, I know," Ahda said, "near the Israeli embassy."

"Oh, man," Ridilson groaned, checking his watch as their wheelman put the van in reverse, whipping the vehicle around in the opposite lane, a cruise ship and the traditional feluccas choking the Nile sweeping by in Bolan's sight.

"How do you know the layout?" Bolan asked Ridilson, who nodded at their driver.

"I've been inside," Ahda volunteered.

"You infiltrated their ranks?"

"As a CIA informant only," the Egyptian said. "I am on probationary status as they run a background check on me."

"Will that hold?"

"It should."

"We live in hope," Bolan said. "If we're walking into a trap…"

"I understand. Listen, I do not wish to see my country become another Beirut because of a few fanatics. Trouble with Americans we do not need."

"And?" Bolan prodded.

"They have a plan to attack both the Israeli and American embassies. They are waiting for this Hahmad animal to deliver the special backpacks. The leader of the EIF intends to fly suicide choppers into the embassies. It is madness. It will ignite more than just an international cry of outrage against Egypt."

And that was understating the matter, the soldier thought. Bolan felt his stomach knot with rage. Terrorism was essentially an invisible empire, the players never known or showing themselves until it was too late and they pulled off some diabolical jihad scheme. If both American and Israeli embassies were blown to smithereens in a double suicide attack, the ramifications would be beyond nightmarish. Egypt would be branded an outlaw state, and that was just for starters. It would come to light that the EIF was sanctioned by certain power players in the government and military infrastructure, and knowing how the Israelis met fire with fire, a war could ignite between the two countries.

"Sounds like we're just in time, huh?" Ridilson said.

"You might say that."

Ahda caught Bolan staring at him, returned the look in the rearview glass. "Sir, I want to see the EIF toppled. Every day, since Egypt has become friendly with the madman of Iraq and are demanding the Americans lift sanctions against them, we are becoming more militant. I wish for peace in my country, and I see that hope slipping away with each growth of these terrorist organizations, like parasites they are. I will help. I will skip saying you can trust me, but I will do as you wish.''

"So far, so good,'' the Executioner said, and knew any amount of trust on his part would have to be earned.

Right then the soldier had an appointment to keep with death.

And after hearing what the EIF had planned, the Executioner wasn't about to disappoint the Grim Reaper.

MAHMUD GHURI WAS tired of waiting.

He stood up from behind his desk in the main office, pacing, staring at the phone, then looking at the radio console in the far corner of the Spartanly furnished room. He was waiting for a call from the Syrian that the special delivery was en route. He was also silently urging his military contact to call and inform him the choppers were secured, prepared to hand them over to be stuffed with the special backpacks of death for the infidels.

He glanced at the blueprints of the American and Israeli embassies, thinking he didn't really need to know the layouts since the choppers would be flown straight into the buildings, human bombs going off before they crashed, clouds of poison spewed over the compounds. He could see the fireballs in his mind when the choppers blew, the horror that would follow when the West learned that nerve gas and germ-laced bombs had killed their people.

He wanted fantasy to become reality. Ghuri was anxious to usher in the new age of jihad.

The waiting was fraying his nerves, though. He knew the Syrian was having problems lately, something about foreign commandos hunting him for his part in murdering the family of a wealthy Frenchman. Well, it wasn't really his problem, but he realized any trouble the Syrian had might find its way to his doorstep.

Which was why the AK-47 was always close by.

He considered taking a stroll around the office complex, but he knew he'd only find his men smoking, sipping tea, playing backgammon as if they didn't have a care in the world. And that would only serve to ratchet up his anxiety, perhaps cause an angry outburst that they really didn't deserve. A leader had to be in control of his emotions.

The phone rang, Ghuri jumping at the sound. He rushed back to his desk, picked it up and heard his military contact inform him, "We have a small problem."

"How come I do not like the sound of that?"

"A source of mine informed me the camp was attacked and that all of our forces down there were slaughtered like sheep."

Ghuri nearly screamed, "What? How? By whom?"

"It is unclear, but I am told the merchandise has been seized by this mystery force."

"How can this be? We have plans, we have—"

"I can get you the choppers, fear not. I can call back in two hours with details on delivery."

It was a rush job, last minute, and with no back-packs...

Well, Ghuri still had plenty of dynamite, plastic explosives he could get his hands on. It wouldn't be the nightmare blow he wanted to deliver, but a massive blast on both embassies could perhaps raze the compound, if they were struck in the heart of the complexes.

His head was spinning with questions, none of which he could be sure his contact was capable of answering.

"I will call you in two hours. Be there."

"Where would I go?" he barked, but the man had already hung up.

Ghuri stood there, visions of disaster and defeat by the hands of some unknown adversary flaming in his mind. He saw blood and fire, yes, but the storm was raging over him.

Ghuri slammed the phone down.

As soon as Bolan entered the alley, he found Cairo was alive with dangers other than terrorists with visions of glorious martyrdom at the expense of innocent lives.

Judging the thickness and length of what was left of the winding black serpent, he figured the cobra was a seven or eight footer. He was rolling on, reaching through the slit in his robe, fisting the mini-Uzi when the serpent vanished, slithering through a crack in the wall.

"Welcome to Cairo," Ridilson said.

Bolan glanced back at the van, Ahda parked in the mouth of the alley.

"He'll be there."

"He'd better be," Bolan said, then reached the double doors of the targeted building.

Fifteen to twenty shooters, Bolan thought, checking the alley, finding it clear of watching eyes. Archways at both ends led to souks where Bolan heard the vendors still going at it, even as the sun began to wane over the Nile.

The Executioner twisted the doorknob and found it open. Mini-Uzi out and leading the way, he marched ahead of Ridilson and into the den of savages.

GHURI FELT his paranoia mounting, his breathing labored as some dark fear began gnawing at him, nerves like sparking electricity. He grabbed his AK-47, but what was he going to do? Who were his enemies? Perhaps the men they greased up the food chain had turned against them?

He decided to check on his men, tell them to tighten up, put the games away, expect the worst, but what was the worst?

He was stepping through the door of his office, sights locked on Nassir, Samir and Abdul, hunched over a backgammon board, when two strangers barged through the doors and opened fire with mini-Uzis.

The trio never knew what hit them, as they went down under the double barrage of autofire, limbs flailing and bits and pieces of wet meat flying through the air.

Ghuri was shocked for a moment, long enough to witness the two smoking muzzles swing his way and flame out his death knell.

The dream of striking a double blow against his hated enemies died with him.

THE EXECUTIONER and Ridilson tagged the four in a matter of eye blinks. The guy in the doorway to his office nearly got it together, raising his AK-47, holding back on the trigger, but his burst hit the ceiling as he toppled back into his office.

By now the house was alerted, and if Ridilson's contact was right there were a half-dozen rooms around the corner where EIF thugs were scrambling, shouting up a storm.

Palming a frag grenade, Bolan raced for the corner, his mini-Uzi up and chopping a hardman off his feet as he dashed into the outer office.

One-handed, Bolan went low at the corner's edge, heard the voices and judged them fifteen to twenty feet down the hall, then ripped loose with a burst of subgun fire, Ridilson on his heels. A cry of pain shot through the racket down there, as curses and shouting mingled with return fire. Bolan gave the steel egg an underhanded pitch, rode out the blast, then rolled out in the open, firing away. Five bodies were stretched out in the hanging pall of cordite and smoke, then armed figures, coughing and hacking, staggered out of doorways. Ridilson by his side, the

Executioner held back on the trigger, and the two men blew another five off their feet.

Now the tricky part, as Bolan reached the first door down the hall, feeding his subgun a fresh clip. Three men were snarling at one another inside the room, voices of panic striking Bolan's ears as he primed a flash-stun, then tossed it into the room.

He looked away as the blinding flash and deafening thunder erupted, then burst through the doorway, tagging the trio as they picked themselves up off the floor. Outside Bolan made out the stutter of Ridilson's subgun, more cries of men getting cut to ribbons reaching his ears, the bittersweet music of death.

The soldier linked up with Ridilson at the next door down, stepping over bodies on the way.

Six rooms checked.

All clear.

Ridilson glanced at his watch. "This time of day..."

"I know what you're going to say. One more stop. We'll make it back even if we have to run."

Retracing their steps, they made the alley, Bolan feeling doubtful their ride had stayed put.

He found Ahda looking around, clearly nervous, then showing the two of them an expression of relief.

"Was there ever any doubt, Colonel Bob?"

The Executioner ignored the grinning Ridilson. They were on Hardball's clock, and it was winding down fast.

CHAPTER TWENTY-TWO

It was the same setup as the hit on the EIF headquarters, likewise the same merciless intent to slaughter the enemy where they stood or sat.

The Executioner led Ridilson up the steps, across the dark landing of the second-floor hall of the apartment while Ahda waited in the van in the alley.

Same deal as the EIF headquarters. Hit and run.

Mini-Uzi out and leading the way, Bolan found the hall clear of human traffic, marking off the numbers of the apartments until he came to the right door. The hall reeked of urine, vomit, spiced food, the sound of a baby squalling from one of the rooms, an eerie, plaintive wail.

For someone other than that child, he thought, the crying had only just begun.

Bolan took up post on the side of the doorway, palmed a flash-stun, mouthed what it was to Ridilson, the soldier nodding the CIA man would take the door-crashing honors. Six or seven EIF flunkies, holed up inside, unaware doomsday was staring them down, and Bolan wanted this wrapped up in seconds flat.

Hit and git.

Ridilson lifted a boot, sent a thundering kick into the door just beside the knob. It splintered and flew open, the Executioner tossing the armed flash-stun inside the room as the familiar tide of voices raised in alarm rolled his way. They were shooting now, autofire raking the door frame, flaying splinters in their faces, and at least that told Bolan the intel was on the money.

Like Ridilson had said, he thought, was there ever any doubt?

They hugged the wall, looking away as the blinding light and sense-shattering bomb ripped through the enemy ranks, ending the barrage of enemy autofire for the moment.

The first one through the door, as agreed upon, Bolan peeled off to the left, holding back on the trigger of his mini-Uzi while Ridilson went right, his compact subgun joining the Executioner's stuttering fusillade. They were spread across the large living room, two going down right away under the double lead sweep of death, a double jig of dancing dead men flying over a divan, all flailing limbs and spurting blood. Wild autofire attempted to track the invaders, but the enemy was blind and deaf, bullets tattooing the wall behind Bolan, a close shave of hot lead nearly scoring his flesh just the same.

Five left, reeling about the living room, and Bolan burned out the clip, hosing them down, left to right, flinging them in all directions. Changing clips, the Executioner rolled for the beaded archway, listening for sounds of life.

The bearded wildman came flying through the

beaded curtain, bellowing something in Arabic, his AK-47 flaming. Hot lead tore past Bolan's scalp, the soldier crouching, darting away, firing his mini-Uzi, the lead storm blowing dangerously close to his side, a lamp blowing up beside the Executioner. A little help from Ridilson and they nailed the wildman, red holes blossoming on the chest of his tunic as he flew back through the curtain.

No sounds from beyond the curtain, but Bolan knew there was no other way than to check the apartment, room by room. With Ridilson covering, Bolan found the first two rooms clear. In the last bedroom, he found a woman, holding a baby to her chest. She was sobbing, rocking the child in her bosom.

Bolan left her to her grief. Whichever husband was among the dead he'd never know, but it pained him just the same to think how one fanatic who would have so blithely snuffed out innocent life had left behind innocents who would be forced to fend for themselves.

"Let's go," Bolan said. "We're finished here."

They were down the steps, outside in the alley.

There was no sign of the van. He searched both ends of the alley, silently cursing, when the van came screeching around the corner.

Bolan raced to the vehicle, opened the side door, hopped in. "I thought I told you to stay put."

When Ridilson took the shotgun seat, Ahda ground the clutch, lurched them ahead, out of the alley. "I apologize. I saw police vehicles, I became nervous. I thought it best to not just be sitting

around, looking suspicious. Cops, here or anyplace
else they have cop's eyes, you understand?''

"Sounds like a good time to get the hell out of
Dodge,'' Ridilson said. "I don't think we'd pass—
even though you're a little on the swarthy side,
Colonel Bob—for your everyday Egyptians. We
kind of fit the profile for ugly American riffraff
mercs.''

Bolan checked his watch. Even if the chopper returned on time it would be cutting it close, mere
minutes actually, and they would be damn lucky to
make the pickup site on schedule.

"Back to the pyramids,'' Bolan told their driver.
"Make it snappy. Don't stop for anybody or anything. Any camels in the way…''

"Run 'em down!'' Ridilson said, and let out a
war whoop. "God, I love this!''

THEY WERE LATE.

Dusk was creeping its dark shroud over the Lib-
yan Desert, Bolan searching the skies to the south,
silently urging the Kiowa to show. Sweating, from
both the heat and the anxiety burning him up inside,
the soldier wheeled, looked at Ridilson's grim expression, the man dwarfed by the three pyramids of
Giza in the background. Bolan walked up to the van,
told Ahda, "You can take off. Our ride's either
coming or it isn't. I appreciate all you did.''

The Egyptian nodded. "I can honestly state it was
my pleasure. You two made Egypt a little better
place to live in after today. Go with God.''

"Back at ya.''

The Egyptian took off, wheels kicking up dust as he headed back for the endless blocks of staggered white buildings that marked the sprawling urban complex comprising a boundary around the pyramids.

"You want to call Hardball?" Ridilson asked.

Bolan was reaching for his tac radio when he spotted the dark speck to the south.

Moments later, the Kiowa landed, Bolan and Ridilson hopping into the fuselage.

"You can thank Hardball when you see him," the helmeted pilot told Bolan. "He insisted I fly back a second time, make sure you guys made the party in Syria. The troops are ready to go, we have the thumbs-up and that includes our Israeli buddies, straight from Mossad. They've tracked this bastard to his home turf. Grab a nap, 'cause what I heard, you won't catch another moment's rest until this is wrapped. Unless..."

The pilot didn't have to finish the statement. Unless, the soldier thought, it was the big sleep.

Bolan nodded, felt the tight smile forming on his lips. A moment later, as he took a seat next to Ridilson, the chopper was up and away, streaking back for the CIA base.

The soldier felt no relief, only a mounting anxiety, aware a surgical strike in Syria loomed, all the marbles on the table, everyone—Marquis, the CIA and the Israelis—going for broke.

Not a problem. The soldier wouldn't have had it any other way.

For all intents and purposes the EIF was finished

in Egypt, the head of the hydra severed by the blitz in Cairo. There were power players who had fronted for the terrorists, giving them free rein, and they would be brought to the light of justice soon enough. He would pass on what he'd learned about the EIF's plot to crash suicide choppers into the American and Israeli embassies to Brognola. From there, it would be the big Fed's responsibility to alert the embassies, beef up security somehow, and Bolan had a few ideas how to do that. It was a hell of a thing, he thought, but the world was changing for the worse every day. It used to be trucks heaped with explosives, bulldozing through the gates of U.S. military barracks, but now the savages were hell-bent on commandeering aircraft.

Hahmad, the Executioner knew, had to go down for good.

The Executioner almost couldn't wait to get into Syria and hunt the savage down. Someone was going to bag the Syrian, and the soldier didn't even care if Marquis scored his blood.

The Frenchman belonged to him anyway. There was the little matter of the Interpol connection in Paris, and the only thing Bolan would insist Hardball and Shaib grant him was a free pass to be the one who bagged Marquis.

"SO WE PARACHUTE, what's the problem?"

The whiskey was fueling his anger and undying craving to taste Hahmad's blood. They were in the war room of the transport bird, eight commandos left, Marquis glaring at the half-empty bottle, then reading the taut faces around him.

"It is suicide," he heard the ship's commander, Chabeaux, say. "We are talking about Syria. We are talking about MiGs perhaps shooting us down as soon as we breach their airspace. So far, we have gotten lucky. I fear our luck will not hold if we fly into Syria. Let us be reasonable, five million dollars or not—"

Enough. Marquis hurled the bottle against the bulkhead, the sound of glass shattering making all of them flinch.

"I see I have your attention now," Marquis snarled. "We have parachutes. We jump. I know, I see you, Anglerre, thinking I'll break my neck since I've never done this before. How hard can it be? Tell me what to do, how to do it. I pull a rip cord, I land on my feet, tuck and roll.

"You!" he barked at their Syrian prisoner. "Come here!"

When the Syrian didn't move fast enough, Martineau rushed to the bench, snatched him to his feet and jacked him along until he was at the conference table.

Marquis stabbed the sat pictures of Syria. "You said here? It is called what?"

"Al-Zhabat."

"How many terrorists?"

"As many as seventy. Half Palestinians, half Syrian. Hahmad, he is protected in this region by the Syrian army."

"Are you telling me I'm crazy?"

"It is...as I heard. Suicide."

"Suicide or not, we're going!"

Marquis looked at the village, circled in red. It was at the foothills of the Anti-Lebanon mountains, northwest of Damascus, due north of the Suq Wadi Barada.

"And what am I supposed to do?"

Marquis scowled at Chabeaux. "You will find a place in the goddamn desert, land and wait!"

"How are we going to take on an army of seventy or more?" Anglerre wanted to know.

"It will be—" Marquis checked his watch "—the dead of night when we jump. We go in, we mine the village with plastique. A simultaneous detonation, then we pick the rats off when they run out of the barrel."

"How do we know Hahmad will even be there?"

"You!" Marquis barked at the Syrian. "Well?"

"It is his home, his primary base of operation."

"And we have the most sophisticated surveillance cameras money can buy," Marquis said. "Scanners. Sensors. We can snap a picture of a steaming pile of camel dung from up here. If his jet is grounded, we fly over, jump and go in. End of discussion. If anyone wants out, grab a parachute now and jump for the Red Sea."

Marquis pinned each and every man with a long burning eye.

"Okay," Anglerre finally said. "Perhaps it can be done. We have enough C-4 left, we slip in, plant it, blow the village, tents, camels, the whole goddamn place on fire and when they come running, shoot them.''

"And earn your five million dollars," Marquis said. "So, it is settled. Anyone want out?''

Marquis saw them look away, a few of the commandos shaking their heads.

"Good. Now, someone find me a fresh bottle of whiskey.''

"YOU HAVE FUN, ladies? How was your little foray into Cairo? I almost gave up on you two.''

Bolan was grateful, though, that Hardball had held on, extending his deadline, waiting on their return.

The turboprops were cranked on, the big Hercules set to fly as Bolan and Ridilson rolled away from the Kiowa, climbing the steps and following Hardball into the belly of the bird.

"Yeah, your boy over there," Hardball said, slamming the hatch shut, nodding at LaPierre. "I caught him sporting a shit-eating grin a while back when he thought I might leave you behind. Like he ever had hope anyway.''

Bolan looked away from the battered face of LaPierre, saw the combined force of CIA-IDF commandos poring over intel and sat pictures on the big metal table bolted to the floor. Shaib had headphones on, talking into the throat mike attached to his sat link.

"What did you do to that guy, anyway, Pollock? Looks like you shoved him through a meat grinder.''

"We were simply getting acquainted.''

"Okay, come on," Hardball said. "We've got a lot of ground to cover, but it's all systems go. Let's just say we're about to get 'acquainted,' Pollock, with some badass Syrian terrorists. Guys want coffee? Whiskey?"

Ridilson opted for a shot or two, while Bolan went and helped himself to a mug of coffee.

Bolan joined the commandos, began perusing the sat pictures, the fax printouts of all pertinent intel from both the CIA and Mossad. He read the numbers of the enemy force waiting for them in Syria, the fact that the Syrian army protected their darling Hahmad.

The Executioner knew it wasn't going to be any walk in the park.

CHAPTER TWENTY-THREE

Syria

Hahmad received a hero's welcome when he stepped off the jet. It was good to be home, even if he wasn't returning to Syria a conquering warrior with the blood of vanquished enemies on his hands. The sorry truth was that he had failed miserably, his warriors crushed by an opposition he still couldn't accurately identify. He still had a few contacts left in Egypt, and a call to Cairo might turn up intelligence on who was after him, although he believed at least some of the attackers had been the Frenchman's commandos.

At least he was on familiar ground, protected by the Syrian army if he chose to call them in. Would he do that if he was attacked in Syria? And to what avail? If Israeli commandos stormed the desert campsite here, would the Syrians roll in tanks, fly in the MiGs just to save his crumbling kingdom?

In the dead of night they came out, howling his name, firing AK-47s into the air. They were a vast sea of shadows before him, shouting and praising him, jihad and God.

"Mohammed! Mohammed!"

"God is great!"

"Praise God!"

Hahmad swiveled his head, seeing but not seeing Abuzah shadowing him toward the rows of tents. His legs felt heavy, the dancing flames from the fire barrels spread around the camp like ghostly apparitions in the haze of a strange unreality he seemed trapped in. The AK-47 in his own hands felt like a great weight. Many of these men had lost brothers, even sons in the ruins of the camp he'd left behind—fled from—in Egypt. What would he say to them? What could he say? They were dead, they had gone to God, martyrs now in Paradise, having sacrificed their lives for the greater good of Islam. That sounded good enough, the usual mantra, he thought, but it was important to keep hope alive. There were future operations to plan, and he needed every single warrior here alive with hunger for blood, pumped with righteous fury, ready to march out and slay the Great Satan. It reminded him he needed to touch base with his cell in the land of the devil. They were waiting for instructions in San Francisco, but he needed to peruse some maps of the city, go over the specific targets again.

He checked the dark heavens, paranoia flaring up, sure the sky would fall any minute now. He had been chased out of Egypt and he found it strange that only a small force had pursued him, when the enemy had gunships at their disposal, could have easily tracked him and blown him off the desert before they had gained any decent altitude.

South, he saw the kerosene lanterns flicker on as the villagers of al-Zhabat awoke to find out what all the noise was about.

The villagers, he thought. If they were attacked here, the women and children of the village could be used as human shields. Perhaps, though, he decided, it was best to contact Major Basri, map out the logistics for getting him into Lebanon. Once there, he could begin staging the next round of attacks against Israel.

Beirut was his second home anyway. He had three sons by two different women in the city. The sons were old enough now to become warriors.

He sensed the packed mob of freedom fighters expected some announcement, a speech that would fan the flames of anticipation of future triumphs against their enemies. He could give them nothing but bad news, inflame the fear of being attacked. He wasn't sure how he knew it was going to happen, assumed it wasn't just paranoia talking to him.

It was gut instinct. His money, his contacts were known to the CIA, Mossad and Interpol. He should have listened to the rumors long ago, when his cutouts informed him he should find safe haven in Pakistan or Afghanistan, mount his operations from a safe distance. He had been warned about venturing out into the field, grooming new contacts and cutouts in person, handing off vast sums of money himself to open new pipelines for the distribution of ordnance and human time bombs.

Hahmad triggered his AK-47 over their heads, one-handed. If nothing else, he could keep up appearances.

The mob went silent.

"Brothers in arms in the holy war against the Great Satan! The hour of truth is upon us! Be vigilant, be strong like the lions you are! There is the chance devils in human skin may come for our blood! Our enemies are everywhere, are those who are not one of us! Take heart! I am not stating absolutely we are going to be attacked, but be ready!"

He searched the crowd, heard a rippling buzz of murmured questions. This was his army, perhaps the last of his immediate holy warriors at his disposal. There were other freedom fighters, cells scattered throughout Beirut, but they were rabble, and without his guidance and direction they were lost, he believed.

"Go with God!" Hahmad said, and circled wide, leaving the mob to howl his name, that God was great.

He saw his second in command, Burqush, stepping toward him.

When they were alone, heading for the main tent, Hahmad heard Burqush ask, "Only you and the pilot? What happened?"

Hahmad debated whether to tell him the truth, then said, "They are dead. All of them."

MARQUIS HEARD Chabeaux tell him they were fifteen minutes from the DZ. He felt his heart hammering now, his face slick with sweat as both his nerves and the whiskey worked up the fire inside. He could feel it was going to happen this time around. Either himself or Hahmad would be dead.

End of game, one way or the other.

"Unless we fly over, I cannot confirm the presence of Hahmad."

"We are going!" Marquis snapped. "Three kilometers north of their camp. Let me know in the cargo hold when you are in position.

"Go!" he barked at Anglerre and the others. "It is time!"

Chabeaux was shaking his head. "I can perhaps set down maybe in this stretch of desert, ten kilometers west of the camp. How long should I wait?"

"As long as necessary. Should you get nervous..."

"I will not leave you behind."

That settled, Marquis looked at their Syrian prisoner, reached for his holstered pistol. The Syrian had to have known what was coming next, since he hit his knees, clasped his hands and began praying in Arabic.

Marquis indulged the man a few moments of prayer, then strode up to him, put the muzzle of the pistol against his temple and squeezed the trigger.

"Throw him out after us," Marquis said, slapping at the blood on his pants leg.

"THAT'S IT, gentlemen. It's slam, bam, wham and thank you, Hahmad. When the smoke clears I don't even want the idea of this asshole still left, not even his ghost left behind in the ashes."

Bolan quickly gave the briefing a silent rehash. Shaib had taken center stage first. The Israeli colonel said they would land at an IDF base near the Syrian border. There, they would transfer to six Black Hawks that would carry them to Hahmad's base of operations at the foot of the Anti-Lebanon Mountains. Shaib stated emphatically Mossad had tracked the jet by satellite and confirmed that the man had landed. Twelve F-15Es would provide cover for the gunships, then they would hammer the camp with doomsday from above while the ground troops disembarked, moved in on foot to clean their clock up close and personal. No mention of Marquis, so Bolan took a moment to ask both men for a favor.

"Yeah, what is it, Pollock?"

"If Marquis turns up, he's mine."

The soldier let his penetrating stare sink in to both Hardball and Shaib.

"This Frenchman, why is he so important to you?" Shaib asked.

"Colonel Pollock here," Hardball volunteered, "came to us from the Justice Department."

Shaib grinned. "I'm sure. And I will sell you oceanfront property in Afghanistan."

"Look, Marquis has an Interpol connection back in Paris."

"You want him as a prisoner?" Hardball asked.

"I'm asking you, Colonel Shaib, to order your pilots to steer clear of his transport plane if Marquis turns up and makes a run back for his plane. Let him fly on, back to Paris. When this is done, I need you," he told Hardball, "to help me get back to France."

"You don't want much," Hardball groused. "I've got more concerns than a few dirty Interpol agents."

"I understand that. First things first. Colonel?"

Shaib seemed to think about something, then nodded. "Very well. Hahmad is who I want. You can have the Frenchman. Depending on how it goes, I can perhaps provide transport for you through Mossad. My country uses Interpol often to track terrorists. If it's true there are corrupt agents..."

"It's true."

"I will help. Traitors are worse than poisonous snakes to me."

"Appreciate that."

Bolan walked to where LaPierre was seated, cuffed and scowling.

"Now what?" LaPierre grumbled.

"It ends soon. Marquis will be history. I need a name from you."

"I heard. The Interpol connection. What about me?"

"Keep helping me out and I'll try to swing you a deal."

"His name is Lassere."

MARQUIS WAS VAGUELY surprised that he didn't break his neck when he hit the ground. It was a three-thousand-foot jump, his assault rifle, hung from a bootstrap, slamming to the earth first. He shed the chute pack and took up his Galil. His eight commandos were spread around the plateau, chutes folding behind them as they stripped out of the packs, armed now and ready to slaughter.

According to Chabeaux's maps, al-Zhabat was two miles east, just beyond the chain of jagged hills, nestled in a valley at the foot of the Anti-Lebanon Mountains.

"Let's go!" Marquis said, NVD goggles dropping over every pair of eyes to lead the way through the thick black heart of night.

It was a tough haul, even with the brisk night air cooling his flesh. Sweat ran as they jogged on, assault rifles out and ready to shoot anything that turned up.

Marquis was no athlete, and his breathing became labored after covering what he figured was a good mile. They were moving up the rise finally, topping the hill, and Marquis nearly howled with angry glee.

The Learjet was parked at the bottom of the slope.

Hahmad was home.

He searched the camp, able to strip off the NVD goggles now, using the light from the fire barrels and the kerosene lanterns hung from wire in front of the tents. There were vehicles of sorts spread around the campsite. A village, much larger than the one he'd seen in Egypt, lay to the south. This one was occupied, as he made out shadows milling around near the rows of stone hovels, some of which were domed. The great black wall of the Anti-Lebanon Mountains loomed to the east, a silent Goliath of a sentry. He made a mental note that once

the explosives went off, Hahmad would either run
once again for his jet or the mountains.

"Mine the jet first," Marquis said. "As many of
the tents as you can." He snugged on the com link.
"Give me the remote box," he ordered Anglerre.

Marquis palmed the small black box, watched as
Anglerre and the others fixed sound suppressors to
their pistols. He counted as many as ten terrorists
meandering around the camp.

Silent kills would have to take them out while the
C-4 was planted.

"I'll let you know when you can light them up,"
Anglerre said, and led the way down the hill.

Marquis watched them go, dark machines of
death sliding off into the night. This was it, he told
himself. There was nowhere left for Hahmad to run,
and in a few minutes he sure as hell wouldn't be
able to hide.

Hahmad would be dead before long. It didn't matter if the blast consumed him in his tent. Marquis
would march down there, shooting whatever survivors were left, right beside his commandos.

All he asked for was an eyeball confirmation of
the big kill.

ANGLERRE USED the dark shadows on the perimeter
of the camp to creep up on the first two sentries.
The sound-suppressed Beretta 92-F up and locking
on, he watched as the other commandos crawled on
their bellies for the back end of the tent row. The
Learjet was already mined, Anglerre grimly aware
it could all go to hell at any second. At least this

time Hahmad couldn't simply fly away. He would be trapped in the conflagration, Marquis tasting vengeance long in coming.

Still it was a suicide run, he knew, and only the hand of God would get them out of Syria.

The two sentries came around the corner of the tent row, smoking and searching the hills, AK-47s hung around their shoulders. Anglerre rose up from his crouch, his commandos snaking toward the tents, planting fat chunks of C-4.

Two taps of the trigger, and Anglerre kicked the sentries off their feet, dark holes blossoming between their eyes.

Silently he urged more speed out of his men. A part of him had nearly defied Marquis, and insisted they simply go back to Paris when the transport plane picked them up in Egypt. The soldier in him told him to go through with it, take his chances.

And then there was the money.

Soon enough the other sentries would discover their fallen comrades, but by then Anglerre would have led his commandos back up the rise to the north behind the tents, radio Marquis to blow the place into the sky.

Then what?

Anglerre sweated out the next few minutes, melting back into the deep shadows, the Galil across his shoulder, but ready to come off and start shooting on full-auto slaughter if they were discovered.

They were.

Two more sentries came around the corner, spotted the bodies and began shouting.

CHAPTER TWENTY-FOUR

Hahmad was discussing an exit strategy into Lebanon with Burqush and a half dozen of his other warriors when he felt an unexplainable chill walking down his spine. He felt paralyzed for a moment by the strange sensation, his ears tuned to the night world beyond the tent, his guts clenching with a fist of ice. What was happening to him? he wondered. It was as if some voice were whispering in his ear, warning him that his own death was on the way.

"Are you listening to me?"

He looked at Burqush. For some reason Hahmad felt strangely, terribly alone right then, and he couldn't explain why. He had told them what happened in Egypt, the possibility they might be attacked any moment, the backpack ordnance that was lost forever. Of course, weapons, even special backpacks, were replaceable for the right amount of money, but jihad warriors who were skilled in weapons, demolitions and who would go the distance weren't so easy to replace. Surprisingly enough there had been no grumbling, no questioning his abandoning the others to a dire fate. Why, though, was it no one but he appeared concerned about an attack? he wondered. Sure, they were in their own country, but that had never stopped the Israelis from flying sorties into Syria, landing commandos, killing freedom fighters, then slipping back into their own country, denying clandestine attacks to the world at large.

It happened.

"Yes," Hahmad said. "Major Basri is not answering his radio."

"Radio silence," Burqush said. "Very strange."

"Static?"

"Nothing. Dead air."

"Perhaps there is something wrong with our unit," Hahmad suggested, but Burqush shook his head.

"I think not."

"Well, then..."

And then Hahmad heard the shouting, the sudden eruption of autofire from somewhere behind the tents.

His worst fear was realized, and he felt his sphincter puckering, bowels quaking, knees trembling. They were under attack—again. And on his own soil.

Cursing, Hahmad snapped up his AK-47, aware he had to do something. What now? Run again? It seemed the logical course of action. It stood to reason the very same black-ops soldiers he'd seen in Egypt had tracked him down, looking to hammer him but good, once and for all. The enemy had a sizable professional force of seasoned killers, gunships that would mow down dozens in a matter of seconds. It was best, once again, to make sure he survived to fight another day.

He was bolting through the flap in the tent, found his troops scrambling all over the camp, when the earth blew up behind him. The shock wave and terrible heat launched him through the air, pounding the wind out of his lungs, the sky appearing to be on fire.

He hit the ground on his face, choking back bitter laughter. The ballsy infidel bastards were going to kill him on his own ground.

It didn't seem right.

MARQUIS SAW the trouble coming before it went to hell. Two terrorists were dropped by Anglerre, but the commando appeared intent on watching the others as they placed the charges at the base of the tents, unaware of the threat until it was too late. Marquis had the urge to shout a warning that two more sentries were coming around the corner when the terrorists started hollering, sounding the alarm, the camp coming alive with darting armed figures, but Anglerre nailed the two shouters with a burst of autofire.

Marquis keyed his com link, ordered, "Fall back! I'm going to light it up!"

They scrambled for the deep cover of the hills to the north, firing on the run.

He thumbed on the red light, saw his commandos engaging in a savage fighting retreat in a backpedal-shuffle for the hills, a little too close to ground zero, Marquis suspected, but there wasn't another second to spare. He saw three of his men going down under a hail of bullets, as two dozen or more terrorists swept around the tents from opposite ends.

Anglerre and the others were locked in a vise of lead death.

The end had come, Marquis realized, then somehow made out the face he saw in his nightmares.

Hahmad was looking around, armed and on the verge of shouting something when Marquis uprooted the tents in a wave of rolling fire.

Marquis laughed next at the sight of the Learjet blown apart in a blossoming ball of flames.

No escape for Hahmad now, but Marquis saw his commandos were taking a drubbing.

Perhaps, he thought, no one was meant to leave here alive.

He was up and moving down the slope when his ears picked up a distant whining noise. Curious, as autofire continued to shred the night, he searched the black skies to the south.

The sound became a shriek in a few moments, as he spotted the fighter jets swooping down for the campsite. It didn't take a genius, he knew, to figure out who was who, what was what.

Those damnable black-ops commandos from Egypt.

Pollock was probably on board, too.

Marquis searched the battlefield, saw Hahmad scraping himself up off the ground.

It was time to finish it, Marquis told himself, and walked down into the valley of the damned.

"WHAT IN THE NAME OF...?"

Bolan was up and moving for the open fuselage doorway of the Black Hawk, followed Hardball's stare.

The camp was going up in flames, the sounds of distant autofire breaking through the rotor wash as the flying armada bore down on the village from the south.

Marquis, Bolan knew, had beaten them to the punch. Behind him the soldier heard Shaib give the order to his fighter pilots to hammer down, one run, then provide cover.

"Drop it down behind those bastards!" Hardball ordered the Israeli pilots over the intercom. "We move in behind! Up through the village, gentlemen! If it moves, if it even gives you guys a dirty look," he roared at Black and Blue teams, "drop it!"

The Executioner, M-16/M-203 combo in hand, watched as the gunships closed on the village, shadows, some armed, scurrying all over the interlacing dirt paths that cut through the stone blocks of al-Zhabat. North of the village the main battle was well under way, but the F-15Es were about to shave the odds dramatically.

The war for the head of Hahmad was only just heating up, Bolan suspected, watching, as twelve jets locked on and streaked ahead, Sidewinder and Sparrow missiles shooting away from the pylons.

Still more hell on earth tore through the camp, and Bolan would be amazed if anyone walked away from that holocaust, but knew there would be survivors.

A few rats always managed to ride out the storm.

ANGLERRE WAS TOO BUSY waxing armed shadows, but he managed to curse Marquis just the same, the damn guy having just lit up the tents, roaring fireballs so close, screaming out for his face, it was a miracle, he knew, that any of them were still alive and kicking.

Anglerre was backpedaling, three of his guys falling, dark sprays of gore splashing his face, when he saw the streaking warbirds in the distance, going for the home run, maybe a dozen fighter jets in all.

Time to duck, he knew.

The sky was falling.

Bullets were snapping all around him as he raked his autofire back and forth, Galil stammering, forced to hose down another four terrorists, then the world before them blew up again.

Anglerre hit the deck. This rolling tidal wave of blasts made the C-4 eruption a firecracker in comparison. The earth shook, the sky turned to fire, screams lost in the deafening peals of explosions. Men, machines, great patches of earth all meshed and vanished in the firestorm.

He couldn't be sure what or who was slamming the earth, but mangled figures appeared to ride the crest of the firewall. Anglerre hugged the ground, thinking there was such seismic force behind those explosions he was amazed the earth didn't break apart beneath him and swallow him whole.

Small comfort, he thought, when those jets roared

overhead, shrieking north over the hills, but certain they were coming back for round two.

Then, incredibly, he found terrorists who had survived the hammering. Fields of fire seemed to converge from several points, Anglerre ordering his commandos to take cover up the hills when he felt the hot stabs of lead eating through his guts.

He went down, but not before he cursed Marquis.

NO AMOUNT of saturation bombing, the Executioner knew, would completely annihilate a large combat force. He'd seen it before, even survived some aerial bombardment himself. Most of the time it was simply luck of the draw, walking away when the world was blowing up around people, holding on, burrowing down for cover.

The soldier found Ridilson by his side. They were moving through the center of the village, as the gunships began hovering over the ruins of the camp, miniguns blazing and chopping up runners.

Shadows, Bolan saw, were standing in the doorways of their domed huts, but no armed resistance was turned their way by the villagers.

The combined CIA-Israeli force charged for the flaming sea ahead, a rolling skirmish line of blacksuits fanning out and blowing terrorists off their feet with long bursts of autofire.

Bolan sighted three terrorists, charging from the lake of fire to his two o'clock, seeking refuge in the village no doubt, flight seeming preferable to fighting under the circumstances. The Executioner hit the trigger of his M-16, bowled them off their feet.

Ahead he heard Shaib barking over his com link for his gunship pilots to clear out.

It was up to the ground troops, Bolan knew, to clean it up from there on.

And where was Hahmad? the soldier wondered. Marquis? If they were in that conflagration, shooting it out, he'd find them.

The night of fury, the soldier knew, still had plenty of scores left to settle.

HAHMAD KNEW he was lucky to have cleared the path of the fighter jets, but he couldn't keep hoping God would save his skin, since sometimes even He got tired of doing all the work.

He wasn't even halfway across the stretch of no-man's-land when the fighter jets, shrieking out of nowhere, unloaded their missiles. He had been thinking he could find Abuzah in this hell, hoping the pilot was racing for the jet when he screamed at the sight of his ride out of there—a flaming heap.

Trapped.

Then he was knocked to the ground by the shock wave of the latest round of hammering.

Once again he was hauling himself off the ground, AK-47 in hand, when the shadow seemed to materialize out of the night.

"Hahmad!"

In the flickering wash of firelight, he read the hatred and rage in the Westerner's eyes, the voice tinged with a European accent.

The Frenchman.

The flames erupted from the darkness before

Hahmad could react to the threat. He felt the bullets ripping into his stomach, groin, every nerve ending on fire as he toppled.

"OH, BUT THE WORLD is full of sorrow and pain. The only cure for it—death."

Marquis strolled up to the Syrian, slapping a fresh clip into his Galil. He wasn't sure why he said what he did, but he saw he had Hahmad's attention. The murdering bastard rolled onto his side, one hand over his stomach, trying to hold in his guts.

Marquis glanced at the raging battle zone. The slaughter appeared confined to the far west edge of the camp, shadows scurrying and dancing all around the crackling bands of firestorms.

He was all alone, his hated enemy stretched out beneath him. Strangely enough he didn't feel good about the moment. Not the way he had envisioned it, standing over the broken body of the man who had murdered his family, alive again in his moment of triumph. The Syrian looked up at him, an odd smile on his lips.

"I know who you are."

"Yes, you do," Marquis told Hahmad.

"Finish it. I will not beg for my life. I will be with God in Paradise."

"You'll be in hell," Marquis growled, and held back on the trigger, pinning the Syrian to the earth with a point-blank crucifixion of autofire.

Marquis stole a moment to stare down at his vanquished enemy. Bile churned in his stomach, a coldness spreading through his chest. This wasn't the way it should have felt, he thought. Why? He felt sick, alone, the firestorms spinning a nausea that draped a haze over his sight.

How many had died because of Hahmad? he wondered. Because of himself, shipping out platoons of commandos, laying waste to entire villages?

Hundreds, could have been in the thousands, but the body count, he suspected, ended with Hahmad. Or did it? Now what?

It was time to find Anglerre and the others, radio Chabeaux. Whatever was happening here was none of his affair any longer. He had what he'd come for, but he was baffled at the strange sick way he felt.

He checked the raging ocean of fire, found a few jeeps, a Humvee still in one piece.

First round up whoever among his commandos was left standing.

Marquis sucked in a deep breath, angling away from the charging commandos.

CHAPTER TWENTY-FIVE

They weren't going out quietly, but Bolan wouldn't have expected anything but a roar from the savages. It was time to crush the poisonous fruits of jihad here, trample whatever vipers were left slithering about the wreckage and the seas of fire.

Bolan, Ridilson and Black and Blue teams bulled ahead, skating past the raging waves of fire, shooting on the run, a feeding frenzy of death descending on the Syrians. The Executioner sensed it was winding down, maybe twenty or so hardmen left standing, but that didn't mean it got any easier.

All it took, Bolan knew, was one bullet, and more often than not the desperate savage could pull off the impossible, find a way to save himself to carry out whatever his evil agenda.

Overhead he heard the Black Hawks buzzing around, but it was up to the combined CIA-IDF shooters to wrap it up. Higher up he made out the shriek of turbofans, no doubt those fighter pilots ordered to lower the boom on the first Syrian patrol that came this way.

A good number of the terrorists appeared bent on fleeing for the Anti-Lebanon Mountains, and if they managed to make it into a gorge or a wadi, Bolan knew it would be a long, hard night of hunting them down, rooting them out of any number of caves, gullies, whatever else.

Not this night.

And Hardball appeared to enjoy the sight of terrorists running for their lives, whooping and hosing down a batch of four or five, drilling autofire up their spines, cracking open skulls. The air was thick with the stink of blood, burning fuel, emptied bowels, the soldier marching on, deeper into the slaughter zone.

Bolan tagged three mangled terror goons as they staggered from the wreckage of the motor pool, his M-16 flaming and tracking on, nailing several wounded terrorists when they attempted to rise from the bloody earth.

The soldier looked east, toward the flaming shell that had been Hahmad's personal jet. He could venture a good guess what happened here. The French commandos had slipped into camp, mining the jet and the tents with C-4, then gone for broke, only they were clearly outnumbered by the Syrians. Which meant Marquis and his commandos could all be dead. So be it. There were plenty of savages left for questing guns.

The Executioner fell in with Black team, M-203s chugging out 40 mm hellbombs now, as they chased down survivors, shredding them apart in groups of three and four, autofire rattling on in a ceaseless cacophony of death knells.

"DID YOU GET HIM?"

Marquis found Anglerre, gut-shot and bleeding out fast, the man clinging to his last breath, the commando making strange choking noises with crimson bubbles frothing on his lips. It took a couple of minutes of walking around the base of the hills, but Marquis discovered every single commando was down and dead.

Marquis thought he was going to puke, the strange feeling of being cold and alone overpowering now that he had no one among his group left. Was it worth it? he wondered. Yes, he told himself.

"Yes," he told Anglerre. "The murdering bastard has gone to hell."

Was that a bitter smile he saw on the man's face?

"Good...I am happy...you are happy."

And Anglerre died.

Marquis vomited, spewing the gore away from Anglerre's limp form, unable to contain his sickness any longer. The sounds of autofire were withering from the direction of the mountains, explosions peppering the night, but the commandos still posed a major threat.

It was time to go, leave the dead where they were.

Marquis stood, shaking, then ran for the fiery ruins of the motor pool. Two jeeps were still intact, and if there were keys in the ignition...

He reached the jeep, hopped in behind the wheel, spotted the keys in the ignition and fired up the engine.

Then he saw a figure, rolling his way from the distance, the commando seeming cloaked in bands

of shimmering fire. He had to peer hard to make out
the face, but the firelight outlined the tall man in
black.

Pollock.

Marquis ground the clutch, whipping the jeep
around, and began racing out across the desert. He
fumbled for his tac radio, but he steadied his hand
long enough to ring up Chabeaux.

"I am on the way!"

"And the others?"

"They didn't make it. Hahmad is dead. I killed
him myself. Start the engines!"

BOLAN PUT A HAND over Ridilson's arm as he lifted
the M-16, sighting on the speeding jeep.

"Let him go."

"You mind if I ask why?"

"I've got a return trip to Paris lined up," the Executioner said.

"Over here!"

Bolan saw Hardball toeing a body in a stretch of
no-man's-land.

"They never look like much when they're dead,
do they?" Hardball said, spitting on Hahmad. "Let
me go tell Shaib someone bagged the bastard. You
did the honors here, Pollock?"

Bolan shook his head. "The Frenchman, I suspect."

"So, Marquis got what he wanted," Hardball
said. "Well, we've got a few stragglers to chase
down, but I'm not spending all night here, shooting
up the mountains. We've got a monitor on the near-

est Syrian army outpost, and I'm sure they're on the way.''

''Makes sense to boogie,'' Ridilson said. ''What about you, Bob?''

''What about me?''

''It's been a hell of a run. This where we say our goodbyes?''

''I need a lift out of here to Paris.''

''Gonna meet Marquis as soon he touches down?''

''I don't know.''

''There's that Interpol mess to clean up?''

''You got it.''

The Executioner listened to the distant and now sporadic retorts of autofire.

''What a mess,'' Ridilson mused.

''Hey, you two want to look alive and give us a hand?'' Hardball growled over his shoulder.

''What did you tell me back in Tunisia, Bob? This ain't no disco...''

''The dance is over here. Let's give our good friend Hardball a little assistance.''

It was over for the moment, Bolan knew, but he had another date with death in Paris. Assuming Marquis made it out of Syria without a few MiGs driving missiles up his tail.

Somehow the soldier believed the man would make it back to Paris. Hole up, hide. Probably grab up a bunch of money, pull a Napoleon.

Only exiling himself.

Marquis was as good as dead if, Bolan thought, he could make it back to Paris in a timely manner.

There were calls to make. Brognola for starters, then SAC Hardin, paving the way for a return visit, watching the store in the City of Lights.

There were still rats scurrying for cover, and Bolan had a feeling it wouldn't end in Paris. It was just a nagging suspicion, but there was something about Bangle in San Francisco that kept bugging him. If the guy was dirty, Bolan intended to find out.

Nothing like terminal jet lag, he thought, and jogged beside Ridilson to help the other commandos nail it down.

It didn't take long before a few possums came groaning from between licking tongues of fire.

Together Bolan and Ridilson started mopping up, hosing them down as they showed, full-auto butchering. Crawling or standing, dying or wounded, it didn't matter. The soldier knew they couldn't afford to leave one potential future suicide machine to rise from the ashes.

MARQUIS PLOPPED in a chair at the conference table in the war room. They were rolling, soon to be gone from Syria. Marquis felt empty, lifeless, and still very much sick to his stomach. He saw but didn't see Chabeaux as the man handed him a bottle of whiskey.

"What happened?"

Marquis shook his head. "The Syrian is dead. That is all you need to know."

"Well, getting out of this country could be a problem."

"What do you mean?"

"I've had to reroute us through Jordanian airspace, according to our intel on radar installations, airfields…"

"Just take us home."

Marquis slugged down a heavy belt, the liquor burning down his throat, but calming the storm raging in his stomach.

"Now what?"

"We go home!" Marquis snapped. "The club, have Ducloux meet me at the club. Radio him! He is to hire twelve or more men. I don't care if they are common criminals. I need shooters!"

"You are not saying…"

"I am saying I am sure trouble will follow us to Paris."

"Who?"

"No more questions! Do what I want!"

Marquis turned away from Chabeaux, stared at the bulkhead, letting the whiskey work its magic, calm his nerves, clear away the sickness in his head.

"We'll have to land in Malta to refuel."

"Whatever it takes to get us home."

And Dante Marquis sat, wondering why he felt like the loneliest, most miserable man to ever walk God's earth.

He had tasted the poisoned fruit of vengeance, and it left a sour taste in his mouth no amount of whiskey would ever wash away.

When he was alone, Marquis hung his head, then slumped his face on the table and wept.

"Where is God?" he cried out loud. "Is this all there is?"

And he heard nothing but the thunder of the plane's engines.

France

"YOU KNOW, you're something else, Belasko. You're truly a piece of work. I mean, what the hell gives here? What am I, a glorified cabbie?"

It was nightfall in Paris the following day by the time Bolan's borrowed Mossad Gulfstream jet touched down in Orly. The soldier was in blacksuit, his side arms concealed by a light windbreaker, the war bag with his M-16/M-203 dumped on the back seat, slits in his pouch filled with an assortment of grenades.

Hardin had the wheel of the sedan, driving them through the congested streets of Paris on the Right Bank, the SAC wearing a scowl that made Bolan wonder if he knew any other expression.

Bolan noted his sat link was on the back seat.

"Oh, you're welcome, Belasko. Thank you, Agent Hardin, for watching my James Bond sat link. Not to mention my own agents keeping an eye on Monsieur Marquis and this Interpol Judas."

"Hey, do you mind?"

"What? You got a headache. You know this is all unorthodox to the point I'm wondering just who the hell Hal Brognola really is, and what you're really all about."

"You wouldn't believe me if I told you."

"Or if you told me, you'd have to kill me? Oh, what the hell, I follow orders. I shouldn't sound off like this, but I don't like playing flunky."

"Who does?"

"Okay, Belasko, do it your way. I guess I sit in the car while you bring the roof down on Dante's Inferno."

Bolan was tired from the long flight, the haggling with Shaib and Mossad to get him airborne, and he wasn't up for a pissing contest. Like Ridilson had put it, there was quite the mess in Syria, but the black-ops warriors had choppered safely back to Israel, all of them debriefed by Mossad. Whatever the international fallout, well, Bolan always left politics to the other guy.

There was still a fair amount of cleaning up to do.

"Hardin, I appreciate all you've done. You're a good man, despite the whining."

Hardin grunted. "That's me. Agent Crybaby."

"I'll let Brognola know you did your job."

"Thanks. I'll be glad when you're gone out of my life. With this Interpol connection, this Lassere having tapped our intel…I've got my hands full enough sorting it all out and figuring out who to arrest that gunplay's the last thing I need."

"That's why I'm here."

"Someone has to do the dirty work?"

"Took the words right out of my mouth."

CHAPTER TWENTY-SIX

Dante Marquis was waiting for the hammer to drop, his life snuffed out, crushed like a bug.

He wasn't sure when it would happen; he only feared the end was on the way.

And his own messenger of doom would come by way of the big commando called Pollock, if that was even his real name.

The waiting. The fear.

The end.

Marquis wasn't even sure he cared anymore if he lived or died. He chuckled to himself, thinking he felt like one of those Arabs he and his late, unlamented commandos had butchered. He would be a martyr, soon to be with God—and his family in Paradise.

"God," he muttered to himself. "He has abandoned me."

He chugged down another shot of whiskey, scowling around the game room at the fourteen pieces of scum Ducloux had dredged up from the gutters of the streets. They were greasy and unkempt for the most part, raggedy clothes, mean, greedy eyes. They were little more than petty criminals, most of them hiding from the law, but he needed gunmen. They were bought and paid for, and he would make damn sure they came through if some black-ops team crashed the club.

They were lounging around, had been drinking his booze and shooting pool and playing cards most of the day, and Marquis had to wonder when it hit the fan if he was just indulging in wishful thinking they could perform.

They were not pros, not like Pollock.

The noise in the dining room began to inflame his ire, his teeth grinding, then he spotted Ducloux giving him a curious look from the end of the bar. Marquis didn't know what to do with himself, how to proceed against an enemy he wasn't even sure was in the city. Was it his imagination, paranoia getting the best of him?

He hated the world right then, didn't even much like himself.

So far, he could count his blessings, searching for something to be grateful about, a reason to live, having flown through the airspace of countries hostile to the West, landing back home, safe, no one cuffing him as soon as he stepped off the plane.

That was the good news.

Who cared? The hell with them, he thought, the hell with them all.

Part of the problem was his lack of intel. Lassere served as his primary eyes and ears but the Interpol man seemed to have disappeared into thin air, running for cover most likely, or it could be the Justice Department had gotten to him. None of the other contacts he had at Interpol were returning his phone calls, either. It was never a good sign when it appeared all his lackeys were AWOL, abandoning what was, essentially, a sinking ship.

San Francisco, it turned out, had been a disaster. The Justice Department had marched in, shutting down his office, seizing his assets, LaPierre, it so happened, snapped up by this Pollock, according to his American source.

He glanced at the three large black nylon bags by the bar stool. During the day, he had cleaned out various accounts, cashing in bonds and stocks until he had accumulated a hundred million francs. Of course, he divvied up the money in different currency, U.S. dollars, dinars, Euros.

There was no telling where he would run to.

He only knew he had to run. But when? Where? Or would he just stay put, see what happened? Certainly he was finished in Paris, the American authorities sure to come knocking on his door anytime, and he had to wonder why they hadn't swarmed over him yet.

Which could only mean one thing as far as he was concerned.

Someone had been sanctioned to take him out.

From where he sat, it made sense. After all, he had run what amounted to a criminal enterprise, paying for the blood of the guilty, as well as the innocent. There were dead bodies all over North Africa and Syria that could be easily linked to his bounty-hunting operation. Interpol was most likely pointing fingers his direction, lackeys scared of going to prison for the rest of their lives, blaming him. And Pollock, like some sorcerer or demon who could rise from the ground, out of nowhere, surely knew where to find him.

The nightmare, he feared, hadn't even begun.

What would he do if they came for his blood? he asked himself. Simple. He would pick up one of the Uzi submachine guns and go out the same way he'd come into this from the beginning.

There would be no whimper, no pleading for his life to be spared. If God had abandoned him to his fate, it was no problem to take his rage and despair out on anything human—or inhuman, the way he saw it.

This was the end. He could feel it. Sitting around, waiting to kill or be killed.

He felt Ducloux watching him and he growled, "What?"

Ducloux shook his head. "I'm wondering who it is exactly we are supposed to fear."

"Right now it's that infernal racket in my dining room."

Marquis slid off the stool, snapping at three of his thugs to follow him. He grabbed up a money bag, muttering on the way past his shooters. He was ready for a scene of some kind, pumped on whiskey, anger and fear.

If he couldn't live it up, he figured, if life as he knew it was over, why should anybody else have a party?

DUCLOUX WAS READY to walk on the man. There was no other way but to leave and not look back.

When? And how to do it, without the madman going berserk and blowing him away on the spot?

The disaster and lack of answers to the questions about the expedition he'd put to Marquis pretty much sealed it.

He wasn't sure why every last one of the men he had known for years—loyal companions he served with in the French foreign legion—were dead, but Marquis was skimpy on facts or maybe the man didn't give a damn any longer. He was over the edge, and Ducloux watched as Marquis began sweeping around the dining room, barking at the crowd to clear out. These were the rich and powerful, the beautiful people of Paris, and he was treating them worse than servants or some beggar on the street.

"Get out of my restaurant! All of you—now! You have shit in your ears! Here, take money, your dinner's paid for! Go! It makes me ill to even look at you, eating my food, drinking my booze! Sit there, stuffing your rich faces, you have no idea how I see you! All of you! You are less than shit to me!"

Ducloux shook his head, Marquis roaring at the bartenders to beat it, every other word the *F* word. He was out of control. Two of the thugs, brazenly and openly lugging their Uzis, were ordered to tell the kitchen staff to go home, don't bother breaking everything down, just get the *F* out of there.

A few more hours, Ducloux told himself. When the man finally passed out, sodden with enough booze to kill a rhino, he would quietly slip out the door, take what money he had earned while under the man's employ and vanish somewhere in the south of France, maybe Belgium.

They were all finished in Paris. He had caught enough whispers from Lassere the other day to know the Justice Department had mounted some operation against them. And they weren't coming to arrest them.

It was most strange, the Americans going clandestine, lurking about, seeking to kill rather than arrest. They were a stubborn, arrogant bunch, those Americans, worse than Germans, in fact. They thought they could do anything, get away with it.

Ducloux walked behind the bar. He needed a stiff drink. The place was clearing out, Marquis shouting in faces, actually kicking a well-known politician in the ass, flinging money in his face.

"What are you doing?"

Ducloux filled a tall glass with straight whiskey. "What does it look like I'm doing?"

Now he was in a mood, watching the dark storm building in the man's eyes again.

"Watch your tone, Ducloux."

Or what? He almost said it, but Marquis suddenly had a pistol in his hand.

Ducloux was killing the drink, Marquis storming back for the game room when he saw the man come through the foyer.

"Hey…"

One of the thugs, Ducloux saw, was heading toward the tall man in black, raising his Uzi when—

It was Pollock, the commando they'd run a background check on, rolling in there, his eyes on fire. He thought he heard Marquis laugh, then shout, "You! Why am I not surprised! Come on, traitor, finish it."

And the big man in black began the finishing, the beginning of the end.

The M-16 was up, out, flaming and spitting death.

BOLAN WAS DONE playing games with Marquis. He was tired of running across one-quarter of the planet, baiting, luring, then letting the man walk so he could shut it all down in Paris, root out the Interpol connection, hoping all the dirty players were gathered under one roof, sweating it out. Bolan was feeling edged out, jacked up and a little on the ugly side.

The Executioner decided to walk straight through the front door. Why bother with anything but a straight crash and crush?

He shouldered his way through the last of the well-heeled crowd, caught the angry buzz from suits and skirts about the indignity of being tossed out of the restaurant in the middle of dinner.

Marquis had flipped out, Bolan figured.

No problem, the soldier decided.

And turned up the heat.

There were three of them, long-haired goons with Uzis, not sure at first what they were looking at, until it was too late and Bolan was knocking them off their feet, a raking burst of M-16 autofire drilling them to crimson sieves. Bodies were flying over white-linen tablecloths splashed with red gore.

Marquis was laughing, running down a hallway,

Bolan glimpsing the man slamming shut two gold-gilded doors.

Ducloux—he believed that was the man's name—was behind the long marble bar, digging inside his jacket.

Bolan hit the trigger of his assault rifle, blew him back into the shelves of bottles, bringing the racks down on his sliced-and-diced frame.

The Executioner marched ahead, slipped a finger around the trigger of the M-203 and sent the door-crasher chugging on.

THE BLAST SENT the doors flying away, bowling down three more thugs Marquis had ordered to man the doors, human dominoes pounded to the floor.

"Come on, Pollock!"

Marquis flew behind the bar, fixed himself a drink, cursing the scumbags who looked uncertain what to do. Cowards!

"Shoot!"

Marquis picked up his own Uzi.

They were shooting, all right, spraying wild sub-gun fire at nothing, he was sure, bullets flying through the boiling smoke, Marquis listening for any cry of pain that signaled they had scored Pollock's flesh.

Then the room started to blow up before his eyes.

Something—two somethings—came bouncing into the game room, and Marquis ducked beneath the bar. Screams knifed the air, the grenades spewing countless lethal steel bits, the mirror coming apart in bits and chunks, raining glass on his head.

Who was this guy? he wondered. Oh, but if he'd had ten commandos like Pollock on his side, not setting him up, not looking to put a blade in his back, life would have been much easier.

He stood, waiting for the man to enter, Uzi aimed toward the cloud of smoke.

Thugs were crawling around, human snakes slithering in blood, only two standing, seeking cover near the pool tables, then a long burst of autofire ripped through the smoke, tearing into their running forms, flinging them through the air on sharp grunts of pain. They twitched, bled out as they draped over the pool tables.

A few thugs staggered to their feet, groaning, faces slashed to meat by shrapnel.

The autofire kept raining death into the game room, the guy like some demon with eyes that could see everything, even when his vision must have been obscured by the smoke.

They were screaming, shot to ribbons, spinning this way and that, falling.

All dead in a matter of seconds.

And then he was alone.

All alone, staring down death somewhere beyond the smoke and running blood.

THE EXECUTIONER LISTENED to the silence, crouched by the doorway, nose filled with smoke and cordite. He smelled the blood and caught a whiff of the fear from inside the room. He couldn't be absolutely positive the goon squad was wiped out, but the silence of death spoke volumes.

"Marquis! It's over! It doesn't have to end like this. Your call."

"You're right, it's my call, my show, my game. It always was! I am taking my toys and going home. You can kiss my ass."

"I don't think so."

"You're judging me?"

"You judged yourself."

"Why? Because I wasted a bunch of terrorist scum?"

"I have no problem with that."

"Right. You're in the same game!"

"Not exactly. I don't go running around, shooting innocent people."

"A hero, you are."

"I never thought of myself that way."

"A man of principle."

"Whatever."

"I deserved to kill Hahmad."

Bolan briefly thought about that. Hadn't he done the same thing, a thousand lifetimes ago, coming home from Vietnam to bury his family who had—indirectly—been slaughtered by the Mafia? His father going berserk over a gambling debt and the prostituting of his...

"That could be, Dante, but there's a difference between you and me."

"What's that?"

"I don't believe in that collateral damage your killers were so fond of!"

He pinned the voice down. Off to the right, two,

maybe three o'clock. Lob in a grenade, charge in after the blast?

The Executioner cracked home a fresh magazine, drew a deep breath.

"They killed innocent people! They got what they deserved! I sanctioned them, me, Dante Marquis! I have more money than God! I played God, and I won! Come on, Pollock! You suckered me once..."

And Bolan went in, shooting.

He dashed to the left, his M-16 spitting out a long burst of 5.56 mm lead, sweeping the line of fire down the bar. It was only a glimpse of the man, but it was enough to tag him. The autofire chopped Marquis across the chest, his Uzi stuttering, bullets tattooing the wall behind Bolan. He held on, roaring and screaming, then the light began to fade in his eyes.

Marquis staggered, crashed into the liquor rack, bottles falling, shattering. The Uzi slipped from his fingers, a stunned look forming his death mask.

If Bolan didn't know better, he would have sworn the man wanted to ask, why?

Why indeed? the Executioner thought, watching as the Frenchman toppled out of sight.

BOLAN HOPPED into the car, ignoring the grim look on Hardin's face. Sirens wailed, the police closing fast on the club.

"What are you waiting for?" Bolan growled.

"Where to?"

"Lassere."

"He's history."

"What?"

"We've been tapping his phones. I sent my guys in before you landed. He didn't go quietly. We were forced to shoot him."

Bolan was too exhausted to debate the matter, why Hardin neglected mentioning that little detail. He didn't like it, but hadn't he also cowboyed the action? Why not give Hardin his moment to shine a little. Still, it would have been better if he could have tried to take the Interpol man alive.

"We're rounding up a few others now," Hardin said, and put the vehicle into Drive. "Something else you might want to know we learned."

"Holding out on me?" Bolan said, showed Hardin a mean smile.

"Hey, come on. I didn't know if you were coming back or what. I've got a job to do, Belasko."

"Fair enough. Get me to the airport. You were saying?"

"We learned who the Justice agent is in America who was feeding Marquis information."

"Let me guess...."

EPILOGUE

Washington, D.C.

"I know, it feels wrong, dirty somehow."

Bolan was stepping off the Gulfstream jet, Brognola waiting for him at Ronald Reagan National Airport. It was the dead of night. The world felt out of kilter to Bolan, jets landing and taking off beyond the reserved Justice Department tarmac little more than noisy blurs in a dream he might have just been waking from.

Bolan had gotten the news while flying back from Paris.

Bangle had opted to eat his gun. Who could explain why Bangle took the easy way out? Greed had gotten the better of him, Brognola digging up fat offshore accounts.

Hell, it was over, and Bangle was gone.

"It's always good to see you after the storm," Brognola said, leading Bolan toward his sedan. "I guess you don't want to hear about my problems?"

There was flak enough flying around, from Washington to Syria, the Arab world up in arms about the attack on Hahmad. Brognola would be taking heat for days, the Man and his minions scrambling for political cover, the usual denials issued.

Things happened.

Hahmad was dead. Marquis was finished. The Interpol rats flushed out and bagged.

"You look like hell," Brognola said.

"Yeah, it's the way I feel. This was an ugly one."

"More so than usual?"

"Understatement."

"I know an all-night diner, we can go sit down, grab a bite."

"Stop and smell the roses?"

"Why not? You earned it."

Strange, Bolan thought, he wasn't sure any man ever earned what he'd done. It was good, just the same, to come out the other side. It always was. Tomorrow would bring another Hahmad, perhaps even another Marquis.

"Well," Bolan said, "let's go smell the roses. Tell me all your woes and concerns."

Brognola smiled, chuckled.

It was good to be home, the soldier thought, with a friend. Tomorrow would arrive soon enough, bringing with it a new crisis. No point in worrying about what hadn't happened yet.

For now it was enough to be with a friend.

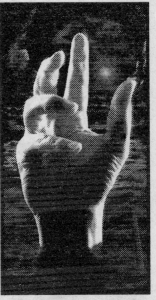

James Axler
Outlanders

FAR EMPIRE

Waging a covert war that ranges from a subterranean complex in the desert to a forgotten colony on the moon, former magistrate Kane, brother-in-arms Grant and archivist-turned-warrior Brigid Baptiste find themselves pawns in a stunning strategy of evil. A beautiful hybrid carries an unborn child—a blueprint for hope in a dark world. She seeks Kane's help, unwittingly leading them into a trap from which there may be no escape....

In the Outlands, the shocking truth is humanity's last hope.